Praise for Cory Doctorow

"Cory Doctorow straps on his miner's helmet and takes you deep into the caverns and underground rivers of Pop Culture, here filtered through SF-colored glasses. Enjoy."

—Neil Gaiman,
author of *American Gods* and *Sandman*

"Time travel made fresh. Pinocchio made haunting. Even the tangential ideas, incidental word choices and minor sub-stories crackle with creativity. If your nerd quotient is high enough, the last story will blow you away."

—Jeff Bezos,
founder and CEO of Amazon.com

"Cory Doctorow is the future of science fiction. An *n*th-generation hybrid of the best of Greg Bear, Rudy Rucker, Bruce Sterling and Groucho Marx, Doctorow composes stories that are as BPM-stuffed as techno music, as idea-rich as the latest issue of *New Scientist*, and as funny as humanity's efforts to improve itself. Utopian, insightful, somehow simultaneously ironic and heartfelt, these nine tales will upgrade your basal metabolism, overwrite your cortex with new and efficient subroutines and generally improve your life to the point where you'll wonder how you ever got along with them. Really, you should need a prescription to ingest this book. Out of all the glittering crap life and our society hands us, craphound supreme Doctorow has managed to fashion some industrial-grade art."

—Paul Di Filippo,
author of *Lost Pages*, *Little Doors*, and *The Steampunk Trilogy*

"Cory Doctorow is one of our best new writers: smart, daring, savvy, entertaining, ambitious, plugged-in, and as good a guide to the wired world of the twenty-first century that stretches out before us as you're going to find."

—Gardner Dozois,
editor, *Asimov's Science Fiction Magazine*

"He sparkles! He fizzes! He does backflips and breaks the furniture! Science fiction needs Cory Doctorow!"

—Bruce Sterling,
author of *The Hacker Crackdown* and *Distraction*

"Cory Doctorow strafes the senses with a geekspeedfreak explosion of gomi kings with heart, weirdass shapeshifters from Pleasure Island and jumping automotive jazz joints. If this is Canadian science fiction, give me more."

—Nalo Hopkinson,
author of *Midnight Robber* and *Brown Girl in the Ring*

"As scary as the future, and twice as funny. In this eclectic and electric collection Doctorow strikes sparks off today to illuminate tomorrow, which is what SF is supposed to do. And nobody does it better."

—Terry Bisson,
author of *The Bears Discover Fire* and *The Fifth Element*

A Place So Foreign and Eight More

Stories

by
Cory Doctorow

FOUR WALLS EIGHT WINDOWS
NEW YORK

"Craphound" originally appeared in *Science Fiction Age*, March 1998.

"A Place So Foreign" originally appeared in *Science Fiction Age,* January 2000.

"To Market, to Market: The Rebranding of Billy Bailey" originally appeared in *Interzone*, August 2000.

"Return to Pleasure Island" originally appeared in *Realms of Fantasy*, August 1999.

"Shadow of the Mothaship" originally appeared in *Amazing Stories*, Winter 2000.

"Home Again, Home Again" originally appeared in *Tesseracts 8* (Tesseract Press, 1999).

"The Super Man and the Bugout" originally appeared in *On Spec*, Fall 2001.

"0wnz0red" originally appeared on Salon.com, August 2002.

Published in the United States by:
Four Walls Eight Windows
39 West 14th Street, room 503
New York, N.Y., 10011

Visit our website at http://www.4w8w.com
First printing September 2003.

Library of Congress Cataloging-in-Publication Data

Doctorow, Cory.
A place so foreign and eight more/by Cory Doctorow; introduction by Bruce Sterling.
p. cm.
ISBN 1-56858-286-2 (pbk.)
1. Science fiction, American. I. Title.
PS3604.O38P58 2003
813'.6–dc21   2003054890

10 9 8 7 6 5 4 3 2

Typesetting by Pracharak Technologies (P) Ltd.
Printed in Canada

Acknowledgements

The stories in this book were written over a six year period, but they represent sixteen years of work in short fiction — more than half my life. In that time, numerous teachers, peers, editors, friends, relatives and employers have stood by me, supported me, blasted me, praised me, tortured me and shored me up.

I'd like to thank them here, in alphabetical order:

The Ad Astra ConComs, Mark Askwith, Darren Atkinson, Jodi BenDavid, Michael Bloom, Grad Conn, the Cecil Street Irregulars, the class of Clarion East 1992 (especially Becky Maines, Janis O'Connor, Cynthia Seelhammer and Cynthia Zender), Avram Doctorow, Gord Doctorow, Neil Doctorow, Roz Doctorow, Gardner Dozois, Scott Edelman, Claire Eddy, Amanda Foubister, Mark Frauenfelder, Greg Frost, Seymour Goldman, Valerie Goldman, James Gunn and the Sturgeon Award team, Glenn Grant, Rusty Halpert, David Hartwell, Patrick Nielsen Hayden, Teresa Nielsen Hayden, John Henson, Al Hoff, Tanya Huff, Michael Jackel, Sandra Kasturi, James Patrick Kelly, Damon Knight, Donald Maass, Tom Marcinko, Judith Merril, The staff of the Merril Collection (especially head librarian Lorna Toolis), the Novellettes, the On Spec editorial board, Bev Pannikar, Brenda Quinn, Lisa Rein, Matthew Rogers, Tom Robe, Spider Robinson, John Rose, Michelle Sagara, Karl Schroeder, Mary Sheridan, Michael Skeet, Martha Soukup, Bertha Starr, Sam Starr, Bruce Sterling, Sean Stewart, Harriet Wolff, Sheila Williams, Roger Wood and Pat York.

Table of Contents

Introduction:
The Kingdom of Magic Junk

Bruce Sterling

I have the pleasure to introduce you to Cory Doctorow and his short story collection.

As a political activist, gizmo freak, junk collector, programmer, entrepreneur and all around Renaissance geek, Cory Doctorow is a science fiction writer who can really drill down.

Cory Doctorow wrote a non-fiction guide to publishing science fiction before he'd published his first science fiction book. Most people into science fiction wouldn't look the business over with an engineer's sobriety, number all its ears, jacks and pulley-belts, and *then* hop into the mess. That is scary, it's like watching people make law and sausage. But Cory Doctorow also watches people make law. That's his day-job. I don't yet know what Cory does about sausage. I didn't dare ask.

Many writers, especially gray, creaky, well-fed ones, have ambivalent feelings about copyrighted ink versus slithering elec-tronica. Me, for instance: I wrote two novels on typewriters, so I still remember the Pleistocene. But Cory possesses an advanced mode of cyber-analysis. Paper versus pixels, that's yesterday's battle, an intriguing archaism for him. It provokes that nose-flaring delight that he takes in old industrial equipment and Howdy Doody dolls.

Cory was born in 1971 and was typing before he was six. I know many science fiction writers engaged in the cyber-world, but Cory Doctorow is a native. There are times when I suspect I've extrapolated Cory Doctorow. Consider Cory's carefree, shoe-shuffling globalism, so typical of vintage 1980s cyberpunk novels. Canada, Mexico, San Francisco, Costa Rica, scuba in Cuba, no change of physical locale can register with the man. The money changes color, maybe. As long as the junk shops are open and Apple is still shipping hardware, Cory's as happy as a clamshell laptop.

Not that he lacks heritage. On the contrary, these are a young man's stories, an artist getting to grip with his regional roots (or, in Cory's case, his aerials). There's a nice introductory cycle of stories here about Earth, or rather Cory Doctorow's Canada, being invaded and conquered by aliens called "Bugouts." Even though these super-aliens have technological dominance and have imposed their own weird notions of world peace, they don't matter all that much. They are rich, distracted, inexplicable aliens. Very much like Americans, I'd be guessing.

Cory Doctorow is obsessed with the Disney corporation. Americans live way too close to the fire there. It takes a clever outsider to get just how peculiar, spooky and otherworldly that enterprise is. In "Return to Pleasure Island" he drags us into a leprous re-imagining of children's commercial entertainment that, really, beggars description.

Cory is a genuine technical expert. He can do most every Mr. Wizard move typical of hard SF. But when he's genuinely engaged, he dumps the conventional genre fripperies. Cory is very into the slice of life, into the moment, into the *sentence*. There are sentences here so far-fetched that they can only arise from a passionate, deeply geekish, imaginative concentration. One gets the firm impression that both the characters *and the author* are hammered into the story with tiny steel finishing nails.

I particularly recommend to your attention two of Cory's newest works, "0wnz0red" and "The Rebranding of Billy Bailey." "The Rebranding of Billy Bailey" is pitiless, but it is also convulsively funny. It's easy to do weird parodies, but to do social satire which is this arch, this plausible, and this aware of our darkest impulses . . . well, that's a gift. It's a fresh gift of hope for science fiction, really. I have high hopes for this writer.

There has been a chunk of science fiction influenced by Silicon Valley, but "0wnz0red" captures the disturbed inner world of the technically sociopathic. For years now I've been searching for a work of science fiction that could only have been written in the 21st century. "0wnz0red" has broken through. This story is fully realized, and it is sarcastic, abrasive, and mind-boggling in a truly novel way. Like Beat writing in its early period, "0wnz0red" has the dual virtues of being both really offensive and genuinely hard for normal people to understand. This work is therefore truly advanced. It deserves an epithet all its own: "Doctorovian." We should all hope and trust that our culture has the guts and moxie to follow this guy. He's got a lot to tell us.

Though I started selling to the semi-professional markets when I was 17, it took nine years before "Craphound," my first professional sale, saw print. Scott Edelman bought it for the late, lamented Science Fiction Age *in the same month that Gardner Dozois bought "At Lightspeed, Slowing" for* Asimov's, *though this story saw print a good eight months before the* Asimov's *story made ink.*

This story remains my best-known. It's been reprinted in best-of anthologies, translated into Japanese, and it gave its name to my domain, craphound.com. It seems to especially resonate with librarians, archivists, collectors and slacker doofuses like me.

I think that there's an increasing sense of the approach of the Singularity, the nonlinearity of human history, the harbinger of which is the extent to which all of our commonsense knowledge is flushed and replaced with brand new memes every five or six years. The quotidian ephemera of our childhoods already seem impossibly naive and silly—did I really once have a "Stereo" the size of a buffet that played 78s? Our parents' crap and tchotchkes are like the fanciful implements littering the tableaux at a local Pioneer Village—girdles and curling irons, typewriters and mimeographs, patent medicine and adding machines.

The original title for this story was "You Ain't Nothin' but a Craphound," but thankfully the writers at the Cecil Street Irregulars workshop in Toronto talked me out of it.

Craphound

Craphound had wicked yard-sale karma, for a rotten, filthy alien bastard. He was too good at panning out the single grain of gold in a raging river of uselessness for me not to like him—respect him, anyway. But then he found the cowboy trunk. It was two months' rent to me and nothing but some squirrelly alien kitsch-fetish to Craphound.

So I did the unthinkable. I violated the Code. I got into a bidding war with a buddy. Never let them tell you that women poison friendships: in my experience, wounds from women-fights heal quickly; fights over garbage leave nothing behind but scorched earth.

Craphound spotted the sign—his karma, plus the goggles in his exoskeleton, gave him the advantage when we were doing 80 kmh on some stretch of back-highway in cottage country. He was riding shotgun while I drove, and we had the radio on to the CBC's summer-Saturday programming: eight weekends with eight hours of old radio dramas: "The Shadow," "Quiet Please," "Tom Mix," "The Crypt-Keeper" with Bela Lugosi. It was hour three, and Bogey was phoning in his performance on a radio adaptation of

The African Queen. I had the windows of the old truck rolled down so that I could smoke without fouling Craphound's breather. My arm was hanging out the window, the radio was booming, and Craphound said "Turn around! Turn around, now, Jerry, now, turn around!"

When Craphound gets that excited, it's a sign that he's spotted a rich vein. I checked the side-mirror quickly, pounded the brakes and spun around. The transmission creaked, the wheels squealed, and then we were creeping along the way we'd come.

"There," Craphound said, gesturing with his long, skinny arm. I saw it. A wooden A-frame real-estate sign, a piece of hand-lettered cardboard stuck over the realtor's name:

EAST MUSKOKA VOLUNTEER FIRE-DEPT

LADIES AUXILIARY RUMMAGE SALE

SAT 25 JUNE

"Hoo-eee!" I hollered, and spun the truck onto the dirt road. I gunned the engine as we cruised along the tree-lined road, trust-ing Craphound to spot any deer, signs, or hikers in time to avert disaster. The sky was a perfect blue and the smells of summer were all around us. I snapped off the radio and listened to the wind rush-ing through the truck. Ontario is *beautiful* in the summer.

"There!" Craphound shouted. I hit the turn-off and down-shifted and then we were back on a paved road. Soon, we were rolling into a country fire-station, an ugly brick barn. The hall was lined with long, folding tables, stacked high. The mother lode!

Craphound beat me out the door, as usual. His exoskeleton is programmable, so he can record little scripts for it like: move left arm to door handle, pop it, swing legs out to running-board, jump to ground, close door, move forward. Meanwhile, I'm still making sure I've switched off the headlights and that I've got my wallet.

Two blue-haired grannies had a card-table set up out front of the hall, with a big tin pitcher of lemonade and three boxes of Tim Horton assorted donuts. That stopped us both, since we share the superstition that you *always* buy food from old ladies and little kids, as a sacrifice to the crap-gods. One of the old ladies poured out the lemonade while the other smiled and greeted us.

"Welcome, welcome! My, you've come a long way for us!"

"Just up from Toronto, ma'am," I said. It's an old joke, but it's also part of the ritual, and it's got to be done.

"I meant your friend, sir. This gentleman."

Craphound smiled without baring his gums and sipped his lemonade. "Of course I came, dear lady. I wouldn't miss it for the worlds!" His accent is pretty good, but when it comes to stock phrases like this, he's got so much polish you'd think he was reading the news.

The biddie blushed and giggled, and I felt faintly sick. I walked off to the tables, trying not to hurry. I chose my first spot, about halfway down, where things wouldn't be quite so picked-over. I grabbed an empty box from underneath and started putting stuff into it: four matched highball glasses with gold crossed bowling-pins and a line of black around the rim; an Expo '67 wall-hanging that wasn't even a little faded; a shoebox full of late sixties O-Pee-Chee hockey cards; a worn, wooden-handled steel cleaver that you could butcher a steer with.

I picked up my box and moved on: a deck of playing cards copyrighted '57, with the logo for the Royal Canadian Dairy, Bala Ontario printed on the backs; a fireman's cap with a brass badge so tarnished I couldn't read it; a three-story wedding-cake trophy for the 1974 Eastern Region Curling Championships. The cash-register in my mind was ringing, ringing, ringing. God bless the East Muskoka Volunteer Fire Department Ladies' Auxiliary.

I'd mined that table long enough. I moved to the other end of the hall. Time was, I'd start at the beginning and turn over each item, build one pile of maybes and another pile of definites, try to strategize. In time, I came to rely on instinct and on the fates, to whom I make my obeisances at every opportunity.

Let's hear it for the fates: a genuine collapsible top-hat; a white-tipped evening cane; a hand-carved cherry-wood walking stick; a beautiful black lace parasol; a wrought-iron lightning rod with a rooster on top; all of it in an elephant-leg umbrella-stand. I filled the box, folded it over, and started on another.

I collided with Craphound. He grinned his natural grin, the one that showed row on row of wet, slimy gums, tipped with writhing, poisonous suckers. "Gold! Gold!" he said, and moved along. I turned my head after him, just as he bent over the cowboy trunk.

I sucked air between my teeth. It was magnificent: a leather-bound miniature steamer trunk, the leather worked with lariats, Stetson hats, war-bonnets and six-guns. I moved toward him, and he popped the latch. I caught my breath.

On top, there was a kid's cowboy costume: miniature leather chaps, a tiny Stetson, a pair of scuffed white-leather cowboy boots with long, worn spurs affixed to the heels. Craphound moved it reverently to the table and continued to pull more magic from the trunk's depths: a stack of cardboard-bound Hopalong Cassidy 78s; a pair of tin six-guns with gunbelt and holsters; a silver star that said Sheriff; a bundle of Roy Rogers comics tied with twine, in mint condition; and a leather satchel filled with plastic cowboys and Indians, enough to reenact the Alamo.

"Oh, my God," I breathed, as he spread the loot out on the table.

"What are these, Jerry?" Craphound asked, holding up the 78s.

"Old records, like LPs, but you need a special record player to listen to them." I took one out of its sleeve. It gleamed, scratch-free, in the overhead fluorescents.

"I got a 78 player here," said a member of the East Muskoka Volunteer Fire Department Ladies' Auxiliary. She was short enough to look Craphound in the eye, a hair under five feet, and had a skinny, rawboned look to her. "That's my Billy's things, Billy the Kid we called him. He was dotty for cowboys when he was a boy. Couldn't get him to take off that fool outfit—nearly got him thrown out of school. He's a lawyer now, in Toronto, got a fancy office on Bay Street. I called him to ask if he minded my putting his cowboy things in the sale, and you know what? He didn't know what I was talking about! Doesn't that beat everything? He was dotty for cowboys when he was a boy."

It's another of my rituals to smile and nod and be as polite as possible to the erstwhile owners of crap that I'm trying to buy, so I smiled and nodded and examined the 78 player she had produced. In lariat script, on the top, it said, "Official Bob Wills Little

Record Player," and had a crude watercolor of Bob Wills and His Texas Playboys grinning on the front. It was the kind of record player that folded up like a suitcase when you weren't using it. I'd had one as a kid, with Yogi Bear silkscreened on the front.

Billy's mom plugged the yellowed cord into a wall jack and took the 78 from me, touched the stylus to the record. A tinny ukulele played, accompanied by horse-clops, and then a narrator with a deep, whisky voice said, "Howdy, pardners! I was just settin' down by the ole campfire. Why don't you stay an' have some beans, an' I'll tell y'all the story of how Hopalong Cassidy beat the Duke Gang when they come to rob the Santa Fe."

In my head, I was already breaking down the cowboy trunk and its contents, thinking about the minimum bid I'd place on each item at Sotheby's. Sold individually, I figured I could get over two grand for the contents. Then I thought about putting ads in some of the Japanese collectors magazines, just for a lark, before I sent the lot to the auction house. You never can tell. A buddy I knew had sold a complete packaged set of "Welcome Back, Kotter" action figures for nearly eight grand that way. Maybe I could buy a new truck . . .

"This is wonderful," Craphound said, interrupting my reverie. "How much would you like for the collection?"

I felt a knife in my guts. Craphound had found the cowboy trunk, so that meant it was his. But he usually let me take the stuff with street-value—he was interested in everything, so it hardly mattered if I picked up a few scraps with which to eke out a living.

Billy's mom looked over the stuff. "I was hoping to get twenty dollars for the lot, but if that's too much, I'm willing to come down."

"I'll give you thirty," my mouth said, without intervention from my brain.

They both turned and stared at me. Craphound was unreadable behind his goggles.

Billy's mom broke the silence. "Oh, my! Thirty dollars for this old mess?"

"I will pay fifty," Craphound said.

"Seventy-five," I said.

"Oh, my," Billy's mom said.

"Five hundred," Craphound said.

I opened my mouth, and shut it. Craphound had built his stake on Earth by selling a complicated biochemical process for non-chlorophyll photosynthesis to a Saudi banker. I wouldn't ever beat him in a bidding war. "A thousand dollars," my mouth said.

"Ten thousand," Craphound said, and extruded a roll of hundreds from somewhere in his exoskeleton.

"My Lord!" Billy's mom said. "Ten thousand dollars!"

The other pickers, the firemen, the blue haired ladies all looked up at that and stared at us, their mouths open.

"It is for a good cause." Craphound said.

"Ten thousand dollars!" Billy's mom said again.

Craphound's digits ruffled through the roll as fast as a croupier's counter, separated off a large chunk of the brown bills, and handed them to Billy's mom.

One of the firemen, a middle-aged paunchy man with a comb-over appeared at Billy's mom's shoulder.

"What's going on, Eva?" he said.

"This . . . gentleman is going to pay ten thousand dollars for Billy's old cowboy things, Tom."

The fireman took the money from Billy's mom and stared at it. He held up the top note under the light and turned it this way and that, watching the holographic stamp change from green to gold, then green again. He looked at the serial number, then the serial number of the next bill. He licked his forefinger and started counting off the bills in piles of ten. Once he had ten piles, he counted them again. "That's ten thousand dollars, all right. Thank you very much, mister. Can I give you a hand getting this to your car?"

Craphound, meanwhile, had repacked the trunk and balanced the 78 player on top of it. He looked at me, then at the fireman.

"I wonder if I could impose on you to take me to the nearest bus station. I think I'm going to be making my own way home."

The fireman and Billy's mom both stared at me. My cheeks flushed. "Aw, c'mon," I said. "I'll drive you home."

"I think I prefer the bus," Craphound said.

"It's no trouble at all to give you a lift, friend," the fireman said.

I called it quits for the day, and drove home alone with the truck only half-filled. I pulled it into the coach-house and threw a tarp over the load and went inside and cracked a beer and sat on the sofa, watching a nature show on a desert reclamation project in Arizona, where the state legislature had traded a derelict mega-mall and a custom-built habitat to an alien for a local-area weather control machine.

The following Thursday, I went to the little crap-auction house on King Street. I'd put my finds from the weekend in the sale: lower minimum bid, and they took a smaller commission than Sotheby's. Fine for moving the small stuff.

Craphound was there, of course. I knew he'd be. It was where we met, when he bid on a case of Lincoln Logs I'd found at a fire-sale.

I'd known him for a kindred spirit when he bought them, and we'd talked afterwards, at his place, a sprawling, two-story ware-house amid a cluster of auto-wrecking yards where the junkyard dogs barked, barked, barked.

Inside was paradise. His taste ran to shrines—a collection of fifties bar kitsch that was a shrine to liquor; a circular waterbed on a raised podium that was nearly buried under seventies bachelor pad-inalia; a kitchen that was nearly unusable, so packed it was with old barn-board furniture and rural memorabilia; a leather-appointed library straight out of a Victorian gentlemen's club; a solarium dressed in wicker and bamboo and tiki-idols. It was a hell of a place.

Craphound had known all about the Goodwills and the Sally Anns, and the auction houses, and the kitsch boutiques on Queen Street, but he still hadn't figured out where it all came from.

"Yard sales, rummage sales, garage sales," I said, reclining in a vibrating naugahyde easy-chair, drinking a glass of his pricey single-malt that he'd bought for the beautiful bottle it came in.

"But where are these? Who is allowed to make them?" Craphound hunched opposite me, his exoskeleton locked into a coiled, semi-seated position.

"Who? Well, anyone. You just one day decide that you need to clean out the basement, you put an ad in the *Star*, tape up a few signs, and voila, yard sale. Sometimes, a school or a church will get donations of old junk and sell it all at one time, as a fundraiser."

"And how do you locate these?" he asked, bobbing up and down slightly with excitement.

"Well, there're amateurs who just read the ads in the weekend papers, or just pick a neighborhood and wander around, but that's no way to go about it. What I do is, I get in a truck, and I sniff the air, catch the scent of crap and *vroom!*, I'm off like a bloodhound on a trail. You learn things over time: like stay away from yuppie yard sales, they never have anything worth buying, just the same crap you can buy in any mall."

"Do you think I might accompany you some day?"

"Hell, sure. Next Saturday? We'll head over to Cabbagetown — those old coach houses, you'd be amazed what people get rid of. It's practically criminal."

"I would like to go with you on next Saturday very much Mr. Jerry Abington." He used to talk like that, without commas or question marks. Later, he got better, but then, it was all one big sentence.

"Call me Jerry. It's a date, then. Tell you what, though: there's a Code you got to learn before we go out. The Craphound's Code."

"What is a craphound?"

"You're lookin' at one. You're one, too, unless I miss my guess. You'll get to know some of the local craphounds, you hang around with me long enough. They're the competition, but they're also your buddies, and there're certain rules we have."

And then I explained to him all about how you never bid against a craphound at a yard-sale, how you get to know the other fellows' tastes, and when you see something they might like, you haul it out for them, and they'll do the same for you, and how you never buy something that another craphound might be looking for, if all you're buying it for is to sell it back to him. Just good form and common sense, really, but you'd be surprised how many amateurs just fail to make the jump to pro because they can't grasp it.

There was a bunch of other stuff at the auction, other craphounds' weekend treasures. This was high season, when the sun comes out and people start to clean out the cottage, the basement, the garage. There were some collectors in the crowd, and a whole whack of antique and junk dealers, and a few pickers, and me, and Craphound. I watched the bidding listlessly, waiting for my things to come up and sneaking out for smokes between lots. Craphound never once looked at me or acknowledged my presence, and I became perversely obsessed with catching his eye, so I coughed and shifted and walked past him several times, until the auctioneer glared at me, and one of the attendants asked if I needed a throat lozenge.

My lot came up. The bowling glasses went for five bucks to one of the Queen Street junk dealers; the elephant-foot fetched $350 after a spirited bidding war between an antique dealer and a collector—the collector won; the dealer took the top-hat for $100. The rest of it came up and sold, or didn't, and at the end of the lot, I'd made over $800, which was rent for the month plus beer for the weekend plus gas for the truck.

Craphound bid on and bought more cowboy things—a box of Super 8 cowboy movies, the boxes mouldy, the stock itself running to slime; a Navajo blanket; a plastic donkey that dispensed cigarettes out of its ass; a big neon armadillo sign.

One of the other nice things about that place over Sotheby's, there was none of this waiting thirty days to get a check. I queued up with the other pickers after the bidding was through, collected a wad of bills, and headed for my truck.

I spotted Craphound loading his haul into a minivan with handicapped plates. It looked like some kind of fungus was growing over the hood and side-panels. On closer inspection, I saw that the body had been covered in closely glued Lego.

Craphound popped the hatchback and threw his gear in, then opened the driver's side door, and I saw that his van had been fitted out for a legless driver, with brake and accelerator levers. A paraplegic I knew drove one just like it. Craphound's exoskeleton levered him into the seat, and I watched the eerily precise way it executed the macro that started the car, pulled the shoulder-belt, put it into drive and switched on the stereo. I heard tape-hiss, then, loud as a b-boy cruising Yonge Street, an old-timey cowboy voice: "Howdy pardners! Saddle up, we're ridin'!" Then the van backed up and sped out of the lot.

I got into the truck and drove home. Truth be told, I missed the little bastard.

Some people said that we should have run Craphound and his kin off the planet, out of the Solar System. They said that it wasn't fair for the aliens to keep us in the dark about their technologies. They say that we should have captured a ship and reverse-engineered it, built our own and kicked ass.

Some people!

First of all, nobody with human DNA could survive a trip in one of those ships. They're part of Craphound's people's bodies, as I understand it, and we just don't have the right parts. Second of all, they *were* sharing their tech with us—they just weren't giving it away. Fair trades every time.

It's not as if space was off-limits to us. We can any one of us visit their homeworld, just as soon as we figure out how. Only they wouldn't hold our hands along the way.

I spent the week haunting the "Secret Boutique," AKA the Goodwill As-Is Center on Jarvis. It's all there is to do between yard sales, and sometimes it makes for good finds. Part of my theory of yard-sale karma holds that if I miss one day at the thrift shops, that'll be the day they put out the big score. So I hit the stores diligently and came up with crapola. I had offended the fates, I knew, and wouldn't make another score until I placated them. It was lonely work, still and all, and I missed Craphound's good eye and obsessive delight.

I was at the cash-register with a few items at the Goodwill when a guy in a suit behind me tapped me on the shoulder.

"Sorry to bother you," he said. His suit looked expensive, as did his manicure and his haircut and his wire-rimmed glasses. "I was just wondering where you found that." He gestured at a rhine-stone-studded ukulele, with a cowboy hat wood-burned into the body. I had picked it up with a guilty little thrill, thinking that Craphound might buy it at the next auction.

"Second floor, in the toy section."

"There wasn't anything else like it, was there?"

"'Fraid not," I said, and the cashier picked it up and started wrapping it in newspaper.

"Ah," he said, and he looked like a little kid who'd just been told that he couldn't have a puppy. "I don't suppose you'd want to sell it, would you?"

I held up a hand and waited while the cashier bagged it with the rest of my stuff, a few old clothbound novels I thought I could sell at a used book-store, and a Grease belt-buckle with Olivia Newton John on it. I led him out the door by the elbow of his expensive suit.

"How much?" I had paid a dollar.

"Ten bucks?"

I nearly said, "Sold!" but I caught myself. "Twenty."

"Twenty dollars?"

"That's what they'd charge at a boutique on Queen Street."

He took out a slim leather wallet and produced a twenty. I handed him the uke. His face lit up like a lightbulb.

It's not that my adulthood is particularly unhappy. Likewise, it's not that my childhood was particularly happy.

There are memories I have, though, that are like a cool drink of water. My grandfather's place near Milton, an old Victorian farm-house, where the cat drank out of a milk-glass bowl; and where we sat around a rough pine table as big as my whole apartment; and where my playroom was the draughty barn with hay-filled lofts bulging with farm junk and Tarzan-ropes.

There was Grampa's friend Fyodor, and we spent every evening at his wrecking-yard, he and Grampa talking and smoking while I scampered in the twilight, scaling mountains of auto-junk. The glove-boxes yielded treasures: crumpled photos of college boys mugging in front of signs, roadmaps of far-away places. I found a guidebook from the 1964 New York World's Fair once, and a lip-stick like a chrome bullet, and a pair of white leather ladies' gloves.

Fyodor dealt in scrap, too, and once, he had half of a carny carousel, a few horses and part of the canopy, paint flaking and sharp torn edges protruding; next to it, a Korean-war tank minus its turret and treads, and inside the tank were peeling old pinup girls and a rotation schedule and a crude Kilroy. The control-room in the middle of the carousel had a stack of paperback sci-fi novels, Ace Doubles that had two books bound back-to-back, and when you finished the first, you turned it over and read the other. Fyodor let me keep them, and there was a pawn-ticket in one from Macon, Georgia, for a transistor radio.

My parents started leaving me alone when I was fourteen and I couldn't keep from sneaking into their room and snooping. Mom's jewelry box had books of matches from their honeymoon in Acapulco, printed with bad palm trees. My Dad kept an old photo in his sock drawer, of himself on muscle-beach, shirtless, flexing his biceps.

My grandmother saved every scrap of my mother's life in her basement, in dusty Army trunks. I entertained myself by pulling it out and taking it in: her Mouse Ears from the big family train-trip to Disneyland in '57, and her records, and the glittery pasteboard sign from her sweet sixteen. There were well-chewed stuffed animals, and school exercise books in which she'd practiced variations on her signature for page after page.

It all told a story. The penciled Kilroy in the tank made me see one of those Canadian soldiers in Korea, unshaven and crew-cut like an extra on M★A★S★H, sitting for bored hour after hour, staring at the pinup girls, fiddling with a crossword, finally laying it down and sketching his Kilroy quickly, before anyone saw.

The photo of my Dad posing sent me whirling through time to Toronto's Muscle Beach in the east end, and hearing the tinny AM radios playing weird psychedelic rock while teenagers lounged on their Mustangs and the girls sunbathed in bikinis that made their tits into torpedoes.

It all made poems. The old pulp novels and the pawn ticket, when I spread them out in front of the TV, and arranged them just so, they made up a poem that took my breath away.

After the cowboy trunk episode, I didn't run into Craphound again until the annual Rotary Club charity rummage sale at the Upper Canada Brewing Company. He was wearing the cowboy hat, six-guns and the silver star from the cowboy trunk. It should have looked ridiculous, but the net effect was naive and somehow charming, like he was a little boy whose hair you wanted to muss.

I found a box of nice old melamine dishes, in various shades of green—four square plates, bowls, salad-plates, and a serving tray. I threw them in the duffel-bag I'd brought and kept browsing, ignoring Craphound as he charmed a salty old Rotarian while fondling a box of leather-bound books.

I browsed a stack of old Ministry of Labor licenses—barber, chiropodist, bartender, watchmaker. They all had pretty seals and were framed in stark green institutional metal. They all had different names, but all from one family, and I made up a little story to entertain myself, about the proud mother saving her sons' framed accreditations and hanging them in the spare room with their diplomas. "Oh, George Junior's just opened his own barbershop, and little Jimmy's still fixing watches . . ."

I bought them.

In a box of crappy plastic Little Ponies and Barbies and Care Bears, I found a leather Indian headdress, a wooden bow-and-arrow set, and a fringed buckskin vest. Craphound was still buttering up the leather books' owner. I bought them quick, for five bucks.

"Those are beautiful," a voice said at my elbow. I turned around and smiled at the snappy dresser who'd bought the uke at the Secret Boutique. He'd gone casual for the weekend, in an expensive, L.L. Bean button-down way.

"Aren't they, though."

"You sell them on Queen Street? Your finds, I mean?"

"Sometimes. Sometimes at auction. How's the uke?"

"Oh, I got it all tuned up," he said, and smiled the same smile he'd given me when he'd taken hold of it at Goodwill. "I can play 'Don't Fence Me In' on it." He looked at his feet. "Silly, huh?"

"Not at all. You're into cowboy things, huh?" As I said it, I was overcome with the knowledge that this was "Billy the Kid," the original owner of the cowboy trunk. I don't know why I felt that way, but I did, with utter certainty.

"Just trying to relive a piece of my childhood, I guess. I'm Scott," he said, extending his hand.

Scott? I thought wildly. *Maybe it's his middle name?* "I'm Jerry."

The Upper Canada Brewery sale has many things going for it, including a beer garden where you can sample their wares and get a good BBQ burger. We gently gravitated to it, looking over the tables as we went.

"You're a pro, right?" he asked after we had plastic cups of beer.

"You could say that."

"I'm an amateur. A rank amateur. Any words of wisdom?"

I laughed and drank some beer, lit a cigarette. "There's no secret to it, I think. Just diligence: you've got to go out every chance you get, or you'll miss the big score."

He chuckled. "I hear that. Sometimes, I'll be sitting in my office, and I'll just *know* that they're putting out a piece of pure gold at the Goodwill and that someone else will get to it before my lunch. I get so wound up, I'm no good until I go down there and hunt for it. I guess I'm hooked, eh?"

"Cheaper than some other kinds of addictions."

"I guess so. About that Indian stuff—what do you figure you'd get for it at a Queen Street boutique?"

I looked him in the eye. He may have been something high-powered and cool and collected in his natural environment, but just then, he was as eager and nervous as a kitchen-table poker-player at a high-stakes game.

"Maybe fifty bucks," I said.

"Fifty, huh?" he asked.

"About that," I said.

"Once it sold," he said.

"There is that," I said.

"Might take a month, might take a year," he said.

"Might take a day," I said.

"It might, it might." He finished his beer. "I don't suppose you'd take forty?"

I'd paid five for it, not ten minutes before. It looked like it would fit Craphound, who, after all, was wearing Scott/Billy's own boyhood treasures as we spoke. You don't make a living by feeling guilty over eight hundred percent markups. Still, I'd angered the fates, and needed to redeem myself.

"Make it five," I said.

He started to say something, then closed his mouth and gave me a look of thanks. He took a five out of his wallet and handed it to me. I pulled the vest and bow and headdress out my duffel.

He walked back to a shiny black Jeep with gold detail work, parked next to Craphound's van. Craphound was building onto the Lego body, and the hood had a miniature Lego town attached to it.

Craphound looked around as he passed, and leaned forward with undisguised interest at the booty. I grimaced and finished my beer.

I met Scott/Billy three times more at the Secret Boutique that week.

He was a lawyer who specialized in alien-technology patents. He had a practice on Bay Street, with two partners, and despite his youth, he was the senior man.

I didn't let on that I knew about Billy the Kid and his mother in the East Muskoka Volunteer Fire Department Ladies' Auxiliary. But I felt a bond with him, as though we shared an unspoken secret. I pulled any cowboy finds for him, and he developed a pretty good eye for what I was after and returned the favor.

The fates were with me again, and no two ways about it. I took home a ratty old Oriental rug that on closer inspection was a 19th century hand-knotted Persian; an upholstered Turkish footstool; a collection of hand-painted silk Hawaiiana pillows and a carved Meerschaum pipe. Scott/Billy found the last for me, and it cost me two dollars. I knew a collector who would pay thirty in an eye-blink, and from then on, as far as I was concerned, Scott/Billy was a fellow craphound.

"You going to the auction tomorrow night?" I asked him at the checkout line.

"Wouldn't miss it," he said. He'd barely been able to contain his excitement when I told him about the Thursday night auctions and the bargains to be had there. He sure had the bug.

"Want to get together for dinner beforehand? The Rotterdam's got a good patio."

He did, and we did, and I had a glass of framboise that packed a hell of a kick and tasted like fizzy raspberry lemonade; and doorstopper fries and a club sandwich.

I had my nose in my glass when he kicked my ankle under the table. "Look at that!"

It was Craphound in his van, cruising for a parking spot. The Lego village had been joined by a whole postmodern spaceport on the roof, with a red-and-blue castle, a football-sized flying saucer, and a clown's head with blinking eyes.

I went back to my drink and tried to get my appetite back.

"Was that an extee driving?"

"Yeah. Used to be a friend of mine."

"He's a picker?"

"Uh-huh." I turned back to my fries and tried to kill the subject.

"Do you know how he made his stake?"

"The chlorophyll thing, in Saudi Arabia."

"Sweet!" he said. "Very sweet. I've got a client who's got some secondary patents from that one. What's he go after?"

"Oh, pretty much everything," I said, resigning myself to discussing the topic after all. "But lately, the same as you—cowboys and Injuns."

He laughed and smacked his knee. "Well, what do you know? What could he possibly want with the stuff?"

"What do they want with any of it? He got started one day when we were cruising the Muskokas," I said carefully, watching his face. "Found a trunk of old cowboy things at a rummage sale. East Muskoka Volunteer Fire Department Ladies' Auxiliary." I waited for him to shout or startle. He didn't.

"Yeah? A good find, I guess. Wish I'd made it."

I didn't know what to say to that, so I took a bite of my sandwich.

Scott continued. "I think about what they get out of it a lot. There's nothing we have here that they couldn't make for themselves. I mean, if they picked up and left today, we'd still be making sense of everything they gave us in a hundred years. You know, I just closed a deal for a biochemical computer that's no-shit 10,000 times faster than anything we've built out of silicon. You know what the extee took in trade? Title to a defunct fairground outside of Calgary—they shut it down ten years ago because the midway was too unsafe to ride. Doesn't that beat all? This thing is worth a billion dollars right out of the gate, I mean, within twenty-four hours of the deal closing, the seller can turn it into the GDP of Bolivia. For a crummy real-estate dog that you couldn't get five grand for!"

It always shocked me when Billy/Scott talked about his job—it was easy to forget that he was a high-powered lawyer when we were jawing and fooling around like old craphounds. I wondered if maybe he *wasn't* Billy the Kid; I couldn't think of any reason for him to be playing it all so close to his chest.

"What the hell is some extee going to do with a fairground?"

Craphound got a free Coke from Lisa at the check-in when he made his appearance. He bid high, but shrewdly, and never pulled ten-thousand-dollar stunts. The bidders were wandering the floor, previewing that week's stock, and making notes to themselves.

I rooted through a box-lot full of old tins, and found one with a buckaroo at the Calgary Stampede, riding a bucking bronc. I picked it up and stood to inspect it. Craphound was behind me.

"Nice piece, huh?" I said to him.

"I like it very much," Craphound said, and I felt my cheeks flush.

"You're going to have some competition tonight, I think," I said, and nodded at Scott/Billy. "I think he's Billy; the one whose mother sold us—you—the cowboy trunk."

"Really?" Craphound said, and it felt like we were partners again, scoping out the competition. Suddenly I felt a knife of shame, like I was betraying Scott/Billy somehow. I took a step back.

"Jerry, I am very sorry that we argued."

I sighed out a breath I hadn't known I was holding in. "Me, too."

"They're starting the bidding. May I sit with you?"

And so the three of us sat together, and Craphound shook Scott/Billy's hand and the auctioneer started into his harangue.

It was a night for unusual occurrences. I bid on a piece, something I told myself I'd never do. It was a set of four matched Li'l Orphan Annie Ovaltine glasses, like Grandma's had been, and seeing them in the auctioneer's hand took me right back to her kitchen, and endless afternoons passed with my coloring books and weird old-lady hard candies and Liberace albums playing in the living room.

"Ten," I said, opening the bidding.

"I got ten, ten, ten, I got ten, who'll say twenty, who'll say twenty, twenty for the four."

Craphound waved his bidding card, and I jumped as if I'd been stung.

"I got twenty from the space cowboy, I got twenty, sir will you say thirty?"

I waved my card.

"That's thirty to you sir."

"Forty," Craphound said.

"Fifty," I said even before the auctioneer could point back to me. An old pro, he settled back and let us do the work.

"One hundred," Craphound said.

"One fifty," I said.

The room was perfectly silent. I thought about my overextended MasterCard, and wondered if Scott/Billy would give me a loan.

"Two hundred," Craphound said.

Fine, I thought. Pay two hundred for those. I can get a set on Queen Street for thirty bucks.

The auctioneer turned to me. "The bidding stands at two. Will you say two-ten, sir?"

I shook my head. The auctioneer paused a long moment, letting me sweat over the decision to bow out.

"I have two—do I have any other bids from the floor? Any other bids? Sold, $200, to number 57." An attendant brought Craphound the glasses. He took them and tucked them under his seat.

I was fuming when we left. Craphound was at my elbow. I wanted to punch him—I'd never punched anyone in my life, but I wanted to punch him.

We entered the cool night air and I sucked in several lungfuls before lighting a cigarette.

"Jerry," Craphound said.

I stopped, but didn't look at him. I watched the taxis pull in and out of the garage next door instead.

"Jerry, my friend," Craphound said.

"WHAT?" I said, loud enough to startle myself. Scott, beside me, jerked as well.

"We're going. I wanted to say goodbye, and to give you some things that I won't be taking with me."

"What?" I said again, Scott just a beat behind me.

"My people—we're going. It has been decided. We've gotten what we came for."

Without another word, he set off towards his van. We followed along behind, shell-shocked.

Craphound's exoskeleton executed another macro and slid the panel-door aside, revealing the cowboy trunk.

"I wanted to give you this. I will keep the glasses."

"I don't understand," I said.

"You're all leaving?" Scott asked, with a note of urgency.

"It has been decided. We'll go over the next twenty-four hours."

"But *why*?" Scott said, sounding almost petulant.

"It's not something that I can easily explain. As you must know, the things we gave you were trinkets to us—almost worthless. We traded them for something that was almost worthless to you—a fair trade, you'll agree—but it's time to move on."

Craphound handed me the cowboy trunk. Holding it, I smelled the lubricant from his exoskeleton and the smell of the attic it had been mummified in before making its way into his hands. I felt like I almost understood.

"This is for me," I said slowly, and Craphound nodded encouragingly. "This is for me, and you're keeping the glasses. And I'll look at this and feel . . ."

"You understand," Craphound said, looking somehow relieved.

And I *did*. I understood that an alien wearing a cowboy hat and six-guns and giving them away was a poem and a story, and a thirtyish bachelor trying to spend half a month's rent on four glasses so that he could remember his Grandma's kitchen was a story and a poem, and that the disused fairground outside Calgary was a story and a poem, too.

"You're craphounds!" I said. "All of you!"

Craphound smiled so I could see his gums and I put down the cowboy trunk and clapped my hands.

Scott recovered from his shock by spending the night at his office, crunching numbers talking on the phone, and generally getting while the getting was good. He had an edge—no one else knew that they were going.

He went pro later that week, opened a chi-chi boutique on Queen Street, and hired me on as chief picker and factum factotum.

Scott was not Billy the Kid. Just another Bay Street shyster with a cowboy jones. From the way they come down and spend, there must be a million of them.

Our draw in the window is a beautiful mannequin I found, straight out of the Fifties, a little boy we call The Beaver. He dresses in chaps and a sheriff's badge and six-guns and a miniature Stetson and cowboy boots with worn spurs, and rests one foot on a beautiful miniature steamer trunk whose leather is worked with cowboy motifs.

He's not for sale at any price.

From the day I read my first novel, "Alice in Wonderland," I was hooked through the bag on narrative. I systematically read my way through my classroom libraries, through the books at home, and finally through the school library and the local branch library. Somewhere along the way, I stumbled on T. D. Fitzgerald's "Great Brain" memoirs, young-adult books that told the story of Fitzgerald's childhood in Adenville, Utah at the turn of the century.

Fitzgerald's wonderful and improbable tales of the pluckiness and cunning of his brothers and playmates stayed with me, and when I decided to write a novella about time-travel, it only seemed natural to revisit Fitzgerald's small-town Utah, with its spirit of limitless possibility, of technological marvels hovering there on the brink, of a frontier freshly tamed and more frontiers opening ahead.

So: "A Place So Foreign." It seems to me that time travel would have a tendency to leak backwards, spinning out alternalities of ever-increasing anachronism and sophistication. 1975 and 1902 are two eras ripe for time-travellers to pitch their tents, times/places filled with boundless optimism for the future and a spirit of adventure.

A Place So Foreign

My pa disappeared somewhere in the wilds of 1975, when I was just fourteen years old. He was the ambassador to 1975, but back home in 1898, in New Jerusalem, Utah, they all thought he was ambassador to France. When he disappeared, Mama and I came back through the triple-bolted door that led from our apt in 1975 to our horse barn in 1898. We returned to the dusty streets of New Jerusalem, and I had to keep on reminding myself that I was supposed to have been in France, and "polly-voo" for my chums, and tell whoppers about the Eiffel Tower and the fancy bread and the snails and frogs we'd eaten.

I was born in New Jerusalem, and raised there till I was ten. Then, one summer's day, my pa sat me on his knee and told me we'd be going away for a while, that he had a new job.

"But what about the store?" I said, scandalized. My pa's wonderful store, the only General Store in town not run by the Saints, was my second home. I'd spent my whole life crawling and then walking on the dusty wooden floors, checking stock and unpacking crates with waybills from exotic places like Salt Lake City and even San Francisco.

Pa looked uncomfortable. "Mr. Johnstone is buying it."

My mouth dropped. James H. Johnstone was as dandified a city-slicker as you'd ever hope to meet. He'd blown into town on the weekly Zephyr Speedball, and skinny Tommy Benson had hauled his three huge steamer trunks to the cowboy hotel. He'd tipped Tommy two dollars, in Wells Fargo notes, and later, in the empty lot behind the smithy, all the kids in New Jerusalem had gathered 'round Tommy to goggle at the small fortune in queer, never-seen bills.

"Pa, no!" I said, without thinking. I knew that if my chums ordered their fathers around like that, they'd get a whipping, but my pa almost never whipped me.

He smiled, and his thick moustache stretched across his face. "James, I know you love the store, but it's already been decided. Once you've been to France, you'll see that it has wonders that beat anything that store can deliver."

"Nothing's better than the store," I said.

He laughed and rumpled my hair. "Don't be so sure, son. There are more things in heaven and earth than are dreamt of in your philosophy." It was one of his sayings, from Shakespeare, who he'd studied back east, before I was born. It meant that the discussion was closed.

I decided to withhold judgment until I saw France, but still couldn't shake the feeling that my pa was going soft in the head. Mr. Johnstone wasn't fit to run an apple-cart. He was short and skinny and soft, not like my pa, who, as far as I was concerned, was the biggest, strongest man in the whole world. I loved my pa.

Well, when we packed our bags and Pa went into the horse barn to hitch up our team, I figured we'd be taking a short trip out to the train station. All my chums were waiting there to see us off, and I'd promised my best pal Oly Sweynsdatter that I'd give him my coonskin cap to wear until we came back. But instead, Pa rode us to the edge of town, where the road went to rutted trail and salt flats, and there was Mr. James H. Johnstone, in his own fancy-pants trap. Pa and me moved our luggage into Johnstone's trap and got inside with Mama and hunkered down so, you couldn't see us from outside. Mama said, "You just hush up now, James. There's parts of this trip that we couldn't tell you about before we left, but you're going to have to stay quiet and hold onto your questions until we get to where we're going."

I nearly said, "To where we're going?" but I didn't, because Mama had never looked so serious in all my born days. So I spent an hour hunkered down in there, listening to the clatter of the wheels and trying to guess where we were going. When I heard the trap stop and a set of wooden doors close, all my guesses dried up and blew away, because I couldn't think of anywhere we would've heard those sounds out in the desert.

So imagine my surprise when I stood up and found us right in our very own horse barn, having made a circle around town and back to where we'd started from! Mama held a finger up to her lips and then took Mr. Johnstone's soft, girlish hand as he helped her down from the trap.

My Pa and Mr. Johnstone started shifting one of the piles of hay-bales that stacked to the rafters, until they had revealed a triple-bolted door that looked new and sturdy, fresh-sawn edges still bright and yellow, and not the weathered brown of the rest of the barn.

Pa took a key ring out of his vest pocket and unlocked the door, then swung it open. Each of us shouldered our bags and walked through, in eerie silence, into a pitch black room.

Pa reached out and pulled the door shut, then there was a sharp click and we were in 1975.

1975 was a queer sight. Our apartment was a lozenge of silver, spoked into the hub of a floating null-gee doughnut. Pa did something fancy with his hands and the walls went transparent, and I swear, I dropped to the floor and hugged the nubby rubber tiles for all I was worth. My eyes were telling me that we were hundreds of yards off the ground, and while I'd jumped from the rafters of the horse barn into the hay countless times, I suddenly discovered that I was afraid of heights.

After that first dizzying glimpse of 1975, I kept my eyes squeezed shut and held on for all I was worth. After a minute or two of this, my stomach told me that I wasn't falling, and I couldn't hear any rushing wind, any birdcalls, anything except Mama and Pa laughing, fit to bust. I opened one eye and snuck a peek. My folks were laughing so hard they had to hold onto each other to stay up, and they were leaning against thin air, Pa's back pressed up against nothing at all.

Cautiously, I got to my feet and walked over to the edge. I extended one finger and it bumped up against an invisible wall, cool and smooth as glass in winter.

"James," said my pa, smiling so wide that his thick moustache stretched all the way across his face, "Welcome to 1975."

Pa's ambassadorial mission meant that he often spent long weeks away from home, teleporting in only for Sunday dinner, the stink of aliens and distant worlds clinging to him even after he washed up. The last Sunday dinner I had with him, Mama had made mashed potatoes and corn bread and sausage gravy and turkey, spending the whole day with the wood-fired cooker back in 1898 (actually, it was 1901 by then, but I always thought of it as 1898). She'd moved the cooker into the horse barn after a week of wrestling with the gadgets we had in our 1975 kitchen, and when Pa had warned her that the smoke was going to raise questions in New Jerusalem, she explained that she was going to run some flexible exhaust hose through the door into '75 and into our apt's air-scrubber. Pa had shook his head and smiled at her, and every Sunday, she dragged the exhaust pipe through the door.

That night, Pa sat down and said grace, and he was in his shirt-sleeves with his suspenders down, and it almost felt like home—almost felt like a million Sunday dinners eaten by gaslight, with a sweaty pitcher of lemonade in the middle of the table, and seasonal wildflowers, and a stinky cheroot for Pa afterwards as he tipped his chair back and rested one hand on his belly, as if he couldn't believe how much Mama had managed to stuff him this time.

"How are your studies coming, James?" he asked me, when the robutler had finished clearing the plates and clattered away into its nook.

"Very well, sir. We're starting calculus now." Truth be told, I hated calculus, hated Isaac Newton and asymptotes and the whole smelly business. Even with the viral learning shots, it was like swimming in molasses for me.

"Calculus! Well, well, well"—this was one of Pa's catch-all phrases, like "How *about* that?" or "What do you know?"— "Well, well, well. I can't believe how much they stuff into kids' heads here."

"Yes, sir. There's an awful lot left to learn, yet." We did a subject every two weeks. So far, I'd done French, Molecular and Cellular Biology, Physics and Astrophysics, Esperanto, Cantonese and Mandarin, and an alien language whose name translated as "Standard." I'd been exempted from History, of course, along with the other kids there from the past—the Chinese girl from the Ming Dynasty, the Roman boy, and the Injun kid from South America.

Pa laughed around his cigar and crossed his legs. His shoes were so big, they looked like canoes. "There surely is, son. There surely is. And how are you doing with your classmates? Any tussles your teacher will want to talk to me about?"

"No, sir! We're friendly as all get-out, even the girls." The kids in '75 didn't even notice what they were doing in school. They just sat down at their workstations and waited to have their brains filled with whatever was going on, and left at three, and never complained about something being too hard or too dull.

"That's good to hear, son. You've always been a good boy. Tell you what: you bring home a good report this Christmas, and I'll take you to see Saturn's rings on vacation."

Mama shot him a look then, but he pretended he didn't see it. He stubbed out his cigar, hitched up his suspenders, and put on his tailcoat and tophat and ambassadorial sash and picked up his leather case.

"Good night, son. Good night, Ulla. I'll see you on Wednesday," he said, and stepped into the teleporter.

That was the last time I ever saw him.

"He died from bad snails?" Oly Sweynsdatter said to me, yet again.

I balled up a fist and stuck it under his nose. "For the last time, yes. Ask me again, and I'll feed you this."

I'd been back for a month, and in all that time, Oly had skittered around me like a shy pony, always nearby but afraid to talk to me. Finally, I'd grabbed him and shook him and told him not to be such a ninny, tell me what was on his mind. He wanted to know how my pa had died, over in France. I told him the reason that Mama and Mr. Johnstone and the man from the embassy had worked out together. Now, I regretted it. I couldn't get him to shut up.

"Sorry, all right, sorry!" he said, taking a step backwards. We were in the orchard behind the schoolyard, chucking rotten apples at the tree-trunks to watch them splatter. "Want to hear something?"

"Sure," I said.

"Tommy Benson's sweet on Marta Helprin. It's disgusting. They hold hands—*in church!* None of the fellows will talk to him."

I didn't see what the big deal was. Back in '75, we had had a two-week session on sexual reproduction, like all the other subjects. Most of the kids there were already in couples, sneaking off to low-gee bounceataria and renting private cubes with untraceable cash-tokens. I'd even tussled with one girl, Katebe M'Buto, another exchange student, from United Africa Trading Sphere. I'd picked her up at her apt, and her father had even shaken my hand—they grow up fast in UATS. Of course, I'd never let on to my folks. Pa would've broken an axle. "That's pretty disgusting, all right," I said, unconvincingly.

"You want to go down to the river? I told Amos and Luke that I'd meet them after lunch."

I didn't much feel like it, but I didn't know what else to do. We walked down to the swimming hole, where some boys were already naked, swimming and horsing around. I found myself looking away, conscious of their nudity in a way that I'd never been before—all the boys in town swam there, all summer long.

I turned my back to the group and stripped down, then ran into the water as quick as I could.

I paddled around a little, half-heartedly, and then I found myself being pulled under! My sinuses filled with water and I yelled a stream of bubbles, and closed my mouth on a swallow of water. Strong hands pulled at my ankles. I kicked out as hard as I could, and connected with someone's head. The hands loosened and I shot up like a cork, sputtering and coughing. I ran for the shore, and saw one of the Allen brothers surfacing, rubbing at his head and laughing. The four Allen boys lived on a ranch with their parents out by the salt flats, and we only saw them when they came into town with their folks for supplies. I'd never liked them, but now, I saw red.

"You pig!" I shouted at him. "You stupid, rotten, pig! What the heck do you think you were doing?"

The Allens kept on laughing—I used to know some of their names, but in the time I'd been in '75, they'd grown as indistinguishable as twins: big, hard boys with their heads shaved for lice. They pointed at me and laughed. I scooped up a flat stone from the shore and threw it at the head of the one who'd pulled me under, as hard as I could.

Lucky for him—and me!—I was too angry to aim properly, and the stone hit him in the shoulder, knocking him backwards. He shouted at me—it was like a roar of a wild animal—and the four brothers charged.

Oly appeared at my side. "Run!" he shouted.

I was too angry. I balled my fists and stood my ground. The first one shot out of the water towards me, and punched me so hard in the guts, I saw stars. I fell to the ground, gasping. I looked up at a forest of strong, bare legs, and knew they'd surrounded me.

"It's the sheriff!" Oly shouted. The legs disappeared. I struggled to my knees.

Oly collapsed to the ground beside me, laughing. "Did you see the way they ran? The sheriff never comes down to the river!"

"Thanks," I said, around gasps, and started to get dressed.

"Anytime," he said. "Now, let's do some swimming."

"No, I gotta go home and help Mama," I lied. I didn't feel like going skinny-dipping anymore—maybe never again.

Oly gave me a queer look. "OK. See you."

I went straight home, pelting down the road as fast as I could, not even looking where I was going. I let the door slam behind me and took the stairs two at a time up to the attic ladder, then bolted the trap-door shut behind me and sat in the dark, with my knees in my chest.

Down below, Mama let out a half-hearted, "James? Is that you?" like she always did since I came back home. I ignored her, like always, and she stopped worrying about it, like always.

Pa's last trip had been to the Dalai Lama's court in 1975. The man from the embassy said that he was going to talk with the monks about a "white-paper that the two embassies were jointly presenting on the effect of mimetic ambassadorships on the reincarnated soul." It was all nonsense to me. He'd never arrived. The teleporter said that it had put him down gentle as you like on the floor of the Lama's floating castle over the Caspian Sea, but the monks never saw him.

And that was that.

It had been a month since our return. I'd ventured out into town and looked up my chums, and found them so full of gossip that didn't mean anything to me; so absorbed with games that seemed childish to me; so *strange,* that I'd retreated home. I'd prowled around our house like a burglar at first, and when I came back to the attic, all the numbness that had enveloped me since the man from the State Department had teleported into our apt melted away and I started bawling.

The attic had always been Pa's domain. He'd come up here with whatever crackpot invention he'd ordered this month out of a catalog or one of the expensive, foreign journals he subscribed to, and tinker and swear and hit his thumbnail and tear his pants on a stray dingus and smoke his cheroots and have a heck of a time.

The muffled tread of his feet and the distant cursing while I sat in the parlor downstairs had been the homiest sound I knew. Mama and I would lock eyes every time a particularly forceful round of hollers shook down, and Mama would get a little smile and her eyes would crinkle, and I felt like we were sharing a secret.

Now, the attic was my private domain: there was the elixir shelf, full of patent medicines, hair-tonics, and soothing syrups. There was the bookcase full of wild theories and fantastic adventure stories. There were the crates full of dangerous, coal-fired machines—an automatic clothes-washing-machine, a cherry-pitter, and other devices whose nature I couldn't even guess at. None of them had ever worked, but I liked to run my hands over them, feel the smooth steel of their parts, disassemble and reassemble them. Back in '75, I'd once tried to take the robut-ler apart, just to get a look at how it was all put together, but it was a lost cause—I couldn't even figure out how to get the cover off.

I walked through the cool dark, the only light coming from the grimy attic window, and fondled each piece. I picked up an oilcan and started oiling the joints and bearings and axles of each machine in turn. Pa would have wanted to know that everything was in good working order.

"I think you should be going to school, James," Mama said, at breakfast. I'd already done my morning chores, bringing in the coal, chopping kindling, taking care of the cows and making my bed.

I took another forkful of sausage, and a spoonful of mush, chewed, and looked at my plate.

"It's time, it's time. You can't spend the rest of your life sulking around here. Your father would have wanted us to get on with our lives."

Even though I wasn't looking at her when she said this, I knew that her eyes were bright with tears, the way they always got when she mentioned Pa. His chair sat, empty, at the head of the table. I had another bite of sausage.

"James Arthur Nicholson! Look at me when I speak to you!"

I looked up, reflexively, as I always did when she used my full name. My eyes slid over her face, then focused on a point over her left shoulder.

"Yes'm."

"You're going to school. Today. And I expect to get a good report from Mr. Adelson."

"Yes'm."

We have two schools in New Jerusalem: the elementary school that was built twenty years before, when they put in the wooden side-walks and the town hall; and the non-denominational academy that was built just before I left for 1975.

Miss Tannenbaum, a spinster lady with a moustache and a bristling German accent, terrorized the little kids in the elementary school—I'd been stuck in her class for five long years. Mr. Adelson, who was raised in San Francisco and who had worked as a roustabout, a telegraph operator and a merchant seaman taught the academy, and his wild stories were all Oly could talk about.

He raised one eyebrow quizzically when I came through the door at 8:00 that morning. He was tall, like my pa, but Pa had been as big as an ox, and Mr. Adelson was thin and wiry. He wore rumpled pants and a shirt with a wilted celluloid collar. He had a skinny little beard that made him look like a gentleman pirate, and used some shiny pomade to grease his hair straight back from his high forehead. I caught him reading, thumbing the handwritten pages of a leatherbound volume.

"Mr. Adelson?"

"Why, James Nicholson! What can I do for you, sonny?" New Jerusalem only had but 2,000 citizens, and only a hundred or so in town proper, so of course he knew who I was, but it surprised me to hear him pronounce my name in his creaky, weatherbeaten voice.

"My mother says I have to go to the academy."

"She does, hey? How do you feel about that?"

I snuck a look at his face to see if he was putting me on, but I couldn't tell—he'd raised up his other eyebrow now, and was looking hard at me. There might have been the beginning of a smile on his face, but it was hard to tell with the beard. "I guess it don't matter how I feel."

"Oh, I don't know about that. This is a school, not a prison, after all. How old are you?"

"Fourteen. Sir."

"That would put you in with the seniors. Do you think you can handle their course of study? It's half-way through the semester now, and I don't know how much they taught you when you were over in," he swallowed, "France."

I didn't know what to say to that, so I just stared at my hard, uncomfortable shoes.

"How are your maths? Have you studied geometry? Basic algebra?"

"Yes, sir. They taught us all that." And lots more besides. I had the feeling of icebergs of knowledge floating in my brain, ready to crest the waves and crash against the walls of my skull.

"Very good. We will be studying maths today in the seniors' class. We'll see how you do. Is that all right?"

Again, I didn't know if he was really asking, so I just said, "Yes, sir."

"Marvelous. We'll see you at the 8:30 bell, then. And James —" He paused, waited until I met his gaze. His eyebrows were at rest. "I'm sorry about your father. I'd met him several times. He was a good man."

"Thank you, sir," I said, unable to look away from his stare.

The first half of the day passed with incredible sloth, as I copied down problems to my slate and pretended to puzzle over them before writing down the answer I'd known the minute I saw the question.

At lunch I found a seat at the base of the big willow out front of the school and unwrapped the waxed paper from the thick ham sandwich Mama had fixed me. I munched it and conjugated Latin verbs in my head, trying to make the day pass. Oly and the fellows were roughhousing in the yard, playing follow-the-leader with Amos Gundersen out front, showing off by walking on his hands and then springing upright. Amos' mother came from circus people in Russia, and all the kids in his family wanted to be acrobats when they grew up.

I tried not to watch them.

I was engrossed in a caterpillar that was crawling up my pants-leg when Mr. Adelson cleared his throat behind me. I started, and the caterpillar tumbled to the ground, and then Mr. Adelson was squatting on his long haunches at my side.

"How are you liking your first day, James?" he asked, in his raspy voice.

"It's fine, sir."

"And the work? You're able to keep up with the class?"

"It's not a problem for me. We studied this when I was away."

"Are you bored? Do you need more of a challenge?"

"It's fine, sir." *Unless you want to assign me some large-prime factoring problems.*

"Right, then. Don't hesitate to call on me if things are moving too slowly or too quickly. I mean that."

I snuck another look at him. He seemed sincere.

"Why aren't you playing with your chums?"

"I don't feel like it."

"You just wanted to think?"

"I guess so." Why wouldn't he just leave me alone?

"It's hard to come home, isn't it?"

I stared at my shoes. What did he know about it?

"I've been around the world, you know that? I sailed with a tramp steamer, the *Slippery Trick*. I saw the naked savages of Polynesia, and the voodoo witches that the freed slaves of the Caribbean worship, and the coolies pulling rickshaws in Peking. It was so *hard* to come home to Frisco, after five years at sea."

To my surprise, he sat down next to me, in the dirt and roots at the base of the tree. "You know, aboard the *Trick*, they called me Runnyguts—I threw up every hour for my first month. I was more reliable than the Watch! But they didn't mean anything by it. When you live with a crew for years, you become a different person. We'd be out at sea, nothing but water as far as the eye could see, and we'd be playing cards on-deck. We'd told each other every joke we knew already, and every story about home, and we knew that deck of cards so well, which one had salt-water stains on the back and which one turned up at the corner and which one had been torn, and we'd just scream at the sun, so bored! But then we'd put in to port at some foreign city, and we'd come down the plank in our best clothes, twenty men who knew each other better than brothers, hard and brown from months at sea, and it felt like whatever happened in that strange port-of-call, we'd come out on top."

"And then I came back to the Frisco, and the Captain shook my hand and gave me a sack of gold and saw me off, and I'd never felt so alone, and I'd never seen a place so foreign.

"I went back to my old haunts, the saloons where I'd gone for a beer after a day's work at the docks, and the dance-halls, and the theatres, and I saw my old chums. That was hard, James."

He stopped then. I found myself saying, "How was it hard, Mr. Adelson?"

He looked surprised, like he'd forgotten that he was talking to me. "Well, James, it's like this: when you're away that long, you get to invent yourself all over again. Of course, everyone invents themselves as they grow up. Your chums there,"— he gestured at the boys, who were now trying, with varying success, to turn somersaults, dirtying their school clothes —"they're inventing themselves right now, whether they know it or not. The smart one, the strong one, the brave one, the sad one. It's going on while we watch."

"But when you go away, nobody knows you, and you can be whoever you want. You can shed your old skin and grow a new one. When we put out to sea, I was just a youngster, eighteen years old and fresh from my pa's house. He was a cable car engineer, and wanted me to follow in his shoes, get an apprenticeship and join him there under the hills, oiling the giant pulleys. But no, not me! I wanted to put out to sea and see the world. I'd never been out of the city, can you believe that? The first port where I took shore leave was in Haiti, and when I stepped onto the dock, it was like my life was starting all over again. I got a tattoo, and I drank hard liquor, and gambled in the saloons, and did all the things that a man did, as far as I was concerned." He had a faraway look now, staring at the boys' game without seeing it. "And when I got back onboard, sick and tired and broke, there was a new kid there, a Negro from Port au Prince who'd signed on to be a cabin boy. His name was Jean-Paul, and he didn't speak a word of English and I didn't speak a word of French. But I took him under my wing, James, and acted like I'd been at sea all my life, and showed him the ropes, and taught him to play cards, and bossed him around, and taught him English, one word at a time.

"And that became the new me. Every time a new hand signed on, I would be his teacher, his mentor, his guide."

"And then I came home."

"As far as the folks back home were concerned, I was the kid they'd said good-bye to five years before. My father thought I was still a kid, even though I'd fought pirates and weathered storms. My chums wanted me to be the kid I'd been, and do all the boring, kid things we'd done before I left—riding the trolleys, watching the vaudeville shows, fishing off the docks.

"Even though that stuff was still fun, it wasn't *me*, not anymore. I missed the old me, and felt him slipping away. So, you know what I did?"

"You moved to New Jerusalem?"

"I moved to New Jerusalem. Well, to Salt Lake City, first. I studied with the Jesuits, to be a teacher, then I saw an ad for a teacher in the paper, and I packed my bag and caught the next train. And here I am, not the me that came home from sea, and not the me who I was before I went to sea, but someone in between, a new me—teaching, but on dry land, and not chasing dangerous adventures, but still reading my old log book and smiling."

We sat for a moment, in companionable silence. Then, abruptly, he checked his pocket watch and yelped. "Damn! Lunch was over twenty minutes ago!" He leapt to his feet, as smoothly as a boy, and ran into the schoolhouse to ring the bell.

I folded up the waxed-paper, and thought about this adult who talked to me like an adult, who didn't worry about swearing, or telling me about his adventures, and I made my way back to class.

It went better, the rest of that day.

In '75, Pa had almost never been home, but his presence was always around us.

I'd call the robutler out of its closet and have it affix its electrode fingertips to my temples and juice my endorphins after a hard day at school, and when I was done, the faint smell of Pa's hair-oil, picked up from the 'trodes and impossible to be rid of, would cling to me. Or I'd sit down on the oubliette and find one of Pa's journals from back home, well-thumbed and open to an article on mental telepathy. We did ESP in school, and it was all about a race of alien traders who communicated in geometric thought pictures that took forever to translate. We'd never learned about Magnetism and Astral Projection and all the other things Pa's journals were full of.

And while I never doubted the things in Pa's journals, I never brought them up in class, neither. There were lots of different kinds of truth.

"James?"

"Yes, Mama?" I said, on my way out to chop kindling.

"Did you finish your homework?"

"Yes, Mama."

"Good boy."

Homework had been some math, and some biology, and some geology. I'd done it before I left school.

The report cards came out in the middle of December. Mr. Adelson sealed them with wax in thick brown envelopes and handed them out at the end of the day. Sealing them was a dirty trick—it meant a boy would have to go home not knowing whether to expect a whipping or an extra slice of pie, and the fellows were as nervous as long-tailed cats in a rocking-chair factory when class let out. For once, there was no horseplay afterwards.

I came home and tossed the envelope on the kitchen table without a moment's worry. I'd aced every test, I'd done every take-home assignment, I'd led the class, in a bored, sleepy way, regurgitating the things they'd stuck in my brain in 1975.

I went up to the attic and started reading one of Pa's adventure stories, *Tarzan of the Apes*, by the Frenchman Jules Verne. Pa had all of Verne's books, each of them crisply autographed on the inside cover. He'd met Verne on one of his diplomatic missions, and the two had been like two peas in a pod, to hear him tell of it—they both subscribed to all the same crazy journals.

I was reading my favorite part, where Tarzan meets the man in the balloon, when Mama's voice called from downstairs. "James Arthur Nicholson! Get your behind down here *now*!"

I jumped like I was stung and rattled down the attic stairs so fast I nearly broke my neck and then down into the parlor, where Mama was holding my report card and looking fit to bust.

"Yes, Mama?" I said. "What is it?"

She handed me the report card and folded her arms over her chest. "Explain that, mister. Make it good."

I read the card and my eyes nearly jumped out of my head. The rotten so-and-so had given me F's all the way down, in every subject. Below, in his seaman's hand, he'd written, "James' performance this semester has disappointed me gravely. I would like it very much if I could meet with you and he, Mrs. Nicholson, at your earliest convenience, to discuss his future at the academy. Signed, Rbt. Adelson."

Mama grabbed my ear and twisted. I howled and dropped the card. Before I knew what was happening, she had me over her knee and was paddling my bottom with her open hand, hard.

"I don't"—whack—"know *what*"—whack—"you think"—whack—"you're doing, James."—whack—"If your *father*"—whack, *whack*—"were here,"—whack—"he'd switch you"—whack—"within an inch of your life." And she gave me a load more whacks.

I was too stunned even to cry or howl. Pa had only beat me twice in all the time I'd known him. Mama had *never* beat me. My bottom ached distantly, and I felt tears come to my eyes.

"Well, what do you have to say for yourself?"

"Mama, it's a mistake —" I began.

"You're durn right!" she said.

"No, really! I did all my homework! I passed all the exams! I showed 'em to you! You saw 'em!" The unfairness of it made my heart hammer in time to the throbbing of my backside.

Mama's breath fumed angrily out of her nose. "You go straight to your room and *stay there*. We're going to see Mr. Adelson first thing tomorrow morning."

"What about my chores?" I said.

"Oh, don't worry about that. You'll have *plenty* of chores to do when I let you out."

I went to my room and stripped down, and lay on my tummy and cracked my window so the icy winter air blew over my backside. I cried a vale of tears, and rained down miserable, mean curses on everyone: Mama, Pa, and especially the lying, snakey, backstabbing Runnyguts Adelson.

Mama didn't get any less mad through the night, but when she came to my door at cock-crow, she seemed to be holding it in better. My throat and eyes were sore as sandpaper from crying, and Mama gave me exactly five minutes to wash up and dress before dragging me out to the horse barn. She'd already hitched up our team and refused my hand when I tried to help her up.

I'd been angry and righteous when I woke, but seeing Mama's towering, barely controlled fury changed my mood to dire terror. I stared out at the trees and farms as we rode into town, feeling like a condemned man being taken to the gallows.

Mama pulled up out front of the academy and marched me around back to the teacher's cottage. She rapped on the door and waited, blowing clouds of steam out of her nose into the frosty morning air.

Mr. Adelson answered the door in shirtsleeves and suspenders, unshaved and bleary. His hair, normally neatly oiled and slicked, stuck out like frayed broom-straw. The muscles on his thin arms stood out like snakes. He blinked at us, standing on his doorstep. "Mrs. Nicholson!" he said.

"Mr. Adelson," my mother said. "We've come to discuss James' report card."

Mr. Adelson smoothed his hair back and stepped aside. "Please, come in. Can I offer you some coffee?"

"No, thank you," Mama said, primly, standing in his foyer. He held out his hand for her coat and kerchief and she handed them to him. I took off my coat and struggled out of my boots. He took them both and put them away in a closet.

"I'm going to have some coffee. Are you sure I can't offer you a cup?"

"No. Thank you, all the same."

"As you wish." He disappeared down the dark hallway, and Mama and I found our way into his tiny parlor. Books were stacked every which way, dusty and precarious. Mama and I sat down in a pair of cushioned chairs, and Mr. Adelson came in, holding two mugs of coffee. He set one down next to Mama on the floor, then smacked himself in the forehead. "You said no, didn't you? Sorry, I'm not quite awake yet. Well, leave it there—there's cream in it, maybe the cat will have some."

He settled himself onto another chair and sipped at his coffee. "Let's start over, shall we? Hello, Mrs. Nicholson. Hello, James. I understand you're here to discuss James' report card."

Mama sat back a little in her chair and let hint of a sardonic smile show on her face. "Yes, we are. Forgive my coming by unannounced."

"Oh, it's nothing."

Mr. Adelson drank more coffee. Mama smoothed her skirts. I kicked my feet against the rungs of my chair. Finally, it was too much for me. "What's the big idea, anyway?" I said, glaring daggers at him. "I don't deserve no F!"

"Any F," Mr. Adelson corrected. "Why don't you think so?"

"Well, because I did all my homework. I gave the right answers in class. I passed all the tests. It ain't fair!"

"Not fair," my mama corrected, gently. She was staring distractedly at Mr. Adelson.

"What you say is true enough, James. What grade do you suppose you should've gotten?"

"Why, an A! An A-plus! Perfect!" I said, glaring again at him, daring him to say otherwise.

"Is that what an A-plus is for, James? Perfection?"

"Sure," I said, opening my mouth without thinking.

Mama shifted her stare to me. She was looking even more thoughtful.

"Why do you suppose you go to school?"

"'Cause Mama says I have to," I said, sullenly.

"James!" Mama said.

"Oh, I suppose it's to learn things," I said.

Mr. Adelson smiled and nodded, the way he did when one of the students got the right answer in class. "Well?"

"Well, what?" I said.

"What did you learn this semester?"

"Why, everything you taught! Geometry! Algebra! Latin! Geography! Biology! Physics! Grammar!"

"I see," he said. "James, what's the formula for determining the constant in the second derivative of an equation?"

I knew that one: it was one of Newton's dirty calculus proofs. "It's a trick question. There's no way to get the constant of a second derivative."

"Exactly right," he said.

"Yes," I said, and folded my arms across my chest.

"Where did you learn that?"

"In —" I started to say 1975, but caught myself. "In France."

"Yes."

"Yes," I said. The fingers of dawn crept across my comprehension. "Oh."

Mama smiled at me.

"But it's not fair! So what if I already knew everything before I started? I still did all the work."

"Why are you in school, James?" Mr. Nicholson asked me again.

"To learn."

"Well, then I think you'd better start learning something, don't you? You're the brightest student in the class. You're certainly smarter than I am—I'm just an old sailor struggling along with the rest of the class. But you, you've *got it*. You've been marking time in class all semester, and I daresay you haven't learned a single thing since you started. That's why you got F's."

"Mr. Adelson," Mama said. "Am I to understand that James performed all his assignments satisfactorily?"

It was Mr. Adelson's turn to squirm. "Yes, but madam, you have to understand —"

Mama waved aside his objections. "If James satisfactorily completed all the work assigned to him, then I think he should have a grade that reflects that, don't you?" She took a sip of her coffee.

"Yes, well —"

"However, you do have a point. I didn't send my son to your school so that he could mark time, as you put it. I sent him there to learn. To be *taught*. Have you taught him anything, Mr. Adelson?"

Mr. Adelson looked so all-fired sad, I forgave him the report card and spoke up. "Yes, Mama."

Mama swiveled her head to me. "Really?"

"Yes. He taught me what I was at school for. Just now."

"I see," Mama said. "This is very good coffee, Mr. Adelson."

"Thank you," he said, and sipped at his.

"James," Mr. Adelson said. "You've learned your first lesson. What do you propose your second should be?"

"I dunno," I said, and went back to kicking the rungs of the chair.

"What is it that you have been doing since you came back to town, son?" he asked.

"Hanging around in the attic, mostly. Reading. Tinkering. Like my pa."

"My husband's machines and journals are up there," Mama explained.

"And his books," I said.

"Books?" Mr. Adelson looked suddenly interested. "What kind of books?"

"Adventure stories. Stevenson. Wells. Some of it's in French. We have all of Verne."

"Well, perhaps that can be your next assignment. I would like to see an original composition of no less than twenty pages, discussing each work of Verne's, charting his literary progress. Due January fifth, please."

"Twenty pages!" I said. "But it's the holidays!"

"Very well. Whatever length the piece turns out is fine. But be sure you do justice to each work."

By the time I got through with the assignment, it was thirty-eight pages long. I never thought I could write that much but it kept on coming, new thoughts about each book, each scene, the different worlds Verne had built: the fantastic slopes of Barsoom, the sinister Island of Dr. Moreau . . . Each one spawned a new insight. I felt like the Verne's detective, Sherlock Holmes, assembling all of the seemingly insignificant details into some kind of coherent picture, finding the improbable links between the wildly different stories the Frenchman told.

Mama was thrilled to see me working, papers spread out all around me on the kitchen table—I could've used Pa's study, but it felt like an invasion, somehow—writing until my wrists cramped. She let me get away without doing my chores, rising early to milk the cow, bringing in the eggs from the henhouse, even chopping the kindling. Just so long as I was writing, she was happy to let me go on shirking my responsibilities.

Even on Christmas Eve, I was too distracted to really enjoy the smells of goose and ham and the stuffing Mama spent days preparing. I was still writing when she told me to go change and set the table for three.

"We're having Mr. Johnston to dinner," she said.

I made a face. Mr. Johnston was the only one in town that I could have talked to about my time in 1975, but I never did. He had a way of bossing a fellow around while seeming to be nice to him. He still ran Pa's store, using ladders to reach the high shelves that Pa had just plucked things off of. I had to see him when Mama sent me on errands there, but I made sure that I left as quickly as I could. Mama kept saying that I should ask him for a job, but I was pretty good at changing the subject whenever it came up.

I put away my papers and changed into my Sunday clothes. I'd been hinting to Mama lately that a boy just wasn't complete without a puppy, so I put an extra shine on my shoes and said a quick prayer that I wouldn't find socks and picture-books under the tree.

Mr. Johnstone arrived with a double-armload of gifts. Well, he *did* run my pa's store, after all, so he could get things wholesale. I took his parcels from him and set them under the tree. Then that dandified sissy actually *kissed* my mama on the cheek, lifting a sprig of mistletoe up with one hand. When Pa and Mama stood together, she'd barely come up to his shoulder, while Mr. Johnstone had to stand on tiptoe to get the mistletoe over their heads. "Merry Christmas, Ulla," he said.

She took his hands and said, "Merry Christmas, James."

I wanted to be sick.

Mr. Johnstone had a whiskey in our parlor before we ate, sitting in my pa's chair, smoking a cigar from my pa's humidor. Mama ordered me to keep him company while she set out the meal.

"Do they call you Jimmy?" he asked me, staring down his long, pointy nose.

"No, sir. James."

"It's a fine name, isn't it? Served me well, man and boy." He made a face that was supposed to be funny, like he'd bit into a lemon.

"I like it fine, sir."

"Are you having any problems adjusting, now that you're home? Finding it hard to relate to the other fellows?"

"No, sir."

"You don't find it strange, after seeing 1975?"

"No, sir. It's home."

"Ha!" he said, as though I'd said something profound. "I guess it is, at that. Say, why don't you come by the store some time? I just got some samples from a new candy company in Oregon, and I need to get an unbiased opinion before I order." He gave me a pinched smile, like he thought he was Santa Claus.

"Mama doesn't like me eating sweets," I said, and stared at my reflection in my shoes.

Mama rescued me by coming into the parlor then, looking young and pretty in her best dress. "Dinner is served, gentlemen."

We followed her into the dining room, and Mr. Johnstone took my pa's seat at the head of the table and carved the goose. Even though the bird was brown and juicy, I found I didn't have any appetite.

"I have word from Pondicherry," Mr. Johnstone said, as he poured gravy over his second helping of mashed potatoes.

"Yes?" Mama said.

"Who's he?" I asked.

"Your father's successor," Mr. Johnstone said. "A British officer from New Delhi. A fat little man, and awfully full of himself."

I repressed a snort. For my money Mr. Johnstone was as full of himself as one man could be. I couldn't imagine a blacker kettle.

"He says that Nussbaum, from 1952 New York, has rolled back relations with extraterrestrials by fifty years. He sold a Centurian half a million defective umbrellas from his brother-in-law's factory. The New Yorkers are all defending him. Caveat emptor."

"I never could keep track of who was friendly and who wasn't," Mama said. "It was all Greek to me. Politics."

Mr. Johnstone opened his mouth to explain, but Mama held up one hand. "No, no, I don't *want* to understand. Les used to lecture me about this from dawn to dusk." She smiled a little sad smile and stared off at the cabbage-roses on our dining-room walls. Mr. Johnstone put one hand over hers.

"He was a good man, Ulla."

Mama stood and smoothed her skirts. "I'll get dessert."

I didn't get a puppy. Mr. Johnstone gave me an air-rifle that I was sure Mama would have fits over, but she just smiled. She gave me a beautiful fountain-pen and a green blotter and a ream of creamy, thick paper.

The pen made the most beautiful, jet-black marks, and the paper drank it up like a thirsty man in the desert. I recopied my essay the next day, sitting with Mama in the parlor while she darned socks. Mr. Johnstone had given her a tin of cosmetics from Paris, that he'd ordered in special. I'd heard Mama say that only dancehall girls wore makeup, but she blushed when he gave it to her. I gave her a carving I'd done, of the robutler we'd had in '75. I'd whittled it out of a block of pine, and sanded it and oiled it until it was as smooth as silk.

Oly Sweynsdatter came by after supper and asked if I wanted to go out and play with the fellows. To my surprise, I found I did. We had a grand afternoon pelting each other with snow-balls, a game that turned into a full-scale war, as all the older boys back from high-school came out and joined in, and then, later, all the men, even the Sheriff and Mr. Adelson. I never laughed so much in all my life, even when I got one right in the ear.

Mr. Adelson led a charge of adults against the fort that most of the academy boys were hiding behind, but I saw him planning it and started laying in ammunition long before they made their go, and we sent them back with their tails between their legs. I hit him smack in the behind with one ball as he dove for cover.

Oly's mother gave us both good, Svenska hot cocoa afterwards, with fresh whipped cream, and Oly and I exchanged gifts. He gave me a tin soldier, a Confederate who was caught in the act of falling over backwards, clutching his chest. I gave him my best marble. We followed his mother around their house, recounting the adventures in the snow until she told me it was time for me to go home.

School started again, and I went in early the first day to turn in my paper. Mr. Adelson took it without comment and scanned the first few paragraphs. "Thank you, James, I think this will do nicely. I'll have it graded for you in the afternoon."

I met Oly out in the orchard, where he was chopping kindling for the school's stove, a job we all took turns at. "I hear you might be getting a new Pa for Christmas," he said. He gave me a smile that meant something, but I couldn't guess what.

"What is that supposed to mean?" I asked.

"My mama says your mama had old man Johnstone over for Christmas dinner. And the widow Ott told my mama that she'd connected one or two calls between your house and the store every day in the last month. My mama says that Johnstone is court-ing your mama."

"Mrs. Ott isn't supposed to talk about the calls she connects," I said, as my mind reeled. "It's like a telegraph operator: it's a confidential trust." Mr. Adelson had told me that, once when he was telling me stories about his life before he went to sea.

"So, is it true?"

"No!" I said, surprising myself with my vehemence. "My mama just didn't want him to be alone at Christmas."

Oly swung the axe a few more times. "Well, sure. But what about all the telephone calls?"

"That's business. The store is still partly ours. Mama's just look-ing after our interests."

"If you say so," he said.

I shoved him hard. I drew a line in the snow with my toe. "I *do* say so. Step across the line if you say otherwise!"

Oly got to his feet and looked at me. "I don't want to fight with you, James. I was just tellin' you what my mama said."

"Well, your mama ought to mind her own business," I said, bait-ing him.

That did it. He stepped over and popped me one, right in the nose. Oly and I had been chums since we could walk, and we'd had a few fights in our days but this time it was different. I was so *angry* at him, at my mama, at my pa, at New Jerusalem, and we just kept on swinging at each other until Mr. Adelson came out to ring the bell and separated us. My nose was sore and I was limping, and I'd torn Oly's jacket and bent his fingers back, so he cradled his hand in the crook of his arm.

"Boys!" Mr. Adelson said. "What the hell do you think you're doing? You're supposed to be friends."

His language shocked me, but I was still plenty angry. "He's no friend of mine!" I said.

"That's fine with me," Oly said and glared at me.

The other kids were milling around, and Mr. Adelson gave us both a look that could melt steel, then rang the bell.

I could hardly concentrate in class that day. My mama getting married? A new pa? It couldn't be true. But in my mind, I kept seeing my mama and that Johnstone kissing under the mistletoe, and him sitting in my pa's chair, drinking his whiskey.

Oly's desk was next to mine, and he kept shooting me dirty looks. Finally, I leaned over and whispered, "Cut it out, you idiot."

Oly said, "You're the idiot. I think you got your brains scrambled in France, James."

"I'll scramble your brains!"

"Gentlemen," said Mr. Adelson. "Do you have something you'd like to share with the class?"

"No sir," we said together, and exchanged glares.

"James, perhaps you'd like to come up to the front and finish the lesson?"

"Sir?" I said, looking at the blackboard. He'd been going through quadratics, an elaborate first-principles proof.

"I believe you know this already, don't you? Come up to the front and finish the lesson."

Slowly, I got up from my desk, leaving my slate on my desk, and made my way up to the front. Some of the kids giggled. I picked up a piece of chalk from the chalk-well, and started to write on the board.

Mr. Adelson walked back to my seat and sat down. I stopped and looked over my shoulder, and he gave me a little scooting gesture that meant *go on*. I did, and by the end of the hour, I found that I was enjoying myself. I stopped frequently for questions, and erased the board over and over again, filling it with steady columns of numbers and equations. I stopped noticing Mr. Adelson in my seat, and when he stood and thanked me and told us we could eat our lunches, it seemed like no time at all had passed.

Mr. Adelson looked up from my essay. "James, I'd like to have a chat with you. Stay behind, please."

"Sit," he said, offering me the chair at his desk. He sat on one of the front-row desks, and stared at me for a long moment.

"What was that mess this morning all about, James?" he asked.

"Oly and I had an argument," I said, sullenly.

"I could see that. What was it about, if you don't mind my asking?"

"He said something about my mama," I said.

"I see," he said. "Well, having met your mother, I feel confident in saying that she's more than capable of defending herself. Am I right?"

"Yes, sir," I said.

"Then we won't see a repeat?"

"No, sir," I said. I didn't plan on talking to Oly ever again.

"Then we'll say no more about it. Now, about this morning's lesson: you did very well."

"It was a dirty trick," I said.

He grinned like a pirate. "I suppose it was. I wouldn't have played it on you if I didn't have every confidence in your abilities, though." He leaned across and picked up my essay from his desk. "It was this that convinced me, really. This is as good as anything I've seen in scholarly journals. I've half a mind to send it to the *Idler*."

"I'm just a kid!"

"You're an extraordinary boy. I'm tempted to let you teach all the classes, and take up whittling."

He said it so deadpan, I couldn't tell if he was kidding me. "Oh, you can't do that! I'm not nearly ready to take over."

He laughed. "You're readier than you think, but I expect the town council would stop my salary unless I did *some* of the work around here. Still, I think that's the most active I've seen you since you came to my class, and I'm running out of ideas to keep you busy. Maybe I'll keep you teaching maths. I'll give you my lesson plan to take home before school's out."

"Yes, sir."

Mr. Adelson gave me a stack of papers tied up with twine after he dismissed the class for the day. I went home and did my chores, then unwrapped the parcel in the parlor. The lesson plans were there, laid out, day by day, and in the center of them was a smaller parcel, wrapped in colored paper. "Merry Christmas," was written across it, in his hand.

I opened it, and found a slim book. *War of the Worlds*, by Verne. For some reason, it rang a bell. I thought that maybe it had been on our bookcase in '75, but somehow, it hadn't made it back home with us. I opened it, and read the inscription he'd written: "From one traveller to another, Merry Christmas."

I forced myself to read the lesson plans for the next month before I allowed myself to start the Verne, and once I started, I found I couldn't stop. Mama had to drag me away for dinner.

My trip back to 1975 wasn't planned, but it wasn't an accident, either. We'd gotten a new load of hay in for our team, and mama added stacking it in the horse barn to my chores. I'd been consciously avoiding the horse barn since Pa had disappeared. Every time I looked at it, I felt a little hexed, a little frightened.

But Mama had a philosophy: a boy should face up to his fears. She'd been terrified of spiders when she was a girl, and she told me that she had made a point of picking up every spider she saw and letting it crawl around on her face. After a year of that, she said, she never met a spider that frightened her.

Mama had been sending me to the store more and more, too, and having Mr. Johnstone over for dinner every Friday night. She knew I didn't like him one little bit, and she said that I would just have to learn to live with what I didn't like, and if that was the only thing I learned from her, it would be enough.

I preferred the horse barn.

I worked close to the door the first day, which is no way to do it, of course: if you blocked the door, it just made it harder to get at the back when the time came. The way to do it is to first clear out whatever hay is left over, move it out to the pasture, and then fill in from the back forward.

Mama told me so, that first night, when she came out to inspect my work. "You sure must love working out here," she said. "If you do it that way, you'll be out here stacking for twice as long. Well, you have your fun, but I still expect you to be getting your home-work and regular chores done. Come in and clean up for supper now."

I jammed the pitchfork into a bale, and washed for supper.

The next afternoon, I resolved to do it right. I moved the bales I'd stacked up by the door to a corner, and then started cleaning out the back. Before long, I'd uncovered the door into 1975. "James," Mama called, from the house. "Dinner!"

I took a long look at the door. The wood on the edges had aged to the silvery-brown of the rest of the barn-boards, and it looked like it had been there forever. I could hardly remember a time when it wasn't there.

I went in for supper.

The next morning, I picked up my lunch and my schoolbooks, kissed Mama good-bye, and walked out. I stood on our porch for a long time, staring at the horse barn. I remembered the brave explorers in Verne's books. I looked over my shoulder at the closed door of our house, then walked slowly to the horse barn. I swung the door open, then walked to the back. The triple-bolts had rusted somewhat and took real shoving to slide back. One of them was stubborn, so I picked up the rake and pried it back with the han-dle, thinking of how ingenious that was.

I gave the door my shoulder and shoved, and it swung back, complaining on its hinges. On the other side was the still-familiar dark of our 1975 apartment. I stepped into it, and closed the door behind me.

"Lights," I said, and they came on.

The old place was just like the day we left it. It wasn't even dusty, and as I heard the familiar trundle of the robutler, I knew why. My pa's easy chair sat in the parlor, with a print-out of the day's *Salt Lake City Bugler* folded on the side table. I walked to one wall and laid my palm against it, the familiar cool glassy stuff it was made of. "Window," I said, and wiped a line across the wall. Wherever my hand wiped went transparent. It was a sunny day in 1975–1980, by then, but it would be '75 in my mind forever. Under the dome, Greater Salt Lake was warm and tranquil. I saw boys my age scooting around in jet-packs, dodging hover-traffic.

Pa liked to open a big, square window when he came home, and sit in his easy chair and smoke a stinky cigar and read the paper and cluck over it —"Well, well, well," he'd say, and "How *about* that?" Sometimes, he'd have a tumbler of whiskey. He'd given me some, once, and the stuff had burned like turpentine and I swore I wouldn't try it again for a long, long time.

I sat in Pa's easy chair and snapped up the newspaper, the way he used to. "Panorama," I said, and Pa's square window opened before me. "Whiskey," I said, and "Cigar," because I was never one for half-measures. The robutler trundled over to me with a tumbler and a White Owl in its hover-field. I plucked them out. Cautiously, I put the cigar between my lips. The robutler extruded a long, snaky arm with a flame, and lit it. I took a deep puff, and coughed convulsively. Unthinking, I took a gulp of whiskey. I felt like my lungs had turned inside-out.

I finished both the whiskey and the cigar before I got up, taking cautious puffs and tiny sips, forcing myself.

My head swam, and nausea nearly drowned me. I staggered into the WC, and hung my head in the oubliette for an eternity, but nothing was coming up. I moved into my old bedroom and splayed out on my bed, watching the ceiling spin. "Lights," I managed to croak, and the room went dark.

When I woke in the morning, the walls were at half-opacity, the normal 0700 schedule, and I dragged myself out of bed.

The robutler had extruded the table and set out my breakfast, ham and eggs and a big bulb of milk. One look at it sent me over the edge, and I left a trail of sick all the way to the WC.

When I was done, I was as wrung-out as a washcloth. My head pounded. The robutler was quietly cleaning up my mess. I started to order it to clear away breakfast, but discovered that I was miraculously hungry. I ate everything on the table and seconds, besides, and had the robutler juice my temples and clear away my headache. I dialed the walls to full transparency, and watched the traffic go by.

The robutler maneuvered itself into my field of vision and flashed a clock on its chest-plate: 0800 0800 0800. It was my old school-alarm. It snapped me back to reality. My mama was going to whip me raw! She must've been worried sick.

I stood up and ran for the door. It was closed. I punched my code into its panel, and waited. Nothing happened. I calmed myself and punched it again. Still nothing. After trying it a hundred times, I convinced myself that it had been changed.

I summoned the robutler and asked it for the code. Its chest-panel lit up: BAD PROGRAM.

That's when I started to really worry. I was near to tears when I remembered the emergency override. I punched it in.

Nothing happened.

I think I started crying around then. I was stuck in 1975!

I'm not a stupid little kid. I didn't spend much time pewling. Instead, I went to the phone and dialed the police. The screen stayed blank. Feeling like I was in a dream, I went to the teleporter and dialed for my old school and stepped in. I failed to teleport.

Reality sank in.

All outside services to the apartment had been shut off when we moved out. The only things that still worked were the ones that ran off our reactor, a squat armored box on the apartment's underbelly. The door in New Jerusalem worked, but on the 1975 side, it needed to communicate with the central office to approve any passage.

I thought about sitting tight and waiting. Mama would be sick with worry, and would check the barn eventually and see the shot bolts. She'd speak to Mr. Johnstone, who would send a telegram to Paris, and they would relay the message to 1975, and voilà, I'd be rescued. I'd get the whipping of my life, and do extra chores until I was seventy, but it was better than starving to death after the apartment's pantry ran out. I felt hungry just thinking about it.

Still, there was a better way. The null-gee doughnut that our apartment was spoked into had a supply of escape-jumpers, single-use jet-packs with a simple transponder that screamed for help on all the emergency channels. I could ride one of these down into Greater Salt Lake, wait for the police. The more I thought about this plan, the better it sounded. Better, anyway, than sitting around like a fairytale princess, waiting for rescue. In my mind, I was the rescuing type, not the kind that needed rescuing.

Besides, there wasn't much better than riding around in one of those jet-packs.

I cycled the emergency lock into the doughnut, unracked a pack and a jumpsuit that looked like it would fit me, and suited up. The pack whined as it powered up and ran through its diagnostics. I checked the idiot-lights to make sure they were all green, feeling like a real man of action, then I stepped into the exterior lock and jumped, arms and legs streamlined, toes pointed.

The jet-pack coughed to life and kicked me gently, then started lowering me to the ground. The emergency beacon's idiot-light came on, and I heaved a sigh of relief and got comfortable.

The flight was peaceful and dreamlike, a slow descent over the gleaming metal city. I was so engrossed with the view that I didn't see the packjackers until they were already on me. They hit me high and low, two kids about my age with tricked-out custom jet-packs with their traffic beacons broken off. One snagged my knees and hugged them to his chest, while the other took me at the armpits. A voice shouted in my ear: "I'm cutting your pack loose. This is a very, very sharp knife, and when I'm done, I'll be the only thing holding you up. *Don't squirm.*"

I didn't even have the chance to squirm. By the time the speech was finished, I was separated from my pack, and I spun over upside-down, and watched it continue its descent, straps dangling in the wind. My hair hung down, and blood filled my head, reawakening my headache. Reflexively, I twisted to get a look at my kidnappers, but stopped immediately as I felt their grips loosen. I squeezed my eyes shut and prayed.

The three of us dove fast and hard, and I tasted that second helping of breakfast again before we leveled off. I risked a peek, then squeezed my eyes shut again. We were speeding through the lower levels of Greater Salt Lake, the unmanned freight corridors, impossibly claustrophobic, and at our speed, dangerous.

We cornered tightly so many times that I lost count, and then we slowed to a stop. They dumped me to the ground, steel traction-plate. The wind was knocked out of me, and I was barely conscious of the hands that untabbed my jumpsuit, then began methodically turning out the pockets of my clothes.

"What the hell are you wearing, kid?" one of them asked. It was the same one who'd warned me about squirming. Hearing his voice a second time, I realized that he was younger than I was, maybe ten or eleven. Even then, it didn't occur to me to fight back—he had a knife sharp enough to cut through the safety strapping on my pack.

"Clothes. I'm from 1898—my pa's an ambassador. I don't have any money." I struggled into a sitting position, and was knocked onto my back again.

"Stay down and you won't get hurt," the same voice said. It was young enough that I couldn't tell if it was a boy or a girl. Small hands pressed into my eyes. "No peeking, now."

Another set of hands systematically rifled my coat and pants, then cut them loose and gave the same treatment to my underpants and shirt. I blushed as they were cut loose, too.

"You really don't have any money!" the voice said.

"I said so, didn't I?"

The voice said a dirty word that would've gotten it beaten black-and-blue back home, and then the hands were gone. I looked up just in time to see two small figures jetting away upwards.

I was naked, sitting on a catwalk above a freight corridor, three-quarters of a century and God-knew-how-many miles from home. I didn't cry. I was too worried to cry. I kicked my ruined clothes down into the freight corridor and pulled on the jumpsuit.

Some hero I was!

It was hard work, climbing staircase after staircase, up to the shopping levels. By the time I reached a level where I could see the sky, I was dripping with sweat and my headache had returned.

Foot traffic was light, but what was there was pretty frightening. I'd gone walking in '75 before of course, but Greater Salt Lake was a big place, and there were parts of it that an ambassador's son would never get to see.

This was one of them. The shopfronts were all iris-open air-locks, and had been painted around to look like surprised mouths, or eyes, or, in one fascinating case, a woman's private parts. Mostly, they were betting shops, or bars, or low-rent bounceaterias. Even in 1975, the Saints had some influence in Salt Lake, and the bars and brothels were pretty shameful places, where no respectable person would be caught.

The other pedestrians on the street were mostly off-worlders, either spacers in uniform or extees. In some cases, it was hard to tell which was which.

I kind of slunk along, sticking to the walls, hands in my pockets. I kept my eyes down, except when I was looking around for a public phone. After several blocks, I realized that no one was paying any attention to me, and I took my hands out of my pockets. The sun filtered down over me, warm through the big dome, and I realized that even though I'd gotten myself stuck in '75, been 'jacked, and left in the worst neighborhood in the whole state, I'd landed on my feet. The thought made me smile. Another kid, say Oly, wouldn't have coped nearly as well.

I still hadn't spied a public phone. I figured that the taprooms would have a phone, otherwise, how could a drunk call his wife and tell her he was going to be late coming home? I picked a bar whose airlock was painted to look like a brick tunnel and walked in.

The airlock irised shut behind me and I blinked in the gloom. My nose was assaulted with sickly sweet incense, and stale liquor, and cigar smoke.

The place was tiny, and crowded with dented metal tables and chairs that were bolted to the floorplates. A woman stood behind the bar, looking hard and brassy and cheap, watching a soap opera on her vid. A spacer sat in one corner, staring at his bulb of beer.

The bartender looked up. "Get lost, kid," she said. "No minors allowed."

"Sorry, ma'am," I said. "I just wanted to use your telephone. I was packjacked, and I need to call the police."

The bartender turned back to her soap opera. "Go peddle it somewhere else, sonny. The phone's for customers only."

"Please," I said. "My father's an ambassador, from 1898? I don't have any money, and I'm stuck here. I won't be a minute."

The spacer looked up from his drink. "Get lost, the lady said," he slurred at me.

"I'll buy something," I said.

"You just said you don't have any money," the bartender said.

"I'll pay for it when the police get here. The embassy will cover it."

"No credit," she said.

"You're not going to let me use your phone?" I said.

"That's right," she said, still staring at her vid.

"I'm a stranger, an ambassador's son, who's been robbed. A kid. Stuck here, broke and alone, and you won't let me use your phone to call the police?"

"That's about the size of things," she said.

"Well, I guess my pa was right. The whole world went to hell after 1914. No manners, no human decency."

"You're breaking my heart," she said.

"Fine. Be that way. Send me back out on the street, deny me a favor that won't cost you one red cent, just because I'm a stranger."

"Shut *up*, kid, for chrissakes," the spacer said. "I'll stand him to a Coke, if that's what it takes. Just let him use the phone and get out of here. He's giving me a headache."

"Thank you, sir," I said, politely.

The bartender switched her vid over to phone mode, poured me a Coke, and handed me the vid.

The policeman who showed up a few minutes later stuck me in the back of his cruiser, listened to my story, scanned my retinas, confirmed my identity, and retracted the armor between the back and front seats.

"I'll take you to the station house," he said. "We'll contact your embassy, let them handle it from there."

"What about the kids who 'jacked me?" I asked.

The cop turned the jetcar's conn over to wire-fly mode and turned around. "You got any description?"

"Well, they had really nice packs on, with the traffic beacons snapped off. One was red, and I think the other was green. And they were young. Ten or eleven."

The cop punched at his screen. "Kid," he said, "I got over three million minors eight to eleven, flying packs less than a year old. The most popular color is red. Second choice, green. Where would you like me to start? Alphabetically?"

"Sorry, sir, I didn't realize."

"Sure," he said. "Whatever."

"I guess I'm not thinking very clearly. It's been a long day."

The cop looked over to me and smiled. "I guess it has, at that. Don't worry, kid, we'll get you home all right."

They gave me a fresh jumpsuit, sat me on a bench, called the embassy, and forgot about me. A long, boring time later, a fat man with walrus moustaches and ruddy skin showed up.

"On your feet, lad," he said. "I'm Pondicherry, your father's successor. You've made quite a mess of things, haven't you?" He had a clipped, British accent, with a hint of something else. I remembered Mr. Johnstone saying he'd been in India. He wore a standard unisex jumpsuit, with his ambassadorial sash overtop of it. He looked ridiculous.

"Sorry to have disturbed you, sir," I said.

"I'm sure you are," he said. "Come along, we'll see about fixing this mess."

He used the station's teleporter to bring me to his apartment. It was as ridiculous as his uniform, and in the same way. He'd taken the basic elegant simplicity of a standard 1975 unit and draped all kinds of silly trophies and models overtop of it: lions' heads and sabers and model ships and framed medals and savage masks and dolls.

"You may look, but not touch, do you understand me?" he said, as we stepped out of the teleporter.

"Yes, sir," I said. If anyone else had said it, I would have been offended, but coming from this puffed-up pigeon, it didn't sting much.

He went to a vid and punched impatiently at the screen while I prowled the apartment. The bookcase was full of old friends, books by the Frenchman, of course, and more, with strange names like Wells and Burroughs and Shelley. I looked over a long, stone-headed spear, and the curve of an elephant's tusk, and a collection of campaign ribbons and medals under glass. I returned to the bookcase: something had been bothering me. There, there it was: *War of the Worlds*, the book that Mr. Adelson had given me for Christmas.

But there was something wrong with the spine of this one: instead of Jules Verne, the author's name was H.G. Wells. I snuck a look over my shoulder; Pondicherry was still stabbing at the screen. I snuck the book off the shelf and turned to the title page: "War of the Worlds, by Herbert George Wells." I turned to the first chapter:

The Eve of the War

No one would have believed in the last years of the nineteenth century that this world was being watched keenly and closely by intelligences greater than man's and yet as mortal as his own; that as men busied themselves about their various concerns they were scrutinized and studied, perhaps almost as narrowly as a man with a microscope might scrutinize the transient creatures that swarm and multiply in a drop of water.

It was just as I remembered it, every word, just as it was in the Verne. I couldn't begin to explain it.

A robutler swung out of its niche with a sheaf of papers. I startled at the noise, then reflexively stuck the book in my jumpsuit. The robutler delivered them to Pondicherry, who stuffed them in a briefcase.

"The embassy will be able to return you home by courier route in three hours. Unfortunately, I don't have the luxury of waiting around here until then. I have an important meeting to attend—you'll have to come along."

"Yes, sir," I said, trying to sound eager and helpful.

"Don't say anything, don't touch anything. This is very sensitive."

"No, sir, I won't. Thank you, sir."

The meeting was in a private room in a fancy restaurant, one that I'd been to before for an embassy Christmas party. Mama had drunk two glasses of sherry, and had flushed right to the neck of her dress. We'd had roast beef, and a goose wrapped inside a huge squash, the size of a barrel, like they grew on the Moon.

Pondicherry whisked through the lobby, and the main dining room, and then up a narrow set of stairs, without checking to see if I was following. I dawdled a little, remembering Pa laughing and raising his glass in toast after toast.

I caught up with Pondicherry just as he was ordering, speaking brusquely into the table. Another man sat opposite him. Pondicherry looked up at me and said, "Have you dined, boy?"

"No, sir."

He ordered me a plate of calf livers in cream sauce, which is about the worst thing you can feed a boy, if you ask me, which he didn't. "Sit down," he said. "Mr. Nussbaum, Master James Nicholson. I am temporarily *in loco parentis*, until he can be sent home."

Nussbaum smiled and extended his hand. He was wearing a grey suit, with a strange cut, and a black tie. His fingers dripped with heavy gold rings, and his hair, while short, still managed to look fancy and a little sissy-fied. "Good to meetcha, son. You Lester's boy?"

"Yes, sir, he was my pa."

"Good man. A damned shame. What are you doing here? Playing hooky?"

"I guess I just got lost. I'm going home, soon as they can get me there."

"Is that so? Well, I'll be sad to see you go. You look like a smart kid. You like chocolate cake, I bet."

"Sometimes," I said.

"Like when?"

"When my mama makes it, with a glass of milk, after school," I said.

He laughed, a strangled har-har-har. "You guys kill me. Your mama, huh? Well, they make some fine chocolate cake here, though it may not be as good as the stuff from home." He thumbed the table. "Sweetie, send up the biggest piece of chocolate cake you got down there, and a glass a milk, willya?"

The table acknowledged his request with a soft green light.

"Thank you, sir," I said.

"That's quite enough, I think," Pondicherry said. "I didn't come here to watch you rot young James's teeth. Can we get to business?"

Pondicherry started talking, in rapid, clipped sentences, punctuated by vicious bites of his food. I tried to follow what it was about—trading buffalo steaks for rare metals, I got that much, but not much more. The calf's liver was worse than I imagined, and I hid as much of it as I could under the potatoes, then pushed the plate away and dug into the cake.

I sneaked a look up and saw that Nussbaum was grinning slyly at me. He hadn't said much, just ate calmly and waited for Pondicherry to run out of steam. He caught my eye and slipped a wink at me. I looked over at Pondicherry, who was noisily cudding a piece of steak, oblivious, and winked back at Nussbaum.

Pondicherry daubed at his mouth with his napkin. "Excuse me," he said, "I'll be right back." He stood and walked towards the WC.

Nussbaum suddenly jingled. Distractedly, he patted his pockets until he located a tiny phone. He flipped it open and grunted "Nussbaum," into it.

"Jules!" he said a moment later. "How're things?"

He scowled as he listened to the answer. "Now, you and I know that there's a difference between *smart* and *greedy*. I think it's a bad idea."

He listened some more and drummed his fingers on the table.

"Because it's not *credible*, dammit! Even the title is anachronistic: no one in 1902 is going to understand what *Neuromancer* means. Think about it, wouldya? Why don't you do some of Twain's stuff? Those books've got *legs*."

My jaw dropped. Nussbaum was talking to the Frenchman—and he was helping him to *cheat*! To steal from Mark Twain! I was suddenly conscious of *War of the Worlds*, down the front of my jumpsuit. I thought back to Mr. Adelson's assignment, and it all made sudden sense. Verne was a *plagiarist*.

Nussbaum hung up just as Pondicherry re-seated himself. He took a sip of his drink, then held up a hand. Pondicherry eyed him coldly.

"Look," Nussbaum said. "We've gone over this a few times, OK? I know where you stand. You know where I stand. We're not standing in the same place. Much as I enjoy your company, I don't really wanna spend the whole day listening to you repeating yourself. All right?"

"Really, I don't think—" Pondicherry started, but Nussbaum held up his hand again.

"That's all right, I'm a rude son-of-a-bitch, and I know it. Let's just take it as read that you and me spent the whole afternoon letting the other fella know how sincere our positions are. Then we can move onto cocktails, and compromise, and maybe have some of the day left over." Pondicherry started to talk again, but Nussbaum plowed over him. "I'll go to six troy ounces per steer. You won't get a better offer. Ninety-eight percent pure ores. Better than anything you'd ever refine back home. It's as far as I go."

"Sir, is that an ultimatum?" Pondicherry asked, his eyes narrowing.

"Call it whatever you please, buster. It's my final, iron-clad offer. You don't like it, I can talk to the Chinaman. He seemed pretty eager to get some good metal home to the Emperor."

"You wouldn't—he's too far back, it would violate the protocols."

"That's what you say. It may be what the trade court decides. I'll take my chances."

"Six and a half ounces," Pondicherry said, in a spoiled-brat voice.

"You don't hear so good, do you? Six ounces is the offer on the table; take it or leave it." Nussbaum pushed some papers across the table.

Pondicherry stared at them for a long moment. "I will sign them, sir, but it is with the expectation of continued trade opportunities. This is a good will gesture, do you understand?"

Nussbaum snorted and reached for his papers. "This is about steaks and metals. This isn't about the future, it's about today, now. That's what's on the table. You can sign it, or you can walk away."

Pondicherry blew air out his nose like a crazy horse, and signed. "If you'll excuse me, I need to use the WC again." He rose and left the room, purple from the collar up.

"What a maroon," Nussbaum said to the closed door. "This's gotta be a real blast for you, huh?" he said.

I grinned. "It's not so bad. I liked watchin' you hogtie him."

He laughed. "I never would've tried that on your father, kid. He was too sharp. But fatso there, he's terrified the Chinaman will give the Middle Kingdom an edge when it faces down his Royal Navy. All it takes is the slightest hint, and he folds like a cheap suit."

That made me chuckle—a cheap suit!

I gave him my best innocent look. "Who else knows about the

Frenchman?" I asked him.

Nussbaum grinned like he'd been caught with his hand in the cookie jar. "I realized about halfway through that conversation that being Lester's boy, you've probably read just about every word old Jules 'wrote.'"

"I have," I said. I took out *War of the Worlds.* "How does Mr. Wells feel about this?" I asked.

"I imagine he's pretty mystified," Nussbaum said. "Would you believe, you're the first one who's caught on?"

I believed it. I knew enough to know that the agencies that policed the protocols had their hands full keeping track of art and gold smugglers. I'd never even thought of smuggling *words.* If the trade courts found out . . . Well, hardly a week went by that someone didn't propose shutting down the ambassadorships; they'd talk about how the future kept on leaking pastwards, and if we thought 1975 looked bad, imagine life in 1492 once the future reached it! The ambassadors had made a lot of friends in high places, though: they used their influence to keep things on an even keel.

Nussbaum raised an eyebrow and studied me. "I think your father may've figured it out, but he kept it to himself. He and Jules got along like a house on fire."

I kept the innocent look on my face. "Well, then," I said. "If Pa didn't say anything, you'd think that I wouldn't either, right?"

Nussbaum sighed and gave me a sheepish look. "I'd *like* to think so," he said.

I turned the book over in my hands, keeping my gaze locked with his. I was about to tell him that I'd keep it to myself, but at the last minute, some instinct told me to keep my mouth shut.

Nussbaum shrugged as though to say, *I give up.* "Hey, you're headed home today, right?" he said, carefully.

"Yes, sir."

"I've got a message that you could maybe relay for me, you think?"

"I guess so . . ." I said, doubtfully.

"I'll make it worth your while. It's got to go to a friend of mine in Frisco. There's no hurry—just make sure he gets it in the next ten years or so. Once you deliver it, he'll take care of you—you'll be set for life."

"Gosh," I said, deadpan.

"Are you game?"

"I guess so. Sure." My heart skipped. Set for life!

"The man you want to speak to is Reddekop, he's the organist at the Castro theatre. Tell him: 'Nussbaum says get out by October 29th, 1929.' He'll know what it means. You got that?"

"Reddekop, Castro Theatre. October 29th, 1929."

"Exac-atac-ally." He slid *War of the Worlds* into his briefcase. "You're doin' me a hell of a favor, son."

He shook my hand. Pondicherry came back in then, and glared at me. "The embassy contacted me. They can set you at home six months after you left—there's a courier gateway this afternoon."

"Six months!" I said. "My mama will go crazy! Can't you get me home any sooner?"

Pondicherry smirked. "Don't complain to me, boy. You dug this hole yourself. The next scheduled courier going anywhere near your departure-point is in five years. We'll send notice to your mother then, to expect you home mid-July."

"Tough break, kiddo," Nussbaum said, and he shook my hand and slipped me another wink.

The courier gateway let me out in an alleyway in Salt Lake City. The embassy had given me ten Wells Fargo dollars, and fitted me out with a pair of jeans and a workshirt that were both far too big for me, so that they slopped around me as I made my way to the train station and bought my ticket to New Jerusalem.

It was Wednesday, the normal schedule for the Zephyr Speedball, so I didn't have too long to wait at the station. I bought copies of the *Salt Lake City Shout*, and the *San Francisco Chronicle* from a passing newsie. The *Chronicle* was a week old, but it was filled with all sorts of fascinating big-city gossip. I read it cover-to-cover on the long ride to New Jerusalem.

Mama met me at the train station. I'd been expecting a switching, right then and there, but instead she hugged me fiercely with tears in her eyes. I remembered that it had been over six months for her since I'd gone.

"James, you will be the death of me, I swear," she said, after she'd squeezed every last bit of stuffing out of me.

"I'm sorry, mama," I said.

"We had to tell everyone you'd gone away to school in France," a familiar male voice said. I looked up and saw Mr. Johnstone standing a few yards away, with our team and trap. He was glaring at me. "I've had the barn gateway sealed permanently on both sides."

"I'm sorry, sir," I said. But inside, I wasn't. Even though I'd only been away for a few days, I'd had the adventure of a lifetime: smoked and drank and been 'jacked and escaped and received a secret message. My mama seemed shorter to me, and frailer, and James H. Johnstone was a puffed-up nothing of a poltroon.

"We'll put it behind us, son," he said. "But from now on, there will be order in our household, do we understand each other?"

Our house? I looked up sharply at my mama. She smiled at me, nervously. "We married, James. A month ago. Congratulate me!"

I thought about it. My mama needed someone around to take care of her, and vice-versa. After all, it wasn't right for her to be all alone. With a start, I realized that in my mind, I'd left my mama's house. I felt the Wells Fargo notes in my pocket.

"Congratulations, mama. Congratulations, Mr. Johnstone."

Mama hugged me again and the Mr. Johnstone drove us home in the trap.

All through the rest of the day, mama kept looking worriedly at me, whenever she thought I wasn't watching. I pretended not to notice, and did my chores, then took my *Chronicle* out to the apple orchard behind the academy. I sat beneath a big, shady tree and re-read the paper, all the curious bits and pieces of a city frozen in time.

I was hardly surprised to see Mr. Adelson, nor did he seem surprised to see me.

"Back from France, James?"

"Yes, sir."

"Looks like it did you some good, though I must say, we missed you around the academy. It just wasn't the same. Have you been keeping up your writing?"

"Sorry, sir, I haven't. There hasn't been time. I'm thinking about writing an adventure story, though—about pirates and space-travellers and airships," I said.

"That sound exciting." He sat down beside me, and we sat there in silence for a time, watching the flies buzz around. The air was sweet with apple blossoms, and the only sound was the wind in the trees.

"I'm going to miss this place," I said, unthinking.

"Me, too," Mr. Adelson said.

Our eyes locked, and a slow smile spread over his face. "Well, I know where *I'm* going, but where are you off to, son?"

"You're going away?" I said.

"Yes, sir. Is that a copy of the *Chronicle*? Give it here, I'll show you something."

He flipped through the pages, and pointed to an advertisement. "The *Slippery Trick* is in port, and they're signing on crew for a run through the south seas, in September. I intend to go as quartermaster."

"You're leaving?" I said, shocked to my boots.

To my surprise, he pulled out a pouch of tobacco and some rolling papers and made himself a cigarette. I'd never seen a school-teacher smoking before. He took a thoughtful puff and blew the smoke out into the sky. "To tell you the truth, James, I just don't think I'm cut out for this line of work. Not enough excitement in a town like this. I've never been happier than I was when I was at sea, and that's as good a reason to go back as any. I'll miss you, though, son. You were a delight to teach."

"But what will I do?" I said.

"Why, I expect your mother will send you back east to go to school. I graduated you from the academy *in absentia* during the last week of classes. Your report card and diploma are waiting on my desk."

"Graduated?" I said, shocked. I had another year to go at the academy.

"Don't look so surprised! There was no earthly reason for you to stay at the academy. I'd say you were ready for college, myself. Maybe Harvard!" He tousled my hair.

I allowed myself a smile—I didn't think I was any smarter than the other kids, but I sure knew a whole lot more about the world—the worlds! And maybe, in my heart of hearts, I knew that I was a *little* smarter. "I'll miss you, sir," I said.

"Call me Robert. School's out. Where are you off to, James?"

I gestured with my copy of the *Chronicle*.

"My hometown! Whatever for?"

I looked at my shoes.

"Oh, a secret. I see. Well, I won't pry. Does your mother know about this?"

I felt like kicking myself. If I said no, he'd have to tell her. If I said yes, I'd only have myself to blame if he spilled the news to her. I looked at him, and he blew a streamer of smoke into the sky.

"No, sir," I said. "No, Robert."

He looked at me. He winked. "Better keep it to ourselves, then," he said.

The ticket-girl at the Castro Theatre wasn't any older than I was, but she wore her hair shorter than some of the boys I'd known back home, and more makeup than even the painted ladies at the saloon. She looked at me like I was some kind of small-town fool. It was a look I was getting used to seeing.

"Reddekop only plays for the *evening* shows, kid. No organ for the *matinee*."

"Who you calling a kid?" I said. I'd kept a civil tongue ever since debarking the train, treating adult and kid with equal respect, but I was getting sick of being treated like a yokel. I'd been farther than any of these dusty slickers would ever go, and I was grown enough that I'd told my mama and Mr. Johnstone that I was going off on my own, instead of just leaving a note like I'd originally planned.

"You. Kid. You want to talk to Reddekop, you come back after six. In the meantime, you can either buy a ticket to the matinee or get lost."

On reflection, telling my mama was probably a mistake. It meant that I was locked in my room for two consecutive Wednesdays so that I couldn't catch the train. On the third Wednesday, I climbed out onto the roof and then went down the rope ladder I'd hidden behind a chimney. The Wells Fargo notes I'd started with were almost gone, mostly spent on the expensive food on the train—I hadn't dared try to sneak any food away from home, my mama was no fool.

I thought about buying a ticket to the matinee. I still had almost five dollars, but a quick look at the menus in the restaurants had taught me that if I thought the food on the train was expensive, I had another think coming. I shouldered my rucksack and wandered away, taking care to avoid the filth from dogs and people that littered the sidewalks. I told myself that I wasn't homesick—just tired.

"October 29, 1929, huh?" Reddekop was a small German with a greying spade beard and a heavily oiled part in his long hair. His fingers were long and nimble, but nearly everything else about him was short and crude. He made me nervous.

"Yes, sir. Mr. Nussbaum thought you'd know what it meant."

Reddekop struck a match off the side of the organist's pit, lighted a pipe, then tossed the match carelessly into the theatre seats. I winced and he chuckled. "Not to worry, kid. The place won't burn down for a few years yet. I have it on the very best authority."

"Now, Nussbaum says October 29, 1929. What else does he say?"

"He said that you'd take care of me."

He gripped the pipe in his yellow teeth and hissed a laugh around the stem. "He did, did he? Well, I suppose I should. Of course, I won't know for sure for more than 25 years—I don't suppose you want to wait that long?"

"No, sir!" I said. I didn't like this little man—he reminded me of some kind of musical rat.

"I thought not. Do you know what a trust is, James?"

We'd covered that in common law—I could rattle off about thirty different kinds without blinking. "I have a general idea," I said.

"Good, good. What I'm thinking is, the best thing is for me to set up a trust through a lawyer I know on Market Street. He'll make sure that you're always flush, but never so filthy that someone will take a notice in you. How does that strike you?"

I thought it over. "How do I know that the trust fund won't disappear in a few years?"

"You're nobody's fool, huh? Well, how about this—you find your own advocate: a lawyer, a bondsman, someone you trust, and he can look over all the books and papers, make sure it's all square-john. How does that strike you?"

Reddekop knew I was a stranger in town, and maybe he was counting on my not being able to find anyone qualified to audit the trust, but I had an ace up my sleeve. I wasn't anybody's fool.

"That sounds fair," I said.

Back at my mama's I'd had long hard days doing chores: chopping wood, stacking hay, weeding the garden, carrying water. I'd go to bed bone-tired, limp as a rag and as exhausted as I thought I could be.

Boy, was I wrong! By the time I found Mr. Adelson's rooming house, I could barely stand, my mouth was dry as a salt flat, and it was hard to keep my eyes open. They've got hills in San Francisco that must've been some kind of joke God played. His landlady, a worn-out gray woman whose sour expression seemed directed at everything and anything, let me in and pointed me up three rickety flights of stairs to Mr. Adelson's room.

I dragged my luggage up with me, bumping it on the stairs, and rapped on the door. Mr. Adelson answered in the same shirtsleeves and suspenders I'd seen him in that Christmas, an age ago, when my mama dragged me to his cottage. "James!" he said.

"Mr. Adelson," I said. "Sorry to drop in like this."

He took my bag from me and ushered me into his room, pulling up a chair. "What on earth are you doing here?" he said. "Do your parents know where you are? Are you all right? Have you eaten? Are you hungry?"

"I'm pretty hungry—I haven't eaten since supper last night on the train," I tried to make it sound jaunty, but I'm afraid it came out pretty tired-sounding.

"I'll fix us sandwiches," he said, and started fishing around his sea-chest. I watched his shoulders move for a moment, and then my eyes closed.

"Well, good morning," Mr. Adelson said, as I sat bolt upright, disoriented in a strange bed with a strange blanket. "Coffee?"

He was leaning over a little Sterno stove, heating up a small tin pot. Morning sun streamed in through the grimy window.

"I wrapped your sandwich up from last night. It's there, on the dresser."

I stood up and saw that except for my shoes, I was still dressed. The sandwich was salt beef and cheese, and the sourdough was stale, and it was the best thing I'd ever eaten. Mr. Adelson handed me a tin cup full of strong coffee, and though I don't much like coffee, I found myself drinking it as fast as I could.

"Thank you, Mr. Adelson," I said.

"Robert," he said, and sat down on the room's only chair. I perched on the bed's end. "Well, you seem to have had quite a day! Let's hear about it."

I told him as much as I could, fudging around some of the details—my mama surely did know where I was, even if she wasn't very happy about it; and of course, I couldn't tell him that I'd met Nussbaum in 1975, so I just moved the locale to France, and hedged around what message he'd asked me to deliver to Reddekop. It still made for a pretty exciting telling.

"So you want me to go to this lawyer's office with you? To look over the papers? James, I'm just a sailor, I'm not qualified."

I'd prepared for this argument, on the long slog to the rooming house. "But *I* know something about this; they won't believe it, though, and will slip all kinds of dirty tricks in if they think that the only fellow who'll be looking at it is just a kid."

"Explain to me again why you don't want to wire Mr. Johnstone to come and look it over? It sounds like an awful lot of money for him not to be involved."

"He's not my pa, Robert. I don't even *like* him, and chances are, he'll hide away all that money until I'm eighteen or *twenty-one*, and try to send me off to school."

"And what's wrong with that? You have other plans?"

"Sure," I said, too loudly—I hadn't really worked that part out. I just knew that the next time I set foot in New Jerusalem, I'd be my own man, a man of the world, and not dependent on anyone. I'd take mama and Mr. Johnstone out for a big supper, and stay in the fanciest room at the Stableman's hotel, and hire Tommy Benson to carry my bags to my room. "Besides, I'm not asking you to do this for *free*. I'll pay you a—an administrative fee. Five percent, *for life!*"

He looked serious. "James, if I do this—mind I said *if*— I won't take a red cent. There are things here that you're not telling me. Now, that's your business, but I want to make sure that if anyone ever scrutinizes the affair, that it's clear that I didn't receive any benefit from it."

I smiled. I knew I had him—if he'd thought it that far through, he wasn't going to say no. Besides, I hadn't even played my trump card yet: that if he didn't help me, I'd be out on the streets on my own, and I could guess that he didn't like that idea.

Mr. Adelson wore his teacher clothes for the affair and I wore the good breeches and shirt I'd packed. We stopped at a barber's before, Mr. Adelson treated me to a haircut from the number-two man while he took a shave and a trim. We boarded the cable car to Market like a couple of proper gentlemen, and if I thought flying in a jetpack was exciting, it was nothing compared to the terror of hanging on the running-board of a cable car as it labored up and then—quickly!—down a monster hill.

The lawyer was a foreigner, a Frenchie or a Belgian, and his offices were grubby and filled with stinking cigar smoke and the din of the trolleys. He asked no embarrassing questions of me. He just sized up Mr. Adelson, then put away the papers on his desk and presented a set from his briefcase, laying out the terms of the trust, and retreated from the office. I read over Mr. Adelson's shoulder, the terms scribbled in a hasty hand, but every word of it legal and binding, near as I could tell.

The amounts in question were staggering. Two hundred dollars, every month! Indexed for inflation, for seventy years or the duration of my natural life, whichever was lesser. The records of the trust to be deposited with the Wells Fargo, subject to scrutiny on demand. Mr. Adelson looked long and hard at me. "James, I can't begin to imagine what sort of information you've traded for this, but son, you're rich as Croesus!"

"Yes, sir," I said.

"Do these papers look legal to you?"

"Yes, sir."

"They seem legal to me, too."

A bubble of excitement filled my chest and I had to restrain myself from bouncing on my heels. "I'm going to sign it," I said. "Will you witness it?"

"I've got a better idea. Let's get that lawyer and take this down to the Wells Fargo and have the President of the Bank witness it himself."

And that's just what we did.

Mr. Adelson had spent the previous night on the floor, while I slept in his bed. My first month's payment was tucked carefully in my pocket, and over his protests, I pried loose a few bills and took my own room in the rooming house, and then the two of us ate out at a restaurant whose prices had seemed impossibly out-of-reach the day before. We had oysters and steaks and I had a slab of apple pie for desert with fresh ice cream and peach syrup, and when I was done, I felt like new man. Mr. Adelson had a bottle of beer with dinner, and a whiskey afterwards, and I insisted on paying.

"Well, then," he said, sipping his whiskey. "You're a very well-set-up young man. What will you do now?"

All throughout my scheming since my second return from '75, the prospect of what to do with all the money had niggled away at the back of my mind. All I knew for sure was that I didn't want to grow up in New Jerusalem. I wanted adventure, exotic places and people, danger and excitement. Over dinner, though, a plan had been forming in my head.

"Does the *Slippery Trick* need a cabin boy?"

He shook his head and smiled at me. "I was afraid it was something like that. Son, you could pay for a stateroom on a proper liner with all the money you have. Why would you want to be in charge of chamber-pots on a leaky old tub?"

"Why do you want to sail off on a leaky old tub instead of teaching in Utah, or working on the trolleys here?"

It took me most of the night to convince him, but there was no doubt in my mind that I would, and when the ship sailed, that I'd be on it, with a big, leather-bound log, writing stories.

This was my first-ever attempt at a "Hard" SF story—that is to say, a story that was primarily about exploring the nature of some scientific or logical theory through a narrative.

Like everyone who grew up reading the cyberpunks, I'm fascinated and repelled at the idea of computer-assisted cognition (though that's not to say that I wouldn't volunteer to beta test a direct brain/machine interface—researchers, take note!). Would computer-assisted skills "Slide in like icebergs of knowledge," as they do in Neuromancer, or would they have to be manually consulted, digital librarians who can answer any question but need be explicitly invoked for each request?

It matters! In the former instance, you'd be able to ask your augmentation to get you out of bed at 4 AM every day, drive your body—still asleep—to the gym for a couple hours' workout, then back home for ablution and evacuation, and finally into the office, where you will awaken, dressed, groomed and exercised, at your desk, having gotten an extra three or four hours' sleep.

On the other hand, how much would it suck to have a know-it-all agent chattering trivialities about every object that enters your sensoria—bacon aroma detected, mass of oncoming auto estimated at 2300 lbs, the door is a ajar, humidity on the rise, 296 toothpicks on the floor, I'm an excellent driver, time for Wapner—a nattering chatterer that you'd have to continually smack down until it learned which factoids you were interested in and which ones were inconsequential?

And what would happen if such an autonomous agent was confronted with something recursively insoluble, like the "knapsack problem," where the puzzle is to optimally arrange a pack of odd-shaped items for maximum free-space, a problem that can't be solved above a trivial threshold of simplicity—once you hit ten or twenty objects, you're in infinite complexity space?

All Day Sucker

"It's a good day to retire," said the weasel to the smartest man alive. The smartest man alive (whose name was Richard) didn't answer, just continued to fume quietly and pack up his desk.

The weasel (whose name was also Richard, but who preferred to be called Dick), was disappointed. His father played golf with the CEO, so *of course* he'd been given a job when he finished his MBA, but that position was essentially fixed, with no room for advancement. But now that he'd stolen the smartest man's brains, he was headed straight to the top, baby, and he wanted a chance to rub it in a little. And Richard just wouldn't rise to the bait.

"Headed back to *el barrio*, Richard?" Dick the weasel asked. The smartest man alive had come from trash, *peones* who would work every day of their lives simply to pay for their shack and their slop and the terminals they logged into Corporate HQ with. Even with his depressing retirement suit and his years behind a desk, Richard still stank of the trash, still looked grizzled and unkempt and unclean. It was only right that he be returned to the garbage.

The smartest man alive shook his head mutely and continued to pack.

Richard packed everything up: the pictures of his sainted parents, his abacus, his densely scribbled notebooks, his datapacks, his collection of Tinkertoys and stackable blocks and twine that he used to represent *n*-space when explaining it to lesser mortals. When it was all done, he turned to the computer on his desk and woke it up for the last time.

Well, he wouldn't miss the computer, that was for sure.

He glanced up at Dick. The weasel was industriously flossing his teeth in the mirror over the sink in Richard's small, homey office. A shaved patch behind Dick's ear, a brown scab in its center, was the only indication of the surgery he'd undergone.

Richard entered his password into the computer and it immediately threw a tricky multibody calculus problem onscreen.

His job, for the last fifteen years, had been solving problems like this one, step by step, explaining patiently to the computer how he simply *knew* the answer to each question. That had been fun, for about ten minutes, when he was seconded from the company betting shop on the corner of his block, a decade and a half ago.

His parents had swollen with pride when he visited home after his first week on the job.

Now, though, the computer had extracted his intuition and successfully duplicated it. The first working unit, an exquisitely engineered chip the size of a pinhead, nestled snug amongst the dendrites of Dick's brain.

And, finally, the smooth, wealthy *jefes* at corporate HQ wouldn't have to endure the stain he made on their lives.

Dick checked his watch. "Ten minutes to the banquet. They do a real nice chicken at these things." He wandered over to Richard's desk and shoulder-surfed.

"The natural logarithm of two," he said, as Richard laboriously pecked the answer into a window onscreen.

That finally got a rise. "I *know*," said Richard.

Dick grinned, mock-sheepishly. "I guess you do, at that."

Of course Richard knew. Richard knew all about that stuff. Dick almost had to respect him for it: the copy of Richard's math-sense that lived in his brain could magick the solution to any math puzzle he saw into his consciousness as fast as he could think of it.

Richard finished typing his answer and clicked the Enter button. Immediately, another question filled the screen: Five boxes of varying sizes were rendered as wireframes in one window, and a larger box was rendered in another. The problem window said, "PACK SMALLER BOXES INTO LARGER BOX IN OPTIMUM CONFIGURATION."

Richard moused around quickly and decisively, neatly packing them.

Richard didn't give any sign that he'd heard the weasel gasping, but he carefully watched the regular, square features of Dick's face distort in the reflected glare of the monitor as the problem came up.

This was a tricky puzzle, more so than at first glance. There was no easy way to solve it: the only answer was to run through all possible configurations until you found the right one.

For five boxes, it took a few seconds, but if you added even a couple more, it could take a very, very long time.

Once you got up to a hundred boxes, it would take more years than the universe has left.

Fifteen years of cloistering at HQ had left Richard a bachelor and a virgin. None of the women here would look at him. On his infrequent visits to the old neighborhood, people watched him with a mixture of fear and envy, and he was always guarded. Lately, he'd been going less and less frequently. How could he return to that?

His duffel and a plastic garment bag were tucked underneath his desk, up against his legs. After the chicken, he'd shoulder them and walk home. His supervisor had given him the address on an official reassignment form that morning. It wasn't too far from the tenement he'd grown up in, not too far from the gnawing hunger and the shouts.

Dick leaned against the wall, trying to breathe normally. What was that? It was like he'd blacked out, standing up. Like his mind had just *gone away*. Not nice. He lived by his wits—he'd tracked down this expert systems program through the corporate rumor mill through a combination of lies, flattery and smooth talk, and had dedicated his every waking moment to becoming the guinea pig.He couldn't afford many of those glitches, for damn sure.

Under his arms, he could feel the sweat stains forming. Damn.

Richard put the computer to sleep for the last time. He reached down and scratched a fleabite on his ankle—the men's dorm at HQ was perpetually infested—then stood and stretched enormously.

"It is time," he said and shouldered his bags. He started for the door, and the corner of his duffel knocked the carton of desk toys and notebooks to the ground.

Dick smacked his palm against his forehead and rolled his eyes as Richard slowly lowered his bags and began to gather up the spilled objects, methodically replacing them one at time, squatting on his haunches.

The smartest man alive moved with deliberate sloth, seeming to slow down every time the weasel clucked his tongue with impatience.

Finally, the weasel cursed and knelt beside him, grabbing an armload of stuff and moving brusquely for the box.

Richard watched Dick's eyes roll back into his head. The armload of objects, at least twenty notebooks, Tinkertoys, spools of twine, datapacks, and stackable blocks, spilled from his arms.

He did a quick mental calculation, factoring in the speed of the microprocessor in Dick's head, the number and irregularity of the objects, and the size of the packing carton.

Twenty years. At least twenty years to solve the problem.

Carefully, the smartest man alive finished repacking the carton, settling for a less-than-optimum configuration. He stepped over the weasel's twitching body and called security from his desk phone.

Then he took his bags and went up to his retirement banquet.

There're a lot of people who sneer at propaganda and branding and marketing, but I'm not one of 'em. Sure, I'm dismayed at the pervasiveness of marketing messages that have invaded every corner of our public spaces, and I use the Mozilla web-browser so that I can shut out banner-ads and pop-up ads, but there has to be a happy medium between no marketing messages and ubiquitous advertising.

I'm an infovore. I consume and excrete interesting factoids for a living. I want to find out about the novel and the odd—preferably before you do, so that my stories will appear to be original!—in great proliferation. Marketing and word-of-mouth are how we discover the stuff whose existence we don't yet suspect but whose utility we will not be able to live without once we acquire them.

Good branding is full of little brain-rewards, a kind of rightness that you get when you see all the matching parts—the logoed cups and lids, the hidden Mickey in the topiary sculpture, the simultaneously exciting and reassuring color scheme picked out on the hotel bedspread, in the elevator's wainscotting, and in the generic painting over the headboard.

So this isn't a straight satire, this story you're about to read. There's at least as much celebration of marketing here as there is damnation.

To Market, to Market:
The Re-Branding of Billy Bailey

Billy and Principal Andrew Alty went all the way back to kindergarten, when Billy had convinced Mitchell McCoy that the green fingerpaint was Shamrock Shake, and watched with glee as the little babyface had scarfed it all down. Billy knew that Andrew Alty knew his style: refined, controlled, and above all, *personal*. Billy never would've dropped a dozen M-80s down the girls' toilet. His stuff was always one-on-one, and possessed of a degree of charm and subtlety.

But nevertheless, here was Billy, along with the sixth-grade bumper-crop of nasty-come-latelies, called on the carpet in front of Andrew Alty's massive desk. Andrew Alty was an athletic forty, a babyface through and through, and a charismatic thought-leader in his demographic.

Hormones. They were the problem.

Billy Bailey was the finest heel the sixth grade had ever seen— a true artisan who kept his brand pure and unsullied, picking and managing his strategic alliances with the utmost care and acumen.

He'd dumped BanginBumpin Fireworks (a division of The Shanghai Novelty Company, Ltd.) in the *fourth* grade, fer chrissakes. Their ladyfingers were too small to bother with; their M-80s were so big that you'd have to be a lunatic to go near them.

But sixth grade was the Year of the Hormone at Pepsi Elementary. Boys who'd been babyfaces since kindergarten suddenly sprouted acne, pubic hair, and an uncontrollable urge to impress girls. Their weak brands were no match for the onslaught of -osterones and -ogens that flooded their brains, and in short order they found themselves switching over to heel.

As a result, the sixth grade was experiencing a heel glut. Last year's Little Lord Fauntleroys were now busy snapping bras, dropping textbooks, cracking grading computers, and blowing up the girls' toilets.

Hormones. They made Billy want to puke.

Andrew Alty gave them his sternest stare, the one over the top of his half-rims that was guaranteed to reduce a fourth-grader to tears. The poseurs alongside of Billy shuffled their feet nervously and looked away. Billy struggled to control his anger, and to meet Andrew Alty's stare with his tried-and-true antidote, a carefree, mischievous grin.

"Ten thousand dollars," Andrew Alty said, for the third time. "What will your parents say, I wonder, when I tell them that it will cost ten thousand dollars to replumb the girls' change-room? Boys, I wouldn't want to be in your shoes when that happens. I imagine that it will go very hard for all of you." He treated them all to another megawatt of stare.

"*But I didn't do it!*" wailed Mitchell McCoy, who'd gotten a Blue Ribbon in the fifth-grade Science Fair for a consumer research report on relative inflammabilities of a range of allegedly fire-proof blue-jeans.

Billy shot him a look of disgust. *But I didn't do it!* Suck.

Andrew Alty looked at him. "So you say. You may be telling the truth. No way to find out, though—not unless we bring the police in to fingerprint you all." The emphasis he put on "police" and "fingerprint" was admirably subtle, Billy thought. He actually liked Andrew Alty, most of the time. The man had a good, strong brand,

and he tended it most carefully. "Of course, once I involve the police, it will be out of my hands. It will be a criminal matter." Again, just the lightest breath of emphasis on "criminal." Billy had to hand it to him.

"It goes without saying that if any of you know how I could resolve this without involving the police, I'd be glad to hear about it. Why don't you take a moment to think about it?"

The boys shuffled their feet. A few of them choked back sobs.

Finally, Mitchell McCoy swung an accusing finger at Billy. "He did it! I saw him sneak in with the M-80s, and matches! He told me if I said anything, he'd beat me up again!"

Billy had seen it coming. Mitchell was almost certainly the culprit—every science-fair project he'd ever done had involved blowing something up or setting something on fire. And Mitchell had nursed a grudge for an entire year, ever since Billy had sent him into the mud during an autumn game of tackle-tag, and then sent him back again and again when he tried to rush Billy.

He stared coolly at Andrew Alty. Billy could practically see the wheels turn in his head. Mitchell McCoy's parents were overbearing, with a hands-on approach to Mitchell McCoy's academic career that often sent one or both to Pepsi Elementary on the pretense of helping out with a bake-sale or fun-faire. Fingering Mitchell McCoy for the incident would surely call down their interminable wrath. Andrew Alty turned his gaze on Billy. "What do you say to this?"

"Consider the source," is what Billy said—it was one of his catch-phrases this term, a tie-in with a kids-only newsfeed. Billy had brought it to Pepsi Elementary, and had spread it beyond the sixth grade into the fifth, with some penetration into the fourth. He liked the sound of it—it was subtly insulting and smart.

Unfortunately, Andrew Alty *was* considering the source—and the source's high-octane-pain-in-the-ass parents. "That's all you have to say, son?" he said, with deadly seriousness.

Until I speak to my agent, it is, Billy thought, and kept mum.

Billy's phone was ringing when he let himself into his parents' place. Billy had paged his agent on the way home from school. He was suspended indefinitely, pending a parent-teacher meeting, but that wasn't what bothered Billy. He was worried about his brand-identity, and that meant talking to Bennie Beasely, endorsement broker and personal agent extraordinaire. Bennie Beasely was chipper to a fault, and made sympathetic noises as Billy related the day's events.

"Well!" he said, finally. "What a *pickle!*"

"What are you going to do about it, Bennie Beasely?"

"Well, it's a really sticky sandwich, Billy Bailey. You could deny it all, call for a police investigation. But I can tell you right now, that's going to mean unspun media coverage, and the sponsors aren't going to like that. In the long run, involving the authorities is going to cost you, big.

"On the other hand, you could admit to everything. The sponsors still won't like that—they like their heels sane and under control. But you've got a *relationship* with them, Billy. You're loyal to them, and they're loyal to you. We could probably hit BanginBumpin up for a post-facto fee, you know. That would salvage things somewhat."

Billy had already figured all this out, even the part about going to the fireworks manufacturer for some money, but there was one thing bothering him. "Who pays the ten thou for the damages, Bennie Beasely?"

Bennie Beasely sighed. "I'm afraid you'd be on the hook for that. We'll take it out of the trust. I know it's a tough jellybean, but you're going to have to chew it."

Billy felt the anger bubble up his chest, and he carefully vented some of it. "No. Way. Never. I'm not going to pay a cent. If it takes a police investigation, fine, so be it. If that costs me down the road, I'll suck it up. But I am not paying out ten grand to cover some half-wit stunt Mitchell McCoy pulled. It'll dilute me. It's not my style." He let the anger give his voice a dangerous edge.

"Billy Bailey! Listen to me! I'm not saying this is a good solution—I'm saying it's the better of two terrible ones. I've got another client who just went though a similar situation. He bit the bacon, swallowed his pie, and toughed it out. You can do that, too. I'm telling you this as your friend, son. If you call the cops, you're through as a heel."

Billy felt a lightbulb flash in his head. He pushed the anger all the way down. "I think I'd better talk it over with my parents," he said, calmly.

"That's my tunafish!" Bennie Beasely said. "You do that, and call me back, anytime. You've got my number."

Billy had three hours until his parents, Barbara and Buford Bailey, came home from the office. He spent it putting together a shareholder presentation. He got out some flip-chart paper and a six-pack of color markers and carefully wrote:

Rebranding Strategy Notes
Problem: *Surplus of amateur heels*
Solution: *Rebrand property—babyface*
Critical Path:

    1) Fire Bennie Beasely

    2) Initiate police investigation

    3) Buckle down on grades

    3a) Seek babyface sponsors (other divisions?)

He surveyed it critically, added some color underlines, then made himself a Skippy SuperChunk on Wonder with Welch's. Then he fleshed out each point, listing pros and cons, using a separate sheet for each, tacking them to the cork-rail that ringed the family room. He finished up by writing out an agenda, just as Barbara and Buford Bailey came home.

Buford Bailey was Billy's VP Operations, so it fell to him to fire Bennie Beasely. Billy supervised him as he downloaded and filled out the Notice of Intent to Terminate, then faxed it off to Bennie Beasely.

Billy and Barbara Bailey went through his things, packing the slingshots and air rifles and gangsta posters into the FedEx boxes they'd arrived in. They piled up all the war comics and t-shirts with rude slogans and bagged them in Hefty Tie-N-Tosses. When they were finished, Billy's room was a pristine expanse of empty Ikea Billy shelves, his wardrobe reduced to his church suit and a few pairs of Levi's whose knees he hadn't gotten around to ripping out yet.

They paged Principal Andrew Alty and gave formal notice of their desire to involve the police. Billy listened in on the extension, and was pleased to hear Andrew Alty groaning in frustration.

Billy did four hours of homework, vetted by Barbara and Buford Bailey: Math, Marketing and Society, Geography, and a special report for Consumer Science on the effects of various bottled waters when used in the preparation of Ramen Noodles. Buford dug out an old soft-sided nylon briefcase, and they packed the hardcopy in it, along with a selections of pens and a new, staid, black-and-silver PDA.

Billy and Barbara Bailey went to the Sears Galleria and bought a few outfits, and then he was ready to go back to school.

Billy kept his head up as he left for school the next day, for Barbara and Buford Bailey's benefit. But once he'd turned the corner at the end of the block, he slowed down, dropped his gaze to his loafers, and fretted.

Billy's brand had been established early on, in the first month of kindergarten. He'd been the first in the category—he'd defined "Heel" for his classmates. Sure, there'd been heels in the upper grades, but they had no interaction with his class.

Billy had been *the* heel. When others followed the trail he'd blazed, pitching spitwads or putting the boot in during a game of British Bulldog, their behavior had been compared to Billy's. More than half of the endorsement dollars that flowed into the sixth grade went straight into Billy's trust account.

As well they should. If you were a sixth-grader looking for a risqué t-shirt, nine times out of ten it'd be a shirt that Billy had worn that week. If you went to see a violent movie, it'd be one that Billy had presented a book-report on. If you wanted a PDA with a shotgun mic attachment for cross-playground spying, what better model than the one that Billy could often be seen holding up to his ear, grinning mischievously?

In the minds of the consumers of Pepsi Elementary, Billy owned the word "Mischief." The immutable wisdom of the ages said that nothing Billy could do would change that. It would be like trying to sell Evian Brake Fluid. A brand-killer.

In the searing light of his anger with Andew Alty and Bennie Beasely and Mitchell McCoy, switching categories had seemed like a bold, sexy move. In the glum winter daylight, it seemed like suicide. *What was he doing?*

As he neared the playground, he saw the earlybirds, babyfaces all, gathered to play their gentle games in the brief calm before the shouting, shoving heels arrived. And he was gobsmacked by revelation.

Billy Bailey, heel, was synonymous with mischief. That would never change. But who wanted to be synonymous with mischief? The world was full of little bastards, getting into their petty troubles. Sponsors couldn't care less about them and their weak, puny brands. At the same time, the few babyfaces remaining in the sixth grade were miserable specimens of the category—snivelling wimps, not child-genius virtuosos. The sponsors barely noticed them, so ineffectual were their brands.

Truth be told, sponsorship was lean in the sixth grade. They were nearly ready for Nintendo Middle School, where they'd be lowly seventh-graders, taking every cue from the wise and savvy eighth-graders, who trembled on the cusp of high-school. In that tough marketplace, heels were jocks or gangstas, the stakes were raised, and real violence was a genuine possibility. The sixth-grade crop of heels was mostly doomed. Billy had gotten out while the getting was good.

Billy's brand had been so strong because he was first in the category. Becoming a babyface, he'd be last in the category—he'd be playing catch-up with the snivelling wimps. He just couldn't stomach the prospect.

But if Billy were to create a *new* category, he would be first to market in it—the automatic leader. And he could leverage the things that had made his brand important to begin with: his native charisma, his understanding of the importance of consistency and caution when managing a brand.

Billy would own a new word in the minds of the consumers at Pepsi Elementary.

That word would be:

Dissent.

And so Billy Bailey, heel, gave way to Billy "Bug" Bailey, dissenter.

His first sponsor came on board a week later.

The promised criminal investigation had fizzled quietly after a fingerprinting session and an intense series of meetings between Principal Andrew Alty and Mitchell McCoy's overbearing parental units. And Billy "Bug" Bailey had attended five days of classes without a single logomark, a single brand, or a single label on his person.

He turned in his homework impeccably and on time, but he refused to incorporate any of the school's approved sponsors into his personal curriculum. His assignments contained no registered trademarks. And they were signed *Bug Bailey*.

In the playground, Bug's new brand met with a great deal of consumer resistance. Mitchell McCoy confronted him during a game of tackle-tag, dropping Billy as he charged for the home-base at the swing-set.

"Got you!" he hissed through clenched teeth. He had a heavy-metal t-shirt on, with more umlauts than the entire Ring Cycle; a TimePuker watch on a studded bracelet; and Doc Marten's ButtKicker 2000s, with the plated shin guards. "You *beetle!*"

Bug wriggled from beneath him, stood and dusted himself off. "Beetle?" he said, wondering if it was a new insult he'd missed.

"Bug, beetle, what's the difference? Either way, you're something disgusting that I squish."

Bug cocked an eyebrow. "The Doc Marten's are a bad idea," he said, off-hand. "Too much line-extension, they've weakened the brand. That's what I told them when they offered me a pair." Of course, no one had ever offered Mitchell McCoy anything—he always paid.

"Bug!" Mitchell McCoy shouted. He looked around to make sure that any heels in range heard him. "Bug!"

Bug kept his cool, confident that Mitchell McCoy couldn't muster the support of any of the heels on the playground. And he was right. The others looked a little embarrassed and moved off. Panic flashed in Mitchell McCoy's eyes.

He charged.

Bug stood perfectly still, let Mitchell McCoy jump on him, force him to the ground. Bug twisted to shield his groin and face, but Mitchell McCoy managed to open a cut over his left eyebrow before a teacher broke it up.

He spent the rest of the day in class, soaking up the blood with one of the janitor's shop rags: he refused to wear the Band-Aids the school nurse had offered him. Mitchell McCoy's parents descended on the principal's office like kingfishers, and left with Mitchell McCoy on a two-week suspension.

When Bug left the schoolyard, a limo was waiting for him.

"Billy, Jesus, you look like you've been in a war," is what Ronnie Ryan, the rep from Polygram, said as Bug approached the limo. Ronnie Ryan had always been good for a half-dozen new CDs every week, gangsta rap and narco-mariachi dance stuff. But they had communicated through Bennie, mostly, never this flashy limousine service.

"Can I give you a ride?" Ronnie Ryan asked.

"Sure," Bug said, and got in the limo.

Ronnie Ryan had an intense cell-phone conversation as they were pulling out, but once they'd hit the highway, he rang off and gave Billy a great big smile. Ronnie Ryan had always reminded Billy of a second-grade heel, more high-strung than mean, with his expensive brand-new casual clothes and his artfully mussed hair.

"I wanted to make a quick stop on the way, I hope you don't mind," Ronnie Ryan said. "I think you'll be interested."

Bug knew that Ronnie Ryan knew that Bug wasn't a heel any longer. He was intrigued by whatever it was that Ronnie Ryan thought would tempt him, but cool enough not to show it. He took a Yoo Hoo from the minibar and settled back for the ride.

They pulled up in front of a warehouse whose broken windows leered at him. From within, he heard wailing guitars and hoarse singing. Ronnie Ryan held the door open for him. "You're going to love these guys," he said.

The band was called Honey-Roasted Landlords. Three B.Comm. grads—a guitar, a bass and a drum kit. They wore faded track pants and plain white t-shirts with off-brand tennis shoes. They weren't bad.

"I thought you'd like them," Ronnie Ryan said, after they'd finished rehearsing. "We're releasing them on our bootleg label, photocopied inserts, home-toasted CDs. They're testing very high in the 11–16 market."

Bug nodded sagely. "My rate has doubled," he said, as offhandedly as he could manage.

Ronnie Ryan swallowed. Bug held his gaze. When you focus a brand down, you end up with a premium product. Rolex makes nothing but watches, and they cost the world; Matsushita makes everything from stereos to space stations, and they have to sell on price, incentives and rebates. Bug knew which camp he was in.

Ronnie Ryan nodded, finally. The B.Comm. with the guitar watched the proceedings with undisguised interest. He snapped Billy a nod that was a salute, one artist to another.

"Let's get you home, huh?" Ronnie Ryan said.

Things were shaky, that first month, but by the end of it, he had a solid seven sponsors lined up, all at double his old rate. He wore "Homemade" band-shirts; did Music Appreciation reports on "Indie" singles he downloaded from "pirate" sites; wore street-vendor styles that had been mass-produced—*sans* label—by DKNY's Chechen facility.

The kids on the playground spent the first week staring in shock; the second, shaking their heads in pity; the third, covertly studying him; and by the fourth, it seemed like a couple were ready to follow his lead. The umlauts dwindled, the hand-drawn t-shirts multiplied. Bug's sponsors were delighted.

Bug knew that it wasn't enough, though. He needed to promote more than himself; he needed to promote the category, to bring some of the stronger heel brands into the fold, to grow the field. Sure, it might decrease his market-share, but it would increase the overall size of the market.

He had to pick his competition.

Mitchell McCoy came off his two-week suspension even more hostile to Bug. He spent the entire morning glaring at Bug while the teacher moused through a PepsiOne multimedia on the Civil War.

Bug made a note of his reaction. He liked to know where he stood. And more and more, it seemed that he stood somewhere very fine indeed. He tried to picture the class seen from overhead, and saw the homemade t-shirts clustered densely around his desk and then thinning in proportion to the distance from it. He could almost see his influence rippling outwards.

Mitchell McCoy sat in the opposite corner of the room, one more black speedmetal t-shirt inside a knot of the same. Bug cocked his head at him and pondered until the recess bell rang.

On the schoolyard, he deliberately distanced himself from the other dissenters, sitting in the shelter of an emergency exit, tapping a game of solitaire on his new PDA, which he'd decorated with "underground" stickers for "Indie" cartoon shows. He peeked up occasionally and watched Mitchell McCoy make his way across the playground to him. He suppressed a grin. This had all started when Mitchell McCoy hadn't had the sense to stay down in a game of tackle-tag, and Mitchell McCoy hadn't learned a thing.

He pretended not to notice Mitchell McCoy's approach, but peripherally watched the oxblood-colored ButtKicker 2000s crunch towards him, kick his PDA into the sky.

"Nice shirt, Bug!"

Bug simulated a cringe. "Why can't you just leave me *alone*, Mitchell McCoy?" he whined.

Mitchell McCoy grinned wolfishly. "Why can't you weave me awone?" he said, in a baby-voice. "Because I don't like you, Bug. You think you're so great—"

"You're just jealous because you don't have any endorsement deals," Bug said, with a calculated amount of petulance.

Mitchell McCoy purpled. "Oh yeah, and I suppose you're just rolling in it these days, with crap like that shirt and those shoes and those nasty CDs you keep bringing in . . ." He trailed off, comprehension crawling with glacial sloth across his acne. "That's it! You've got deals with these guys! Independent, my butt!"

"No I don't," Bug said, too quickly.

"Oh yes you do! Wait'll I tell everyone! You're a dead man, Bug." Mitchell McCoy rubbed his hands and did a little ButtKicker 2000 dance.

"Don't!" Bug said. "Please! I'll do anything." Bug consciously didn't hold his breath, tried to play the part to its utmost. This was the moment of truth.

"What can you do?"

"Well, I could hook you up with my sponsors," Bug said, forcing misery into his voice. "Then you'd be in on it, too."

"What makes you think I'd *want* to endorse any of your low-rent sponsors, Bug?"

"How else are you going to pay for the girl's toilet?" Bug wondered if he was showing too much premeditation, but Mitchell McCoy was hooked.

"How do I know they'll want to sign me?" he asked, almost drooling.

"I'll tell them. They'll consider the source."

"It's a deal," Mitchell McCoy said. "I'll meet you at the back gate after school." He walked away, pausing to crush Bug's PDA underfoot.

They met Ronnie Ryan in an alley a block from the school. Once they were in the limo, Bug dropped the pretense that he was scared of Mitchell McCoy. He and Ronnie Ryan tag-teamed Mitchell McCoy, giving him pointers on dress, speech, comportment and behavior. Mitchell McCoy's eyes, already bugged out from the moment he'd seen the stretch limo, grew wider with every moment, and he nodded unconsciously as they tore apart his brand.

Finally, Ronnie Ryan passed him a neatly folded bundle: non-name sneakers, homemade CDs, track-pants, a t-shirt with Honey-Roasted Landlord written in Magic Marker. He dug out a Hefty Tie-N-Toss and shook it open. "Toss everything in," he commanded. "The boots, the shirt, anything in your pockets. You're not a heel anymore."

Bug and Ronnie Ryan politely turned their heads while Mitchell McCoy changed. Ronnie Ryan had him sign a nondisclosure and a noncompete, then sent him packing.

"You're sure about this?" he asked Bug once they were alone.

"I'm growing the category," Bug said. "It's the natural next-step."

"But that kid —" Ronnie Ryan gave a dramatic shudder. "Ugh."

"Don't worry about it," Bug said. "I'll make sure he does his part. He's the perfect number-two brand—dumb and easy to figure out."

"Take this, will you?" Ronnie Ryan said, holding out the Tie-N-Toss. "I can't even bear to hold it."

Mitchell McCoy was a loser. Bug knew that. But he'd underestimated how much of a loser he was. When he dumped out the Tie-N-Toss in his bedroom that night, he nearly laughed out loud.

Mitchell McCoy's pockets had been filled with BanginBumpin M-80s. Some people never learn.

Bug got a couple of Zip-Loc bags from the kitchen and put them on like gloves. He picked up the M-80s and carefully slipped them into his pocket.

He set the alarm for 7 AM, so that he could get to school nice and early. Early enough to drop the M-80s—covered in Mitchell McCoy's fingerprints—down the newly rebuilt girls' toilets.

As he nestled under the covers, he felt a tremor of doubt. He wasn't a heel anymore, so wasn't setting up Mitchell McCoy off-strategy?

He pondered it while sleep overtook him, and in the morning he knew the answer.

Billy "Bug" Bailey could act like a heel if he wanted to. He was a category-killer.

The most striking thing about cunning artifice is its sudden absence. While the actors are on stage, they can command our complete attention, still the nattering voices in our minds, suspend our disbelief to the rafters. But no matter how magical the action onstage is, it can't touch the shocking and wildly dissonant moment when the curtain rings down and the lights come up, returning the theatre from a house of wonders to a mundane place of people and things. In that interstitial moment, the hot second when the world slides from fantasy to reality, our brains do a kind of flip-flop that is more interesting than anything on the stage or off it.

If you ever have the good fortune to be on a Disney ride when it really thoroughly breaks down, you'll get to experience this. The safety bar comes forward, the lights come up, the animatronics slide to a halt, and secret doorways are revealed leading to utilitarian service corridors tagged with old graffiti and scars from illicit cigarettes. In the moment where you walk from the "Onstage" area of the park to the "Offstage," your brain undergoes exactly the same kind of flip-flop. It's addictive.

What would it be like to live in that interstitial zone, to be a cast-member at a theme-park, constantly traversing the equator girding the real and fantastic hemispheres?

And on a slightly different subject: What the hell did Stromboli want to turn Pinocchio and Lampwick into donkeys for, anyway?

(All the above notwithstanding, this entire story materialized in my head during a trip through the Pinocchio ride in Disneyland's Fantasyland).

Return to Pleasure Island

George twiddled his thumbs in his booth and watched how the brown, clayey knuckles danced overtop of one another. Not as supple as they had once been, his thumbs—no longer the texture of wet clay on a potter's wheel; more like clay after it had been worked to exhausted crackling and brittleness. He reached into the swirling vortex of the cotton-candy machine with his strong right hand and caught the stainless-steel sweep-arm. The engines whined and he felt them strain against his strong right arm, like a live thing struggling to escape a trap. Still strong, he thought, still strong, and he released the sweep-arm to go back to spinning sugar into floss.

A pack of boys sauntered down the midway, laughing and calling, bouncing high on sugar and g-stresses. One of them peeled off from the group and ran to his booth, still laughing at some cruelty. He put his palms on George's counter and pushed against it, using them to lever his little body in a high-speed pogo. "Hey, mister," he said, "How about some three-color swirl, with sprinkles?"

George smiled and knocked the rack of paper cones with his strong right elbow, jostled it so one cone spun high in the air, and he caught it in his quick left hand. "Coming *riiiiiight* up," he sang, and flipped the cone into the floss-machine. He spun a beehive of pink, then layered it with stripes of blue and green. He reached for the nipple that dispensed the sprinkles, but before he turned its spigot, he said, "Are you sure you don't want a dip, too? Fudge? Butterscotch? Strawberry?"

The boy bounced even higher, so that he was nearly vaulting the counter. "All three! All three!" he said.

George expertly spiraled the floss through the dips, then applied a thick crust of sprinkles. "Open your mouth, kid!" he shouted, with realistic glee.

The boy opened his mouth wide, so that the twinkling lights of the midway reflected off his back molars and the pool of saliva on his tongue. George's quick, clever left hand dipped a long-handled spoon into the hot fudge, then flipped the sticky gob on a high arc that terminated perfectly in the boy's open mouth. The boy swallowed and laughed gooily. George handed over the dripping confection in his strong right hand, and the boy plunged his face into it. When he whirled and ran to rejoin his friends, George saw that his ears were already getting longer, and his delighted laugh had sounded a little like a bray. A job well done, he thought, and watched the rain spatter the spongy rubber cobbles of the midway.

George was supposed to go off-shift at midnight. He always showed up promptly at noon, but he rarely left as punctually. The soft one who had the midnight-to-six shift was lazy and late, and generally staggered in at twelve thirty, grumbling about his tiredness. George knew how to deal with the soft ones, though—his father had brought him up surrounded by them, so that he spoke without his father's thick accent, so that he never inadvertently crushed their soft hands when he shook with them, so that he smiled good-naturedly and gave up a realistic facsimile of sympathy when they griped their perennial gripes.

His father! How wise the old man had been, and how proud, and how *stupid*. George shucked his uniform backstage and tossed it into a laundry hamper, noting with dismay how brown the insides were, how much of himself had eroded away during his shift. He looked at his clever left thumb and his strong right thumb, and tasted their good, earthy tastes, and then put them away. He dressed himself in the earth-colored dungarees and workshirt that his own father had stolen from a laundry line when he left the ancestral home of George's people for the society of the soft ones.

He boarded a Cast Member tram that ran through the utilidors underneath Pleasure Island's midway, and stared aimlessly at nothing as the soft ones on the tram gabbled away, as the tram sped away to the Cast housing, and then it was just him and the conductor, all the way to the end of the line, to the cottage he shared with his two brothers, Bill and Joe. The conductor wished him a good night when he debarked, and he shambled home.

Bill was already home, napping in the pile of blankets that all three brothers shared in the back room of the cottage. Joe wasn't home yet, even though his shift finished earlier than theirs. He never came straight home; instead, he wandered backstage, watching the midway through the peepholes. Joe's Lead had spoken to George about it, and George had spoken to Joe, but you couldn't tell Joe anything. George thought of how proud his father had been, having three sons—three! George, the son of his strong right thumb, and Bill, the son of his clever left thumb, and Joe. Joe, the son of his tongue, an old man's folly, that left him wordless for the remainder of his days. He hadn't needed words, though: his cracked and rheumy eyes had shone with pride every time they lit on Joe, and the boy could do no wrong by him.

George busied himself with supper for his brothers. In the little wooded area behind the cottage, he found good, clean earth with juicy roots in it. In the freezer, he had a jar of elephant-dung sauce, spiced with the wrung-out sweat of the big top acrobats' leotards, which, even after reheating, still carried the tang of vitality. Preparing a good meal for his kind meant a balance of earthy things and living things, things to keep the hands supple and things to make them strong, and so he brought in a chicken from the brothers' henhouse and covered it in the sloppy green-brown sauce, feathers and all. Bill, being the clever one, woke when the smell of the sauce bubbling in the microwave reached him, and he wandered into the kitchen.

To an untutored eye, Bill and George were indistinguishable. Both of them big, even for their kind—for their father had been an especially big specimen himself—whose faces were as expressive as sculptor's clay, whose chisel-shaped teeth were white and hard as rocks. When they were alone together, they went without clothing, as was the custom of their kind, and their bodies bulged with baggy, loose muscle. They needed no clothing, for they lacked the shame of the soft ones, the small thumb between the legs. They had a more civilized way of reproducing.

"Joe hasn't returned yet?" Bill asked his strong brother.

"Not yet," George told his clever brother.

"We eat, then. No sense in waiting for him. He knows the supper hour," Bill said, and since he was the clever one, they ate.

Joe returned as the sun was rising, and burrowed in between his brothers on their nest of blankets. George flung one leg over his smallest brother, and smelled the liquor on his breath in his sleep, and his dreams were tainted with the stink of rotting grapes.

George was the first one awake, preparing the morning meal. A maggoty side of beef, ripe with the vitality of its parasites, and gravel. Joe came for breakfast before Bill, as was his custom. Bill needed the sleep, to rest his cleverness.

"God-*damn*, I am *hungry!*," Joe said loudly, without regard for his sleeping brother.

"You missed dinner," George said.

"I had more important things to do," Joe said. "I was out with an Imagineer!"

George stared hard at him. "What did the Imagineer want? Is there trouble?"

Joe gave a deprecating laugh. "Why do you always think there's trouble? The guy wanted to chat with me—he likes me, wants to get to know me. His name is Woodrow, he's in charge of a whole operations division, and he was interested in what I thought of some of his plans." He stopped and waited for George to be impressed.

George knew what the pause was for. "That's very good. You must be doing a good job for your Lead to mention you to him."

"That little prick? He hates my guts. Woodrow's building a special operations unit out of lateral thinkers—he wants new blood, creativity. He says I have a unique perspective."

"Did you talk to Orville?" Orville was the soft one who'd brought them from their father's shack to the Island, and he was their mentor and advocate inside its Byzantine politics. Bill had confided to George that he suspected Orville was of a different species from the soft ones—he certainly seemed to know more about George's kind than a soft one had any business knowing.

Joe tore a hunk from the carcass on the rickety kitchen table and stuffed it into his mouth. Around it, he mumbled something that might have been yes and might have been no. It was Joe's favorite stratagem, and it was responsible for the round belly that bulged out beneath his skinny chest.

Joe tore away more than half of the meat and made for the door. "Woodrow wants to meet with me again this morning. Don't wait up for me tonight!" He left the cottage and set off toward the tram-stop.

Bill rolled over on his bedding and said, "I don't like this at all."

George kept quiet. Bill's voice surprised him, but it shouldn't have. Bill was clever enough to lie still and feign sleep so that he could overhear Joe's conversations, where George would have just sat up and started talking.

"Orville should know about this, but I can't tell if it would make him angry. If it made him angry and he punished Joe, it would be our fault for telling him."

"Then we won't tell him," George said.

Bill held up his hand. "But if we don't tell him and he finds out on his own, he may be angry with us."

"Then we should tell him," George said.

"But Joe and this Woodrow may not get along after all, and if that happens, the whole thing will end on its own."

"Then we won't tell him," George said.

"But if they do get along, then they may do something that would make Orville angry," Bill looked expectantly at George.

"Then we should tell him?" George said, uncertainly.

"I don't know," Bill said. "I haven't decided."

George knew that this mean that Bill would have to think on it, and so he left him. He had to catch the tram to make it to his shift, anyway.

The soft one with the six-to-noon shift left as soon as George arrived, without a word. George was used to soft ones not having anything to say to him, and preferred it that way. He was better off than Bill—soft ones always wanted to talk to Bill, and he hated it, since they never had anything to say that Bill wanted to know. The weather needed no discussion, Bill said. And as for the complaints about the shift's Lead, well, one soft one was just about the same as any other, and Orville had told them that at the end of the day, they worked for him, not for any Lead.

Joe liked talking to the soft ones. Joe liked to talk, period. He told the soft ones lies about their childhood in the shack with their father, and told them about how his brothers tormented him, and even talked about the weather. When he got back home, he told his brothers all over again, everything he'd told the soft ones.

George had memorized the SOP manual when they came to the Island, five years before. It clearly said that the floor of the booth would be disinfected every three hours, and the surfaces polished clean, and the pots and machines refilled. The soft one with the six-to-noon shift never did any of these things, which could get him disciplined by their Lead, but George didn't complain. He just wiped and disinfected and re-stocked when he arrived, even though he had to be extra careful with the water, so that he didn't wash any of himself away.

Boys ran up and down the midway, baking in the mid-day sun. They reminded George of the boys he'd gone to school with, after the social worker had come to his father's shack. They'd teased him to begin with, but he'd just stood with his hands at his sides until they stopped. Every time he started a new grade, or a new kid came to the school, it was the same: they'd tease him, or hit him, or throw things at him, and he'd stand strong and silent until they stopped, even if it took months. His teachers quickly learned that calling on him in class meant standing in awkward silence, while he sat stoic and waited for them to call on someone else. The social worker could make him go to school with the soft ones, but she couldn't make him act like one.

George watched the boys carefully, as carefully as he had when he stood silently in the schoolyard, not seeming to watch anything. He was better at spotting a donkey than any of the soft ones. When a boy was ready to turn, George could almost see the shape of the donkey superimposed on the boy, and he radioed a keeper to pick up the donkey come morning. He got a bonus for each one he spotted, and according to Bill, it had accumulated to a sizable nest-egg.

George looked at the inventory and decided that the fudge was getting a little long in the tooth. He'd start pushing fudge-nut dips, and by the end of his shift, the tub would be empty and he'd be able to give it a thorough cleaning and a refill from fresh stock. "Hey guys!" he called to three boys. "Is anybody *hungry?*" He dipped a floss and held it up, so that it oozed fudge down his wrist. The boys shyly approached his booth. George knew from their manner that they were new to the Island: probably just picked up from a video-arcade or lasertag tent on the mainland that afternoon. They didn't know what to make of their surroundings, that was clear.

"Step right up," he said, "I don't bite!" He smiled a smile he'd practiced in the mirror, one that shaped his soft, flexible features into a good-natured expression of idiotic fun. Cautiously, the boys came forward. They were the target age, eleven-to-fourteen, and they'd already accumulated some merch, baseball hats and fanny packs made from neoprene in tropical-fish colors, emblazoned with the Island's logomarks and character trademarks. They had the beginnings of dark circles under their eyes, and they dragged a little with low blood-sugar. George dipped two more and distributed them around. The eldest, a towheaded kid near the upper age range, said, "Mister, we haven't got any money—what do these cost?"

George laughed like a freight train. "It's all free, sonny, free as air! Courtesy of the Management, as a reward for very *special* customers like you." This was scripted, but the trick was to sell the line like it was fresh.

The boys took the cones from him timidly, but ate ravenously. George gave them some logoed serviettes to wipe up with and ground the fudge into his wrists and forearms with one of his own. He looked at his watch and consulted the laminated timetable taped to the counter. 1300h, which meant that the bulk of the Guests would be migrating towards Actionland and the dinosaur rides, and it was time to push the slightly down-at-the-heels FreakZone, to balance the crowds. "You boys like rollercoasters?" he said.

The youngest—they were similar enough in appearance and distant enough in ages to be brothers—spoke up. "Yeah!" The middle elbowed him, and the youngest flipped the middle the bird.

"Well, if you follow the midway around this curve to the right, and go through the big clown-mouth, you'll be in the FreakZone. We've got a fifteen-storey coaster called 'The Obliterator' that loops fifty times in five minutes—running over *ninety-five miles per hour!* If you hurry, you can beat the line!" He looked the youngest in the eye at the start of the speech, then switched to the middle when he talked about the line.

The youngest started vibrating with excitement, and the middle looked pensive, and then to the eldest said, "Sounds good, huh, Tom?"

The eldest said, "We haven't even found out where we're sleeping yet—maybe we can do the ride afterwards."

George winked at the youngest, then said, "Don't worry about it, kids. I'll get that sorted out for you right now." He picked up the white house phone and asked the operator to connect him with Guest Services. "Hi there! This is George on the midway! I need reservations for three young men for tonight—a suite, I think, with in-room Nintendo and a big-screen TV. They look like they'd enjoy the Sportaseum. OK, I'll hold," he covered the mouthpiece and said to the boys, "You'll love the Sportaseum—the chairs are shaped like giant catcher's mitts, and the beds are giant Air Jordans, and the suite comes with a regulation half-court. What name should I put the reservation under?"

The eldest said, "Tom Mitchell."

George made the reservation. "You're all set," he said. "The monorails run right into the hotel lobby, every ten minutes. Anyone with a name tag can show you to the nearest stop. Here's

a tip—try the football panzerotto: it's a fried pizza turnover as big
as a football, with beef-jerky laces. It's *my* favorite!"

"I want a football!" the youngest said.

"We'll have it for dinner," the eldest said, looking off at the skyline of coaster-skeletons in the distance. "Let's go on some rides
first."

George beamed his idiot's grin at them as they left, then his face
went slack and he went back to wiping down the surfaces. A
moment later, a hand reached across the counter and plucked the
cloth from his grip. He looked up, startled, into Joe's grinning face.
Unlike his brothers', Joe's face was all sharp angles and small teeth.
Nobody knew what a child of a tongue was supposed to look like,
but George had always suspected that Joe wasn't right, even for a
third son.

"Big guy!" Joe shouted. "Workin' hard?"

George said, "Yes." He stood, patiently, waiting for Joe to give
him the cloth back.

Joe held it over his head like a standard, dancing back out of
reach, even though George hadn't made a grab for it. George
waited. Joe walked back to his counter and gave it back.

"We're dozing the FreakZone," Joe said, in a conspiratorial
whisper. He put a spin on *We're*, making sure that George knew he
was including himself with the Island's management.

"Really," George said, neutrally.

"Yeah! We're gonna flatten that sucker, start fresh, and build us a
new theme land. I'm a Strategic Project Consultant! By the time
it's over, I'll be an Imagineer!"

George knew that the lands on Pleasure Island were flattened
and rebuilt on a regular basis, as management worked to stay ahead
of the lightspeed boredom-threshold of the mainland. Still, he said,
"Well, Joe, that's marvelous. I'm sure you'll do a fabulous job."

Joe sneered at him. "Oh, I know I will. We all do just *fabulous*
jobs, brother. Just some of us *have* fabulous jobs to do."

George refused to rise to the bait. He could always outwait Joe.

Joe said, "We're thinking of giving it a monster theme—
monsters are testing very high with eleven-to-fourteens this
year. Dragons, ogres, cyborgs, you know. We may even do a

walk-through—there hasn't been one of those here since the sixties!"

George didn't know what Joe wanted him to say. He said, "That sounds very nice."

Joe gave him a pitying look, and then his chest started ringing. He extracted a slim phone from his shirt-pocket and turned away. A moment later, he turned back. "Gotta go!" he said. "Meeting with Woodrow and Orville, down at Ops!"

Alarm bells went off in George's head. "Shouldn't Bill go along if you're meeting with Orville?"

Joe sneered at him, then took off at a fast clip down the midway. George watched him until he disappeared through one of the access doors.

Bill was clearly upset about it. George couldn't help but feel responsible. He should have called Bill as soon as Joe told him he was meeting with Orville, but he'd waited until he got home.

He'd been home for hours, and Joe still wasn't back. Bill picked absently at the dinner he'd made and fretted.

"He didn't say how Orville found out?" Bill asked.

George shook his head mutely.

"Why didn't he invite me?" Bill asked. "I always handle negotiations for us."

George couldn't eat. The more Bill fretted, the more he couldn't eat. It was long dark outside, hours and hours after Joe should've been home. Bill fretted, George stared out the window, and Joe didn't come home.

Then, an electric cart's headlights swept up the trail to their cabin. The lights dazzled George, so he couldn't see who was driving. Bill joined him at the window and squinted. "It's Joe and Orville!" he said. George squinted too, but couldn't make anything out. He took Bill's word for it and joined him outside.

It was indeed Orville and Joe. Orville was driving, and Joe was lolling drunkenly beside him. Orville shook hands with Bill and nodded to George, who lifted Joe out of the cart and carried him inside.

When he got back, Orville and Bill were staring calmly into each other's eyes, each waiting for the other to say something.

Orville was dressed in his working clothes: a natty white suit with a sport-shirt underneath. His bald head gleamed in the moonlight. His fleshy, unreadable face was ruddy in the glow from the cabin's door. George bit his tongue to keep from speaking.

"He's drunk," Orville said, at last. Orville didn't beat around the bush.

"I can see that," Bill said. "Did you get him drunk?"

"Yes, I did. We were celebrating."

Bill's eyes narrowed. "So you know."

Orville smiled. "Of course I know. I set it up. I thought you'd approve: Joe clearly needed something to keep him out of trouble."

Bill said, "This will keep him out of trouble?"

Orville leaned against the cart's bumper, pulled out a pipe, stuffed it and lit it. He puffed at it, and watched the smoke wisp away in the swamp breezes. "I think that Joe's going to really like life with the Imagineers. They're Management's precious darlings who can do no wrong. Anything they ask for, they get. There won't be any more discipline problems."

Bill said, "Why not?"

Orville grinned without showing his teeth. "Where there's no discipline, there're no discipline problems. He can work whatever hours he wants. He'll have access to anything he needs: budget, staff, an office, whatever. It's his dream job."

Bill said, "I don't like this."

George wondered why not. It sounded pretty good to him.

Orville puffed at his pipe. "Like it or not, I think you'll have a hard time convincing Joe not to do it. He's sold."

Bill went back into the cabin and closed the door.

"He took that well, don't you think?" Orville asked.

George said, "I suppose so."

Orville said, "Is everything working out all right for you? Shifts OK? Co-workers?"

George said, "Everything's fine. Thank you."

Orville tapped his pipe out on the bumper, then got back into the cart. "All right then. Good night, George."

George started cooking dinner for two. More and more, Joe spent the night in a suite at one of the hotels, "Working late." George didn't know what sort of work he was doing, but he sure seemed to enjoy it. He hardly came back to the cabin at all. The first time he'd stayed out all night, Bill had gone back to the Island and gotten Orville out of bed to help him search. After that, Joe started sending out a runner, usually some poor Ops trainee, to tell them he wasn't coming back for dinner. Eventually, he stopped bothering, and Bill stopped worrying.

One night, a month after Orville had come out to the cabin, George slathered a muskrat's carcass with mayonnaise and lemon and dragonfly eggs and set it out for him and Joe.

Bill hardly ate, which was usually a signal that he was thinking. George left him half of the dinner and waited for him to speak. Bill picked his way through the rest, then pushed his plate away. George cleared it and brought them both mason jars full of muddy water from the swamp out back. Bill took his jar out front of the cabin and leaned against the wall and stared out into the night, sipping. George joined him.

"We're getting old," Bill said, at last.

"Every night, the inside of my uniform is black," George said.

"Mine, too. We're getting very old. I think that you're at least thirty, and I'm pretty sure that I'm twenty-five. That's old. Our father told me that he thought he was fifty, the year he died. And he was very old for one of us."

George thought of their father on his deathbed, eating the food they chewed for him, eyes nearly blind, skin crazed with cracks. "He was very old," George said.

Bill held his two whole hands up against the stars. "When father was my age, he had two sons. Can you remember how proud he was of us? How proud he was of himself? He'd done well enough that he could lose both his thumbs, and still know that his sons would take care of him."

George shifted and sighed. He'd been thinking about sons, too.

"I've wanted a son since we came to the Island," Bill said. "I never did anything about it because I couldn't take care of Joe and a son." Bill turned to look at George. "I think Joe's finally taking care of himself."

George didn't know what to say. If Bill had a son, then he couldn't. They couldn't both stop working to raise their sons. But Bill always made the decisions for them. George didn't know what to say, so he said nothing.

"I'm going to have a son," Bill said.

Bill did it the next night. He told Orville that he'd need a month off, and after eating the dinner George made for them, he made a nest of earth and blankets on the floor of their cabin.

George sat in the corner and watched Bill as he stared at his thumbs. It was the most important decision one of their kind ever made: a clever son of the left hand, or a strong son of the right. George knew that his son would come from the left hand. In the world his father had brought them to, cleverness was far more important than strength. After all, Bill was having the first son.

Bill put his clever left thumb in his mouth and slowly, slowly, bit down. George felt muddy tears pricking at his eyes. Bill's hand coursed with silty blood. He ignored it, and used his strong right hand to take the severed thumb from his mouth and bed it down with infinite care in the nest he'd built.

George cautiously moved forward to peer at the thumb, which was already moving blindly in its nest, twisting like a grub. Bill looked on, his eyes shining.

"It's perfect," George breathed.

George felt an uncharacteristic welling up inside him, and he put his arm around Bill's shoulders. Bill leaned into him, and said, "Thank you, George. This family wouldn't exist without you."

They both slept curled around the nest that night.

By morning, the thumb had sprouted tiny arm- and leg-buds, and it inched itself blindly around the nest. George marveled at it before going to work.

Joe stopped by his stand that day. His belly was bigger than ever, and his skin was cracking like their father's had. "Big guy!" he shouted, vaulting the counter into George's stand. "Where's Bill today? He wasn't at his post."

George said, "Bill had a son last night. From his left hand."

Joe rolled his eyes, which had gone the murky yellow of swamp water. "Wonderful, right? Ugh. There are better ways to achieve immortality, bro. I'm designing a crawl-through for HorrorZone: you're an earthworm crawling underneath a graveyard. It's gonna be huge: maggots as big as horses, chasing the Guests through the tunnels; huge ghost hands grabbing at them. We're building a giant tombstone as the weenie, you'll be able to see it from anywhere on the Island. We'll build out over the midway for HorrorZone—it's the biggest rehab we've done since they brought in electric power."

As usual, George didn't know what to say to Joe. "That sounds very nice," he said.

Joe rolled his eyes again and started to say something, but stopped when three Guests came up to George's booth. George hardly recognized the Mitchell brothers. The youngest was already three-quarters donkey, so dangerously close that it was a miracle he hadn't been picked up already. He was hunched over, and his hands were fused into fists. His hair had grown down over his shoulders in a coarse mane, and his lips bulged around his elongated jaws.

The middle and eldest were well on their ways, too. The points of their ears poked out from under their hair, and they carried themselves painfully, forcing their legs and hips upright.

George flipped over his phone and punched 911, but left it out of sight below the counter. Loudly, he said, "Come on over, boys! You look like you could use one of George's triple-dips, the best on the midway!"

From the phone, he heard the security operator say, "Thank you, George, we'll be along in a moment." Surreptitiously, he racked the receiver and smiled at the boys.

"How are you enjoying your stay, boys?" he said.

"It'th aw-thome!" the youngest said around his clumsy teeth.

George handed him a cone piled high with floss, then started building two more for his brothers. Joe smirked at them. George hoped he wouldn't say anything before security got there.

The eldest said, "I don't think my brother's feeling too good. Is there a doctor here I can take him to?"

The youngest, face sticky with confection, kicked his brother.

"I'm fine!" he said. "I wanna go on more rideth!"

His brother said, "We'll go on more rides after we see a doctor."

The youngest dropped to his knees and cried. "No!" he said, hammering his fists on the ground. "No no no no!" George watched in alarm as the boy went all the way over to donkey. His cries turned to brays, and his shorts split around his haunches and tail. His shirt went next, and George smoothly vaulted the counter and stood in front of the donkey, blocking him from passers-by. The other two made a run for it. George snagged the middle by his collar, but the boy tore free and took off down the midway. George looked about wildly for security, but they still hadn't arrived.

Then Joe tore past him, moving faster than George had ever seen him go. He caught the boys and stuffed one under each arm, kicking and squirming. He grinned ferociously as he pinned them beneath his knees at George's feet. He clamped his hands over their mouths. "Got 'em!" he said to George.

A security team emerged from the utilidor beside George's booth, wearing clown makeup and baggy pants. Two of them tranquilized the boys and the third fitted the donkey out with a halter and bit. The clown slapped the donkey's haunch appreciatively. "He's a healthy one."

The security team disappeared down the utilidor with the Mitchell brothers: two boys and a donkey.

Joe smacked George on the back. "Did you see me catch them? Like greased lightning! Bounty, here I come!"

George didn't mind sharing his bounty with Joe, so he just smiled and nodded and went back around to his booth.

Bill named his son Tom. Names weren't very important to their people, but the soft ones' world demanded them. Within a week, Tom was eagerly toddling through their cabin, tasting everything, exploring everything. His eyes shone with curious brilliance. The clever son of a clever son.

George loved Bill's son. He loved to watch Tom as he gnawed at their bedding, as he dug at the floor in search of grubs. Tom was clearly delighted with his surroundings, and George basked in Tom's delight. Bill could barely restrain himself from picking Tom up and hugging him every moment. The only time he left George alone with Tom was a few precious moments after each evening's meal, when he would duck into the woods to find some new toy for Tom: a crippled chipmunk; a handful of pretty rocks; a discarded beer can. The son built bizarre towers out of them, then knocked them down in a fit of giggles. Tom ate all day long, and spoke a steady stream of adorable nonsense.

Bill hardly spoke to George. Their evening meals were given over to watching the son eat. George didn't mind. Talking to the Guests all day wore him out.

When Tom was two months old, Joe came by George's booth.

"Well, it's final. Tomorrow, we shut down the midway. Too old-fashioned—it's only stood this long because some of the older Imagineers had an emotional attachment to it. I told 'em: 'that's *your* demographic, not the *target* demographic.' So we're knocking it down. HorrorZone's gonna be *huge*." He skipped off before George could say anything. His ears were long and pointed. It wasn't the first time George noticed it, but now, he could see that Joe's hunched-over gait wasn't just because of his belly.

George built a dozen cones for the Guests, but his heart wasn't in it. Besides, most of the Guests already had their hands full of gummi spiders and snakes, from the Actionland Jungle Treats buffet. His thoughts were full of Joe, and he turned them over in his slow, cautious manner. Joe was turning into a donkey. He didn't think that one of their kind could turn into a donkey, but this was Pleasure Island. Indulging your vices was a dangerous pastime here. He should tell Bill, but there was no phone at the cabin. He couldn't send a runner for him, because this was family business. His shift wouldn't end for hours yet, and this was too important to wait.

Finally, he called his Lead. "I have to get offstage. I'm having a bad day."

Technically, this was allowed. Management didn't want anyone onstage who wasn't 100 percent. But it was something that none of the brothers, not even Joe, had ever done. The Lead was surprised, but he sent over a soft one to relieve George.

Orville and Bill were sitting out front of the cabin, watching Tom, when George got back. He wrung his hands as he approached them, not sure of what to say, and whether he should talk in front of Orville at all. He held his left thumb in his right hand, and it comforted him, a little.

Bill and Orville were so engrossed in Tom's antics that they didn't even notice George until he cleared his throat. Orville raised his eyebrows and looked significantly at Bill.

"I just saw Joe," George said. "On the midway. His ears are pointed, and he's walking all hunched over. I give him a few days at the most before he's all the way gone." George held his breath, waiting for Bill's reaction.

"Too bad," Bill said. "It was inevitable, I suppose. A child of the tongue! What was father thinking?"

Orville smiled and puffed at his pipe. "Don't you worry about it, George. Joe's going to be much, much happier. Focused. If you'd like, I can bring him out here to live. Little Tom could have pony rides."

Bill said, "I don't think that's such a good idea. Joe's too wild to play with a child."

Orville put a hand on his shoulder. "You'd be amazed at how docile he'll become."

Bill scooped up Tom, who was up to his waist now, and who liked to grab onto Bill's nose. "We'll see, then." He retreated into the cabin with his son.

Orville turned to George and said, "You've probably heard that we're taking down the midway tomorrow. The others are all being reassigned until the rehab is done, but I thought I'd see if I could get you a couple months off. You could stay here and play with Tom—it's not every day you get to be a new uncle."

Orville had always taken obvious pleasure in the transformation of boys into donkeys. It was the whole why of Pleasure Island, after all. Orville seemed especially pleased tonight, and George thought that he was as surprised about Bill as George was.

George, not knowing what to say to any of it, said nothing.

It didn't take long for George to start missing the midway. Stuck at the cabin with Bill and Tom, he sat against an outside wall and tried not to get in the way. He prepared meals in silence, taking a long time in the woods, gathering up choice morsels. Bill and Tom ate on the floor, away from the table. Bill chewed the tougher morsels first, and then put them in Tom's mouth with his crippled left hand. Most of the time, neither of them took any notice of George.

One day, he prepared a whole day's worth of meals and left them on the table, then walked to the utilidor at the other side of the woods. He boarded a tram and rode to the old midway entrance.

The midway was fenced in with tall plywood sheets, and construction crews bustled over the naked skeletons of the new HorrorZone. Heavy machinery groaned and crashed. Nothing but the distant silhouettes of Actionland's skyline were familiar. George tried to imagine working here for years to come. An overwhelming tiredness weighed him down.

He took the tram back to the cabin and stripped off his clothes. They were browner than ever. His arms felt weak and tired. He suddenly knew that he would never have a son of his own.

Bill and Tom were playing out front of the cabin. He sat in his usual spot against the wall and watched them. "Bill," he said, softly.

"Yes?" Bill said.

"When will I have a son of my own?" Bill always knew the answers.

Bill gathered Tom up to his chest unconsciously while he thought. "I suppose that once Tom is grown, you could take some time off and have a son of your own."

To his own surprise, George said, "I want to have a son now."

Bill said, "That's out of the question, George. We're too busy with Tom." On hearing Bill's annoyed tone, Tom leaned into him.

George said, "I'm not busy. I am old, though. If I don't have a son soon, I won't be able to care for it until it's old enough to care for me."

Bill said, "You're thinking like Father. We're living with the soft ones now. Orville will make sure that you and your son will be fine until he's grown."

George never won arguments with Bill. He went inside the

cabin and set out dinner.

Orville visited the brothers the next morning. He chucked Tom under the chin and shook hands with Bill. Then he took George out into the woods for a walk.

"Your brother tells me you want a son of your own," he said.

George nodded, and stooped to put a small, mossy log in his basket.

"Bill doesn't want you to, huh?"

George didn't feel very comfortable discussing the family with Orville. That was Bill's job. After some thought, he said, "Not right now."

Orville said, "I can see that that makes you unhappy. No one should be unhappy here. I'll see what I can do. Come down to Ops tomorrow morning, we'll talk more."

When George got back to the cabin, Bill was lying on his back on the floor, laughing while Tom climbed all over him. Tom still babbled, but they were real words now, though nonsensical. With his constant talking, he reminded George of Joe, and that made him even sadder.

George had never been to Ops before, but he knew where it was, in a collection of low-slung prefab buildings hidden behind the topiary sculptures near MagicLand. He clutched his right thumb nervously as he stood and waited in the reception area for Orville to come and get him. The secretary had taken his name and buzzed Orville, and now kept sneaking him horrified looks. George's family were the only of their kind to leave their homeland and join the soft ones, and here at Ops, there were any number of low-ranking babus who'd never heard tell of them.

Orville was all smiles and effusion as he breezed through the glass security-door and pounded George on the back. "George! I'm so *glad* you came down!"

He took George by the arm and led him away, stopping to wink at the secretary, who looked at him with a mixture of disgust and admiration.

Orville's office was buried in a twisting maze of door-lined, fluorescent-lit corridors, where busy soft ones talked on telephones and clattered on keyboards. He led George through his door, into an office as big as George's cabin.

Orville paced and talked. "Did I say I was glad you came? I'm glad you came. Now, let's talk about Bill. Bill's happy. He's got what he wants. A son. He doesn't have to take care of Joe. It's good for him."

He paused and looked at George. George nodded.

"OK. There's a problem, though. You want a son, too, only Bill won't allow it."

It didn't need any comment, so George kept quiet.

"My thinking is, Bill's so busy with Tom, he wouldn't really notice if you were there or not. You're an adult, you can take care of yourself. Do you see where I'm going with this?"

George assumed it was a rhetorical question.

"Right. What I'm thinking is, there's no reason that both of you shouldn't have your own son. This is Pleasure Island, after all. No one should be sad on Pleasure Island. You've worked hard and well for us for a long time here. We can take care of you."

George felt an uncomfortable sensation in his stomach, a knot of guilt like rising vomit.

"I thought about having another cabin built in the woods, but that's no good. I think that you and Bill need your own space. So let me bounce my current thought off you: we'll put you up in the new Monster's Arms, that's the hotel we're building for HorrorZone. It's way ahead of schedule, almost finished now. There's a penthouse suite that you can take for as long as you like. It's only temporary, just until you and Bill have had some time to raise up your sons. Then, we'll get the whole family together back at the cabin."

The guilt rose higher, choking George.

"Don't worry about eating, either. I've briefed the house chef on your tastes, and he'll send up three squares every day; everything a growing boy needs." He flashed a grin.

"And forget about Bill. I'll smooth things over with him. He'll see that it's for the best."

Finally, George had something to say. "What about Joe?"

Orville had been almost dancing as he spoke, enchanted with

his own words. He pulled up short when George spoke. "What about him?"

"I want to live with him again," George said.

"He's gone, you know that." Orville pointed his fingers alongside his ears. "Hee-haw, hee-haw. The monthly ferry will take him to the mainland tomorrow."

"I don't care about that," George said. "I want him there."

Orville said, "I don't think that's such a good idea, George. You're going away to concentrate on *you*—Joe's a handful, even now. I don't want you distracted."

George said, "I want Joe."

Orville stared at him. George set his face into a blank mask. Finally, Orville said, "If that's what you want, that's what you'll get."

George didn't have anything to fetch from the cabin, and Orville thought it would be best if he spoke to Bill alone, so he sent George to the stables to get Joe.

The donkey stables were beyond Ops, at the very edge of the island, opposite the docks where the ferries brought new boys in. A different kind of boat docked there, large utility freighters that brought in everything the Island needed and took away braying, kicking herds of jackasses.

The donkeys shifted nervously in their stalls. George smelled horse-apples and hay, and heard fidgeting hooves and quiet, braying sobs. He wasn't clear on what happened to donkeys when they went back to the mainland, but he had an idea that it wasn't very pleasant. On the Island, donkeys were prizes, a sign that a boy's every wish had been gratified. What happened afterwards wasn't something that they were encouraged to think about.

He walked down the clean, wooden aisles, peering into the stalls, looking for Joe. Finally, in a dark stall in the very darkest corner of the stables, he found him. A large, pot-bellied jackass, who leapt up and brayed loudly at him when he clucked his tongue at it.

"Joe?" he asked softly.

The donkey brayed again and kicked at the stall's door. It was already splintered from many such kicks. George opened the catch and was nearly trampled beneath Joe's hooves as he ran out and away, braying loudly. George chased his brother. He didn't start very fast, but once he got going, inertia made him unstoppable.

He cornered Joe at the door that led out to the Island. The donkey was kicking at it, trying for escape. George locked his strong right arm around Joe's neck. "Stop it, Joe," he said. "I'm taking you out with me, but you have to stop it."

Joe's eyes rolled madly, and he struggled against George, kicking and biting. George waited in silence until the donkey tired, then used a bridle hanging on the wall to lead Joe out of the stables.

When Joe saw Orville waiting for them, he went wild again. George caught him by the hind leg and dragged him to the ground, while Orville danced back with a strange grace.

Orville grinned and said, "I guess he doesn't like me very much." He came forward and darted an affectionate pat on Joe's haunch.

Joe brayed loudly and George kept his own counsel. Orville led them down a utilidor and into an electric tram with an open car. George led Joe in and held onto his neck while Orville sped down the utilidor. He drove up a service ramp and out into HorrorZone, then to the doors of the newly completed Monster's Arms.

George and Joe lived in the Monster's Arms. Every morning, Orville paid them a visit and snuck looks at George's thumbs. They were intact.

George wanted to have a son, but he couldn't bring himself to do it. Orville's visits grew shorter, and Orville's manner grew more irritated. Still, George had no son.

One day, he waited until Joe was napping, and slipped out through the iron-maiden elevator, right down into the utilidor.

The tram driver recognized him and took him out to the cabin. The last mile of the utilidor was dusty and disused. George leaped off the tram and walked quickly to the cabin, his heart racing. It had been so long since he'd seen Bill and little Tom. He missed them terribly.

The little cabin was even smaller than George remembered it, and it looked sad, sagging and ramshackle. He hesitated at the door, then, feeling a stranger, knocked.

There was movement inside, but no voices, and the door stayed shut. George opened the door.

It was a disaster. The kitchen cupboards were smashed in, the little table knocked over and splintered, the bedding scattered and soiled. Deep shadows collected in the corners.

"Bill?" George called, softly. A shadow stirred, an indistinct figure within its depths.

"Bill, it's George. I missed you. I need to talk with you. I'm confused."

The shadow stirred again. George crept forward, peering, his old eyes night-dimmed.

Bill huddled in the corner, wracked and wasted. He stared up at George through eyes filmed with tears. He held up his hands. They had already begun to shape themselves into hooves, but George could still see that both his thumbs were gone. His ears were pointed and long.

"Oh, Bill," George said.

His brother let out a braying sob, and George saw he had no tongue.

Orville came looking for them the next morning.

"Where are the sons?" George asked him, while stroking the donkey's head in his lap.

Orville smiled a slightly abashed smile. "I'm keeping them safe. I didn't think that Bill was in any shape to take care of them."

George said, "I'll take care of them. Bring them here. Joe, too— he's in the room. I'll take care of them all."

Orville smiled his abashed smile again, then gave George an ironic salute. "Yes, sir," he said. He patted Bill's haunch and smiled to himself.

George didn't know how to respond to irony, so he held his brother more tightly. Eventually, Orville went away, and then came back a while after that. He drove an electric cart. In the front seat, three sons bounced—Tom, bright and curious; another, strong and big; a third, whose little pot belly jiggled as he talked and talked and talked. In a trailer, Joe kicked and fought against his bonds.

George let him out first, then took the sons to the porch. Joe and Bill stared at each other for a long moment, then Bill brayed out a long, donkeyish laugh.

Orville looked with proprietary satisfaction at the donkeys, then at the sons, then at George. He waggled a finger at George, as if to say, *I'll be back for you, someday.* Then he got into his tram and drove off. George went back inside and made dinner for his family.

This story almost didn't get written. The way I write stories is really stupid: I write the first two-thirds without any particular idea of how it's all going to end, but with a general sense that the ending is going to have to tie together all the memelets and idealings from the first two-thirds of the text. I get to feeling like the person who's going to finish the story is a collaborator, some other writer who's going to be faced with figuring out how it all ties together. When I'm on a roll, I really get into it, chuckling nastily at the thought of this other poor bastard being handed this 16-car-pileup popcult salmagundi, wondering how he's going to bring it all home.

Then, of course, I get to the ending, and I'm standing at the base of this giant, sheer cliff I've erected, figuring out how I'm going to scale it. Usually, I get derailed at this point, and take three or four months off while I work it out in my subconscious.

That's what happened with this story, only it was a couple of years, and I decided I'd take it with to a writer's retreat in Colorado Springs and finish it off there. I had my only copy of it on my PowerBook 145, the latest in a series of hand-me-down laptops, and I stuck it in my carry-on and took a cab to Toronto's Pearson International Airport.

When I got to security, they made me boot up the machine, and when I was done, the officer handed it back to me—and fumbled it. It smashed to the hard poured-concrete floor and broke into many bits. The officer maintained that he'd given it to me and I'd dropped it. I didn't see it that way, but all of his co-workers backed him up. The duty-supervisor smirkingly offered to let me file a report, but warned that it would take a couple hours to go through the paperwork, knowing full well my flight was leaving in twenty minutes.

Fuming, I flew to Colorado Springs, borrowed an old Mac Classic and rekeyed the first twenty-some pages from memory, finished the thing in a huff, and turned it in to the group for dissection.

For all that, I think it came out pretty well!

Shadow of the Mothaship

It's the untethering of my parents' house that's on my plate today. The flying of a kite on a windy Toronto Halloween day and the suspension of worry for a shiny moment.

And sail surface isn't even a problemette when it comes to my parents' home—the thing is a three-story bat whose narrow wings contain the trolleycar-shaped bedrooms and storages. Mum and Dad built it themselves while I tottered in the driveway, sucking a filthy shred of blanket, and as I contemplate it today with hands on hips from the front yard, I am there on that day:

Dad is nailgunning strips of plywood into a frame, Mum stands where I am now, hands on her hips (and I take my hands from my hips hastily, shove them deep in pockets). She squints and shouts directions. Then they both grab rolls of scrim and stapleguns and stretch it loosely across the frames, and fast-bond pipes and prefab fixtures into place. Mum harnesses up the big tanks of foam and aims the blower at the scrim, giving it five fat coats, then she drops the blower and she and Dad grab spatulas and tease zillions of curlicues and baroque stuccoes from the surface, painting it with catsup, chutney, good whiskey and bad wine, a massive canvas covered by centimeters until they declare it ready and Mum switches tanks, loads up with fix-bath and mists it with the salty spray. Ten minutes later, and the house is hard and they get to work unloading the U-Haul in the drive.

And now I'm twenty-two again, and I will untether that house and fly it in the stiff breeze that ruffles my hair affectionately.

Firstly and most foremost, I need to wait for the man. I hate to wait. But today it's waiting and harsh and dull, dull, dull.

So I wait for the man, Stude the Dude and the gentle clip-clop of Tilly's hooves on the traction-nubbed foam of my Chestnut Ave.

My nose is pressed against the window in the bat's crotch, fingers dug into the hump of fatty foam that runs around its perimeter, fog patches covering the rime of ground-in filth that I've allowed to accumulate on my parents' spotless windows.

Where the frig is Stude?

The man has cometh. Clop-clip, clip-clop, Stude the Dude, as long as a dangling booger, and his clapped-out nag Tilly, and the big foam cart with its stacks of crates and barrels and boxes, ready to do the deal.

"Maxes!" he says, and I *know* I'm getting taken today—he looks genuinely glad to see me.

"Stude, nice day, how's it?" I say, as cas and cool as I can, which isn't, very.

"Fine day! Straight up fine day to be alive and awaiting judgment!" He power-chugs from the perpetual coffee thermos at his side.

"Fine day," I echo.

"Fine, fine day." Like he's not in any hurry to get down to the deal, and I know it's a contest, and the first one to wheel gets taken.

I snort and go "Yuh-huh." It's almost cheating, since I should've had something else nice to say, but Stude gives me a conversational Get-Out-of-Jail-Free.

"Good night to tricky treat."

I concede defeat. "I need some stuff, Stude."

Give it to him, he doesn't gloat. Just hauls again from Mr. Coffee and pooches his lips and nods.

"Need, uh, spool of monofilament, three klicks, safety insulated. Four liters of fix bath. Liter, liter and a half of solvent."

"Yeah, okay. Got a permit for the solvent?"

"If I had a permit, Stude, I'd go and buy it at the friggin' store. Don't pull my dick."

"Just askin'. Why for the solvent? Anything illegal?"

"Just a project, Stude. Nothing to worry."

"What kinda project?"

"Art project. Fun-friggin'-tastic. You'll love it."

"Cause you know, they tag the shit with buckyballs now, one molecule in a million with a serial number and a checksum. You do something stupid, I get chopped."

I hadn't known. Didn't matter, my parents' house was legally mine, while they were up confabbing with their alien buds on the mothaship. "No worries."

"That'll be, uh, sixty-eight cents."

"Thirty."

"Sixty, firm."

"Fifty-four."

"Fifty-eight."

"Take it in trade?"

"Fricken Maxes! Tradesies? You're wastin' my time, lookin' for bootleg solvent, looking for trade and no cash? Get fucked, Maxes."

He starts to haw-up Tilly and I go, "Wait-wait-wait, I got some good stuff. Everything must go, moving sale, you know?"

He looks really pissed and I know it hard now, I'm gonna get *taken*. I hand him up my bag, and he does a fast-paw through the junk. "What's this?" he asks.

"Old video game. Atari. Shoot up the space aliens. Really, really antisocial. Needs a display, but I don't got it anymore." I'd sold it the month before on a bored day, and used the eight cents to buy good seats behind home plate at the Skydome and thus killed an entire afternoon before Judgment Day.

There are some of the artyfarty "Freestyle" kitchen utensils Mum used to sell for real cash until Dad founded his Process for Lasting Happiness and she found herself able to pursue "real art." There are paper books and pictures and assorted other crap.

Stude clucks and shakes his head. "If I just gave you the monofil and the fix-bath for this shit, it'd be a favor. Look, I can *get* real money for solvent. I *pay* real money for solvent. This just don't cut it."

"I'll get more, just hang a sec."

He haws-up Tilly but reigns her in slow, and I dash back to my place and fill a duffel with anything I lay hands to, and run out, dragging it behind me, catching the cart before it turns the corner. "Here, here, take this too."

Stude dumps it out in front of him and kicks at the pile. "This is just crap, Maxes. There's lots of it, sure, but it's still crap."

"I need it, Stude, I really need some solvent. You already *got* all my good stuff."

He shakes his head, sad, and says, "Go ask Tilly."

"Ask?"

"Tilly. Ask her."

Stude likes to humiliate you a little before he does you a favor. The word is *capricious*, he told me once.

So I go to his smelly old horse and whisper in her hairy ear and hold my breath as I put my ear next to the rotten jumbo-chiclets she uses for teeth. "She says you should do it," I say. "And she says you're an asshole for making me ask her. She says horses can't talk."

"Yeah, okay," and he tosses me the goods.

With stage one blessedly behind me, I'm ready for stage two. I take the nozzle of the solvent aerosol and run a drizzle along the fatty roll of the windowsills and then pop them out as the fix bath runs away and the windows fly free and shatter on the street below.

Then it's time to lighten the ballast. With kicks and grunts and a mantra of "Out, out, out," I toss everything in the house out, savoring each crash, taking care to leave a clear path between the house and the street.

On the third floor, I find Dad's cardigan, the one Mum gave him one anniversary, and put it on. She carved it herself from foam and fixed it with some flexible, dirt-shedding bath, so by the time I'm done with the third floor, my arms and chest are black with dust, and the sweater is still glowing with eerie cleanliness.

I know Dad wouldn't want me to wear his sweater now. They say that on the mothaship, the bugouts have ways to watch each and every one of us, and maybe Mum and Dad are there, watching me, and so I wipe my nose on the sleeve.

When the ballast is done, phase three begins. I go to work outside of the house, spritzing a line of solvent at the point where the foam meets the ground, until it's all disconnected.

And then I got to kick myself for an asshole. A strand of armored fiber-optic, a steel water pipe, and the ceramic gas line hold it all down, totally impervious to solvent.

Somewhere, in a toolbox that I ditched out the second floor window, is a big old steel meat-cleaver, and now I hunt for it, prying apart the piles of crap with a broomstick, feeling every inch the post-apocalyptic scrounger.

I finally locate it, hanging out of arm's reach from my neighbor Linus's rose trellis. I shake the trellis until it falls, missing my foot, which I jerk away and swear at.

The fiber cleaves with a single stroke. The gas line takes twenty or more, each stroke clanging off the ceramic and sending the blade back alarmingly at my face. Finally it gives, and the sides splinter and a great jet of gas whooshes out, then stops.

I could kick myself for an asshole. Praise the bugouts for civil engineers who made self-sealing pipes. I eye the water line warily and flip open my comm, dial into the city, and touch-tone my way through a near-sexy woman reading menus until I find out that the water, too, self-seals.

Whang, whang, whang, and I'm soaked and blinded by the water that bursts free, and *I could kick myself for an asshole!*

The house, now truly untethered, catches a gust of wind and lifts itself a few meters off the ground, body-checking me on my ass. I do a basketball jump and catch the solvent-melted corner, drag it down to earth, long-arm for the fix bath and slop it where the corner meets the driveway, bonding it there until phase four is ready.

I bond one end of monofilament to the front right corner of the house, then let it unwind, covered in eraser-pink safety goop, until I'm standing in my deserted Chestnut Ave. I spray a dent in the middle of the road with my solvent, plunk the reel into it, bond it, then rush back to the house and unbond that last one corner.

I hit the suck button on the reel and the house slowly drags its way to the street, leaving a gap like a broken tooth in the carefully groomed smile of my Chestnut Ave.

The wind fluffs at the house, making it settle/unsettle like a nervous hen and so I give it line by teasing the spit button on the reel until it's a hundred meters away. Then I reel it in and out, timing it with the gusts until, in a sudden magnificent second, it catches and sails up-and-up-and-up and I'm a friggin' genius.

It's nearly four and my beautiful kite is a dancing bird in the sky before the good little kiddies of my Chestnut Ave start to trickle home from their days of denial, playing at normalcy in the face of Judgment.

Linus is the first one home, and he nearly decapitates himself on the taut line as he cruises past on his bicycle. He slews to a stop and stares unbelieving at me, at the airborne house, at the gap where he had a neighbor.

"Maxes Fuentes Shumacher! What is this?"

"Flying a kite, Linus. Just flyin' a kite. Nice day for it, yeah?"

"This," he says, then sputters. Linus is a big devotee of Dad's Process for Lasting Happiness, and I can actually watch him try to come up with some scripture to cover the situation while he gulps back mouthsful of bile. "This is an Irresponsible Wrong, Maxes. You are being a Feckless Filthy. This is an abuse of property, a Lashing Out at a Figure in Absentia. You are endangering others, endangering aircraft and people and property below that. I insist that you Right-Make this now, this instant."

"Yeah, uh-huh, yeah." And I squint up at my kite, the sun coming down behind it now, and it's just a dot in the big orange fire. The wind's more biting than friendly. I pull the foam sweater a little closer, and do up one of the buttons in the middle.

"Maxes!" Linus shouts, his happiness dissipating. "You have thirty seconds to get that down here, or I will Right-Make it myself."

I didn't live with my dad for twenty years without picking up some Process-speak. "You seem to be Ego-Squeezing here, Lin. This Blame-Saying is a Barrier to Joy, bud, and the mark of a Weekend Happyman. Why don't you go watch some TV or something?"

He ignores me and makes a big show of flipping open his comm and starting a timer running on it.

Man, my kite is a work of art. Megafun.

"Time's up, Feckless Filthy," Linus says, and snakes out and punches the suck button on my monofilament reel. It whizzes and line starts disappearing into its guts.

"You can't bring down a kite *that* way, frickface. It'll crash." Which it does, losing all its airworthiness in one hot second and plummeting like a house.

It tears up some trees down Chestnut, and I hear a Rice Crispies bowl of snap-crackle-pops from further away. I use a shear to clip the line and it zaps away, like a hyperactive snake.

"Moron," I say to Linus. The good kiddies of Chestnut Ave are now trickling home in twos and threes and looking at the gap in the smile with looks of such bovine stupidity that I stalk away in disgust, leaving the reel bonded to the middle of the road forever.

I build a little fort out of a couch and some cushions, slop fix bath over the joints so they're permanent, and hide in it, shivering.

Tricky-treaters didn't come knocking on my pillow-fort last night. That's fine by me. I slept well.

I rise with the sun and the dew and the aches of a cold night on a mattress of clothes and towels.

I flip open my comm, and there's a half-doz clippings my agent's found in the night. Five are about the bugouts; I ignore those. One is about the kite.

It crashed around Highway 7 and the 400 in Vaughan, bouncing and skidding. Traffic was light, and though there were a few fender-benders, nothing serious went down. The city dispatched a couple-three guys to go out with solvent and melt the thing, but by the time they arrived, an errant breeze had lofted it again, and it flew another seventy kay, until it crossed the antidebris field at Jean Paul Aristide International in Barrie.

I'm hungry. I'm cold. My teeth are beshitted with scum. Linus comes tripping Noel Coward out of his front door and I feel like kicking his ass. He sees me staring at him.

"Did you have a good night, Maxes?"

"Spiff, strictly nift. Eat shit and die."

He tsks and shakes his head and gets on his bicycle. He works down at Yonge and Bloor, in the big Process HQ. His dad was my dad's lieutenant, and since they both went to the confab on the mothaship (along with all the other grownups on my Chestnut Ave), he's sort of in charge. Shit-eating prick. He lisps a little when he talks, and he's soft and pudgy, not like Dad, who could orate like a Roman tyrant and had a washboard for a gut.

I hope he gets hit by a semi.

I pass the morning with my comm, till I come to the pict of Mum and Dad and their Process buds on the jetway to the shuttle at Aristide, ascending to the heavens as humanity's reps. They're both naked and arm-in-arm and as chaste as John and Yoko, and my eyes fill up with tears. I crawl back into my fort and sleep and dream about buzzing Chestnut Ave in a shuttle with a payload of solvent, melting down all the houses into trickles that disappear into the sewers.

I wake for the second time that day to the sound of a gas engine, a rarity on Chestnut Ave and the surrounding North Toronto environs. It's a truck, from the city, the kind they used to use to take away the trash before the pneuma was finished—Dad pointed out how it was a Point of Excellence, the plans for the subterranean pneuma, and his acolytes quietly saw to it. Three men in coveralls and reflective vests ride on the back. It pulls up into my drive, and my comm chimes.

It's a text-only message, signed and key-crypted from Linus, on Process letterhead. The first thing it does is flash a big message about how by reading it, I have logged my understanding of its contents and it is now officially served to me, as per blah blah blah. Legal doc.

I scroll down, just skimming. ". . . *non compos mentis* . . . anti-social destruction of property . . . reckless endangerment of innocent life . . . violation of terms . . . sad duty of the Trustees . . ."—and by the time I'm finished the message, I'm disinherited. Cut off from the Process trust fund. Property stripped. Subpoenaed to a competency hearing.

The driver of the truck has been waiting for me to finish the note. He makes eye contact with me, I make eye contact with him. The other two hop out and start throwing my piles of ballast into the back of the truck.

I take my bicycle from the shed out back, kick my way through the piles of crap, and ride off into the sunset.

For Christmas I hang some tinsel from my handlebars and put a silver star on the big hex-nut that holds the headset to the front forks.

Tony the Tiger thinks that's pretty funny. He stopped into my sickroom this morning as I lay flat on my back on my grimy, sweaty futon, one arm outflung, hand resting on the twisted wreckage of my front wheel. He stood in the doorway, grinning from striped shirt to flaming red moustache, and barked "Hah!" at me.

Which is his prerogative, since this is his place I'm staying at, here in a decaying Rosedale mansion gone to spectacular Addams Family ruin, this is where he took me in when I returned on my bike from the ghosttown of Niagara Falls, where I'd built a nest of crap from the wax-museums and snow-globe stores until the kitsch of it all squeezed my head too hard and I rode home, to a Toronto utterly unlike the one I'd left behind. I'd been so stunned by it all that I totally missed the crater at Queen and Brock, barreling along at forty kay, and I'd gone down like a preacher's daughter, smashing my poor knee and my poor bike to equally dismal fragments.

"Hah!" I bark back at Tony the Tiger. "Merry happy, dude."

"You, too."

Which it is, more or less, for us ragtags who live on Tony the Tiger's paternal instincts and jumbo survivalist-sized boxes of Corn Flakes.

And now it's the crack of noon, and my navel is thoroughly contemplated, and my adoring public awaits, so it's time to struggle down bravely and feed my face.

I've got a robe, it used to be white, and plush, with a hood. The hood's still there, but the robe itself is the sweat-mat gray of everything in Tony the Tiger's dominion. I pull it on and grope for my cane. I look down at the bruisey soccerball where my knee used to be and gingerly snap on the brace that Tony fabbed up for me out of foam and velcro. Then it's time to stand up.

"Friggin'-mother-shit-jesus-fuck!" I shout and drown out my knee's howls of protest.

"Y'okay?" floats Tony's voice up the stairs.

"Peachy keen!" I holler back and start my twenty-two-year-old old-fogey shuffle down the stairs: step, drag.

On the ground-floor landing, someone's used aerosol glitter to silver the sandbags that we use to soak up bullets randomly fired into our door. It's a wonderful life.

I check myself out in the mirror. I'm skinny and haunted and stubbly and gamey. Num.

There's a pair of size-nine Kodiaks in a puddle of melting slush and someone's dainty wet sock-prints headed for the kitchen. Daisy Duke's home for the holidays. Off to the kitchen for me.

And there she is, a vision of brave perseverance in the face of uncooperative climate. She's five-six average; not-thin, not-fat average; eyes an average hazel; tits, two; arms, two; legs, two; and skin the color of Toronto's winter, sun-deprived-white with a polluted grey tinge. My angel of mercy.

She leaps out of her chair and is under my arm supporting me before I know it. "Maxes, hi," she says, drawing out the "Hi" like an innuendo.

"Daisy Duke, as I live and breathe," I say, and she's got the same mix of sweat and fun-smell coming off her hair as when she sat with me while I shouted and raved about my knee for a week after coming to Tony the Tiger's.

She puts me down in her chair as gently as an air-traffic controller. She gives my knee a look of professional displeasure, as though it were swollen and ugly because it wanted to piss her off. "Lookin' down and out there, Maxes. Been to a doctor yet?"

Tony the Tiger, sitting on the stove, head ducked under the exhaust hood, stuffs his face with a caramel corn and snorts. "The boy won't go. I tell him to go, but he won't go. What to do?"

I feel like I should be pissed at him for nagging me, but I can't work it up. Dad's gone, taken away with all the other Process-heads on the mothaship, which vanished as quickly as it had appeared. The riots started immediately. Process HQ at Yonge and Bloor was magnificently torched, followed by the worldwide franchises. Presumably, we'd been Judged, and found wanting. Only a matter of time, now.

So I can't get pissed at Tony for playing fatherly. I kind of even like it.

And besides, now that hospitals are turf, I'm as likely to get kakked as cured, especially when they find out that dear ole Dad was the bull-goose Process-head. Thanks, Pop.

"That right? Won't go take your medicine, Maxes?" She can do this eye-twinkle thing, turn it off and on at will, and when she does, it's like there's nothing average about her at all.

"I'm too pretty to make it in there."

Daisy turns to Tony and they do this leaders-of-the-commune meaningful-glance thing that makes me apeshit. "Maybe we could get a doc to come here?" Daisy says, at last.

"And perform surgery in the kitchen?" I say back. All the while, my knee is throbbing and poking out from under my robe.

Daisy and Tony hang head and I feel bad. These two, if they can't help, they feel useless. "So, how you been?" I ask Daisy, who has been AWOL for three weeks, looking for her folks in Kitchen-Waterloo, filled up with the holiday spirit.

"Baby, it's cold outside. Took highway 2 most of the way—the 407 was drive-by city. The heater on the Beetle quit about ten minutes out of town, so I was driving with a toque and mittens and all my sweaters. But it was nice to see the folks, you know? Not fun, but nice."

Nice. I hope they stuck a pole up Dad's ass and put him on top of the Xmas tree.

"It's good to be home. Not enough fun in Kitchener. I am positively fun-hungry." She doesn't look it, she looks wiped up and wrung out, but hell, I'm pretty fun hungry, too.

"So what's on the Yuletide agenda, Tony?" I ask.

"Thought we'd burn down the neighbors', have a cheery fire." Which is fine by me—the neighbors split two weeks before. Morons from Scarborough, thought that down in Florida people would be warm and friendly. Hey, if they can't be bothered to watch the tacticals fighting in the tunnels under Disney World, it's none of my shit.

"Sounds like a plan," I say.

We wait until after three, when everyone in the happy household has struggled home or out of bed. We're almost twenty when assembled, ranging from little Tiny Tim to bulldog Pawn-Shop Maggie, all of us unrecalcitrants snagged in the tangle of Tony's hypertrophied organizational skills.

The kitchen at Tony's is big enough to prepare dinner for forty guests. We barely fit as we struggle into our parkas and boots. I end up in a pair of insulated overalls with one leg slit to make room for my knee/soccerball. If this was Dad and Mum, it'd be like we were gathered for a meeting, waiting for the Chairman to give us the word. But that's not Tony's style; he waits until we're approaching ready, then starts moving toward the door, getting out the harness. Daisy Duke shoulders a kegger of foam and another full of kerosene, and Grandville gets the fix-bath. Tiny Tim gets the sack of marshmallows and we trickle into the yard.

It was a week and a half after Halloween when the vast cool intelligences from beyond the stars zapped away. The whole year since they'd arrived, the world had held its breath and tippytoed around on best behave. When they split, it exhaled. The gust of that exhalation carried the stink of profound pissed-offedness with the Processors who'd acted the proper Nazi hall-monitors until the bugouts went away. I'd thrown a molotov into the Process center at the Falls myself, and shouted into the fire until I couldn't hear myself.

So now I'm a refugee on Xmas Eve, waiting for fearless leader to do something primordial and cathartic. Which he does, even if he starts off by taking the decidedly non-primordial step of foaming the side of our squat that faces the neighbors', then fixing it, Daisy Duke whanging away on the harness's seal with a rock to clear the ice. Once our place is fireproofed, Daisy Duke switches to kero, and we cheer and clap as it laps over the neighbors', a two-story coach-house. The kero leaves shiny patches on the rime of frost that covers the place. My knee throbs, so I sit/kneel against the telephone pole out front.

The kids are getting overexcited, pitching rocks at the glass to make holes for the jet of kero. Tony shuts down the stream, and I think for a minute that he's pissed, he's gonna take a piece out of someone, but instead he's calm and collected, asks people to sort out getting hoses, buckets and chairs from the kitchen. Safety first, and I have to smile.

The group hops to it, extruding volunteers through a non-obvious Brownian motion, and before long all of Tony's gear is spread out on the lawn. Tony then crouches down and carves a shallow bowl out of the snow. He tips the foam-keg in, then uses his gloves to sculpt out a depression. He slops fix-bath on top, then fills his foam-and-snow bowl with the last of the kero.

"You all ready?" he says, like he thinks he's a showman.

Most of us are cold and wish he'd just get it going, but Tony's the kind of guy you want to give a ragged cheer to.

He digs the snow out from around the bowl and holds it like a discus. "Maestro, if you would?" he says to Daisy Duke, who uses long fireplace match to touch it off. The thing burns like a brazier, and Tony the Tiger frisbees it square into the middle of the porch.

There's a tiny *chuff* and then all the kero seems to catch at once and the whole place is cheerful orange and warm as the summer.

We pass around the marshmallows and Tony's a friggin' genius.

The flames lick and spit, and the house kneels in slow, majestic stages. The back half collapses first, a cheapie addition that's fifty years younger than the rest of the place. The front porch follows in the aftershock, and it sends a constellation of embers skittering towards the marshmallow-roasters, who beat at each other's coats until they're all extinguished.

As the resident crip, I've weaseled my way into one of the kitchen chairs, and I've got it angled to face the heat. I sit close enough that my face feels like it's burning, and I turn it to the side and feel the delicious cool breeze.

The flames are on the roof, now, and I'm inside my own world, watching them. They dance spacewards, and I feel a delicious thrill as I realize that the bugouts are not there, that the bugouts are not watching, that they took my parents and my problems and vanished.

I'm broken from the reverie by Daisy Duke, who's got a skimask on, the mouth rimmed in gummy marshmallow. She's got two more marshmallows in one three-fingered cyclist's glove.

"Mmm. Marshmallowey," I say. It's got that hard carboniferous skin and the gooey inside that's hot enough to scald my tongue. "I *like* it."

"Almost New Year's," she says.

"Yuh-huh."

"Gonna make any resolutions?" she asks.

"You?"

"Sure," she says, and I honestly can't imagine what this perfectly balanced person could possibly have to resolve. "You first," she says.

"Gonna get my knee fixed up."

"That's *it?*"

"Yuh-huh. The rest, I'll play by ear. Maybe I'll find some Process-heads to hit. How'bout you?"

"Get the plumbing upstairs working again. Foam the whole place. Cook one meal a week. Start teaching self-defense. Make sure your knee gets fixed up." And suddenly, she seems like she's real *old*, even though she's only twenty-five, only three years older than me.

"Oh, yeah. That's real good."

"Got any *other* plans for the next year, Maxes?"

"No, nothing special." I feel a twinge of freeloader's anxiety. "Maybe try and get some money, help out around here. I don't know."

"You don't have to worry about that. Tony may run this place, but I'm the one who found it, and I say you can stay. I just don't want to see you," she swallows, "You know, waste your life."

"No sweatski." I'm not even thinking as I slip into *this* line. "I'll be just fine. Something'll come up, I'll figure out what I want to do. Don't worry about me."

Unexpectedly and out of the clear orange smoke, she hugs me and hisses in my ear, fiercely, "I *do* worry about you, Maxes. I *do*." Then Bunny nails her in the ear with a slushball and she dives into a flawless snap-roll, scooping snow on the way for a counterstrike.

Tony the Tiger's been standing beside me for a while, but I just noticed it now. He barks a trademarked Hah! at me. "How's the knee?"

"Big, ugly and swollen."

"Yum. How's the brain?"

"Ditto."

"Double-yum."

"Got any New Year's resolutions, Tony?"

"Trim my moustache. Put in a garden, here where the neighbors' place was. Start benching in the morning, work on my upper-body. Foam the house. Open the rooms in the basement, take in some more folks. Get a cam and start recording house meetings. Start an e-zine for connecting up squats. Some more things. You?"

"Don't ask," I say, not wanting to humiliate myself again.

He misunderstands me. "Well, don't sweat it: if you make too many resolutions, you're trying, and that's what counts."

"Yuh-huh." It feels good to be overestimated for a change.

Tony used to work in the customer-service dept at Eatons-Walmart, the big one at Dundas and Yonge where the Eaton Center used to be. They kept offering him promotions and he kept turning them down. He wanted to stay there, acting as a guide through the maze of bureaucracy you had to navigate to get a refund when you bought the dangerous, overpriced shit they sold. It shows.

It's like he spent thirty years waiting for an opportunity to grab a megaphone and organize a disaster-relief.

The neighbors' is not recognizable as a house anymore. Some people are singing carols. Then it gets silly and they start singing dirty words, and I join in when they launch into Jingle Bells, translated into Process-speak.

I turn back into the fire and lose myself in the flickers, and I don't scream at all.

Fuck you, Dad.

Someone scrounged a big foam minikeg of whiskey, and someone else has come up with some chewable vitamin C soaked in something *up*, and the house gets going. Those with working comms—who pays for their subscriptions, I wonder—micropay for some tuneage, and we split between the kitchen and the big old parlor, dancing and Merry Xmassing late.

About half an hour into it, Tony the Tiger comes in the servant's door, his nose red. He's got the hose in one hand, glove frozen tiff from blow-back. I'm next to the door, shivering, and he grins. "Putting out the embers."

I take his gloves and toque from him and add them to the drippy pile beside me. I've got a foam tumbler of whiskey and I pass it to him.

The night passes in the warmth of twenty sweaty, boozy, speedy bodies, and I hobble from pissoir to whiskey, until the whiskey's gone and the pissoir is swimming from other people's misses, and then I settle into a corner of one of the ratty sofas in the parlor, dozing a little and smiling.

Someone wakes me with a hard, whiskey-fumed kiss on the cheek. "How can you *sleep* on *speed*, Maxes?" Daisy shrieks into my ear. I'm not used to seeing her cut so loose, but it suits her. That twinkle is on perma-strobe and she's down to a sportsbra and cycling shorts. She bounces onto the next cushion.

I pull my robe tighter. "Just lucky that way." Speed hits me hard, then drops me like an anvil. My eyelids are like weights. She wriggles up to me, and even though she's totally whacked, she manages to be careful of my knee. Cautiously, I put my arm around her shoulders. She's clammy with sweat.

"Your Dad, he musta been some pain in the ass, huh?" She's babbling in an adrenalized tone, and the muscles under my hand are twitching.

"Yeah, he sure was."

"I can't imagine it. I mean, we used to watch him on the tube and groan—when the bugouts got here and he told everyone that he'd been invited to explain to them why they should admit humanity into the Galactic Federation, we laughed our asses off. My sister, she's thirty, she's somewhere out west, we think, maybe Winnipeg, she had a boyfriend in highschool who ended up there. . . ."

It takes her four more hours to wind down, and I think I must be picking up a contact-high from her, because I'm not even a little tired. Eventually, she's lying with her head in my lap, and I can feel my robe slip underneath her, and I'm pretty sure my dick is hanging out underneath her hair, but none of it seems to matter. No matter how long we sit there, I don't get cramps in my back, none in my knee, and by the time we both doze away, I think I may be in love.

I should have spent the night in my bed. I wake up nearly twenty hours later, and my knee feels like it's broken into a million pieces, which it is. I wake with a yelp, catch my breath, yelp again, and Daisy is up and crouching beside me in a flash. Tony arrives a moment later and they take me to bed. I spend New Year's there, behind a wall of codeine, and Daisy dips her finger into her glass of fizzy nauga-champagne and touches it to my lips at midnight.

I eat four codeine tabs before getting up, my usual dose. Feb is on us, as filthy and darky as the grime around the toilet bowl, but I accentuate the positive.

By the time I make it downstairs, Tony's in full dervish, helping unload a freshly-scrounged palette of brown bread, lifted from the back of some bakery. He grins his trademark at me when I come into the kitchen and I grin back.

"Foo-oo-ood!" he says, tearing the heel of a loaf and tossing it my way. A half-doz of my housemates, new arrivals whose names I haven't picked up yet, are already sitting around the kitchen, stuffing their faces.

I reach into my robe-pocket for my comm and shout "Smile!" and snap a pict, then stash it in the dir I'm using for working files for the e-zine.

"What's the caption?" said Tony.

"*Man oh manna*," I say.

I eat my heel of bread, then stump into the room that Daisy calls the butler's pantry, that I use for my office and shut the door. Our e-zine, *Sit/Spin*, went from occasional to daily when I took it over after New Year's, and I commandeered an office to work in. Apparently, it's de rigueur cafe reading in Copenhagen.

Whatever. The important things are:

1) I can spend a whole day in my office without once remembering to need to take a pill;

2) When I come out, Daisy Duke is always the first one there, grabbing my comm and eating the ish with hungry eyes.

I start to collect the day's issue, pasting in the pict of Tony and Daisy under the masthead.

I'm on a Harbourfront patio with a pitcher of shandy in front of me, dark shades, and a fabbed pin in my knee when the mothaship comes back.

I took the cure in February, slipped out and left a note so Daisy wouldn't insist on being noble and coming with, lying about my name and camping out in the ER for a week in the newly recaptured Women's College Hospital before a doc could see me.

Daisy kissed me on the cheek when I got home and then went upside my head, and Tony made everyone come and see my new knee. While I was in, someone had sorted out the affairs of the Process, and a government trustee had left a note for me at general delivery. I got over fifty dollars and bought a plane-ticket for a much-deserved week in the Honduras. I tried to take Daisy, but she had stuff to do. I beach-fronted it until the melanomas came out, then home again, home again, only to find the house crime-scene taped and Tony the Tiger and Daisy Duke nowhere to be found in a month of hysterical searching.

So now, on the first beautiful day of spring after a friggin' evil, grey winter of pain and confusion, I work on my tan and sip beer and lemonade until the sirens go and the traffic stops and every receiver is turned to the Emergency Broadcast System—*This is not a test*.

I flip open my comm. There's a hubble of the mothaship, whirlagig and widdershins around our rock. The audio track is running, but it's just talking heads, not a transmission from the mothaship, so I tune it out.

The world holds its breath again.

The first transmission comes a whole pitcher later. They speak flawless English—and Spanish and Cantonese and Esperanto and Navajo, just pick a channel—and they use a beautiful bugout contralto like a newscaster who started out as an opera singer. Like a Roman tyrant orating to his subjects.

My stomach does a flip-flop and I put the comm down before I drop it, swill some shandy and look out at Lake Ontario, which is a preternatural blue. Rats-with-wings seagulls circle overhead.

"People of Earth," says the opera-singer-cum-newscaster. "It is good to be back.

"We had to undertake a task whose nature is . . . complex. We are sorry for any concern this may have caused.

"We have reached a judgment."

Lady or the tiger, I almost say. Are we joining the bugout UN or are we going to be vaporized? I surprise myself and reach down and switch off my comm and throw a nickel on the table to cover the pitchers and tip, and walk away before I hear the answer.

The honking horns tell me what it is. Louder than the when the Jays won the pennant. Bicycle bells, air-horns, car-horns, whistles. Everybody's smiling.

My comm chimes. I scan it. Dad and Mum are home.

They rebuild the Process centers like a bad apology, the governments of the world suddenly very, very interested in finding the arsonists who were vengeful heroes at Xmastime. I smashed my comm after the sixth page from Dad and Mum.

Sometimes, I see Linus grinning from the newsscreens on Spadina, and once I caught sickening audio of him, the harrowing story of how he had valiantly rescued dozens of Process-heads and escaped to the subway tunnels, hiding out from the torch-bearing mobs. He actually said it, "Torch-bearing mobs," in the same goofy lisp.

Whenever Dad and Mum appear on a screen, I disappear.

I've got over fifteen dollars left. My room costs me a penny a night, and for a foam coffin, it's okay.

Someone stuck a paper flyer under my coffin's door this morning. That's unusual—who thinks that the people in the coffins are a sexy demographic?

My very own father is giving a free lecture on Lasting Happiness and the Galactic Federation, at Raptor Stadium, tomorrow night.

I make a mental note to be elsewhere.

Of course, it's not important where I am, the friggin' thing is simulcast to every dingy, darky corner of the world. Pops, after all, has been given a Governor General's award, a Nobel Prize, and a UN Medal of Bravery.

I pinball between bars, looking for somewhere outside of the coffin without the Tyrant's oration.

Someone's converted what was left of Roy Thompson Hall into a big booming dance club, the kind of place with strobe lights and nekkid dancers.

It's been so long since I was at a bar. Last summer. When they first ascended to the mothaship. I feel like an intruder, though I notice about a million half-familiar faces among the dancers, people who I met or shook hands with or drank with or fought with, some time in another life.

And then I see Daisy Duke. Six months have been enough for her to grow her hair out a little and do something to it that makes it look *expensive*. She's wearing a catsuit and a bolero jacket, and looks sexy and kind of scary.

She's at one of the ridiculously small tables, drinking and sparkling at a man in a silver vest and some kind of skirt that looks like the kind of thing I laugh at until I catch myself trying one on.

We make eye-contact. I smile and start to stand. I even point at my knee and grin. Her date says something, and I see, behind the twinkle, a total lack of recognition. She turns to him and I see myself in the mirror behind her.

My hair's longer. I'm not wearing a bathrobe. I've got some meat on my bones. I'm not walking with a cane. Still, I'm *me*. I want to walk over to her and give her a hug, roll up my pants and show her the gob of scar tissue around my knee, find out where Tony the Tiger's got to.

But I don't. I don't know why, but I don't. If I had a comm, I might try calling her, so she'd see my name and then I wouldn't have to say it to her. But I don't have a comm.

I feel, suddenly, like a ghost.

I test this out, walk to the bar, circling Daisy's table once on the way and again on the way back. She sees me but doesn't recognize me, both times. I overhear snatches of her conversation, "— competing next weekend in a black-belt competition—oh, man, I can't *believe* what a pain in the ass my boss was today—want another drink —" and it's her voice, her tones, but somehow, it doesn't seem like *her*.

It feels melancholy and strange, being a ghost. I find myself leaving the bar, and walking off towards Yonge Street, to the Eatons-Walmart store where Tony the Tiger worked.

And fuck me if I don't pass him on the street out front, looking burned and buzzed and broke, panning for pennies. He's looking down, directly addressing people's knees as they pass him, "Spare-change-spare-change-spare-change."

I stand in front of him until he looks up. He's got an ugly scar running over his eyebrow, and he looks right through me. *Where you been, Tony?* I want to ask it, can't. I'm a ghost. I give him a quarter. He doesn't notice.

I run into Stude the Dude and hatch my plan at Tilly the horse's funeral. I read the obit in the Globe, with a pict of the two of them. They buried her at Mount Pleasant Cemetery, with McKenzie King and Timothy Eaton and Lester Pearson. Stude can afford it. The squib said that he was going aboard the mothaship the day after the ceremony.

Lots of people are doing that. Now that we're members of the Confederation, we've got passports that'll take us to *wild* places. The streets get emptier every day. It's hard to avoid Dad's face.

Stude scares the shit out of me with his eulogy. *It's all in Process-speak.* It is positively, friggin' eerie.

"My Life-Companion goes into the ground today."

There's a long pause while he stares into the big hole and the out-sized coffin.

"My Daily Road has taken me far from the Points of Excellence, and I feel like my life has been a Barrier to Joy for myself and for many others. But Tilly was a Special Someone, a Lightning Rod for Happiness, and her presence graced me with the Vision of Joy."

And so on.

I wait near the back until Stude finishes, then follow at a discreet distance as he makes his way back to his place. It's not something I ever would have considered doing last Halloween—the Stude I knew would've spotted a tail in hot second. But now the world has gone to jargon-slinging harmony and I'm brazen as I ride along behind on my bike, down Yonge to Front, and up to a new building made of foam.

I feel like a ghost as I watch him look straight through me, and I mark the address.

I spend a day kicking at everything foam.

The foam is hard, and light, and durable, and I imagine the houses of my parent's suburb, the little Process enclave, surviving long past any of us, surviving as museum pieces for arsenic-breathing bugouts, who crawl over the mummified furniture and chests of clothes, snapping picts and chattering in their thrilling contraltos. I want to scream.

Here and there, pieces of the old, pre-Process, pre-foam Toronto stick out, and I rub them as I pass them by, touchstones for luck.

Spring lasted about ten days. Now we're into a muggy, 32 degrees Toronto summer, and my collar itches and sweat trickles down my neck.

I'd be wearing something lighter and cooler, except that today I'm meeting my Dad, at Aristide. They've got a little wire-flown twin-prop number fuelled up and waiting for me at the miniature airstrip on Toronto Island. Dad was *so* glad when I got in touch with him. A real Milestone on his Personal Road to Lasting Happiness. There's even one of the Process-heads from Yonge and Bloor waiting for me. He doesn't even comment on all my friggin' luggage.

I hit Stude's place about ten minutes after he left for his trip to the mothaship. I had the dregs of the solvent that he'd sold me, and I used that to dissolve a hole in his door, and reached in and popped the latch.

I didn't make a mess, just methodically opened crates and boxes until I found what I was looking for. Then I hauled it in batches to the elevator, loaded it, and took it back to my coffin in a cab.

I had to rent another coffin to store it all.

The Process-head stays at the airport. Praise the bugouts. If he'd been aboard, it would've queered the whole deal.

I press my nose against the oval window next to the hatch, checking my comm from time to time, squinting at the GPS readout. My stomach is a knot, and my knee aches. I feel great.

The transition to Process-land is sharp from this perspective, real buildings giving way to foam white on a razor-edged line. I count off streets as we fly low, the autopilot getting ready to touch down at Aristide, only 70 kay away.

And there's my Chestnut Ave.

God *damn* the wind's fierce in a plane when you pop the emergency hatch. It spirals away like a maple key as the plane starts soothing me over its PA.

I've got a safety strap around my waist and hooked onto the front row of seats, and the knots had better be secure. I use my sore leg to kick the keg of solvent off the deck.

I grab my strap with both hands and lie on my belly at the hatch's edge and count three hippopotami, and then the charge on Stude's kegger goes bang, and the plane kicks up, and now it's not the plane coming over the PA, but the Roman tyrant's voice, shouting, but not loud enough to be understood over the wind.

The superfine mist of solvent settles like an acid bath over my Chestnut Ave, over the perfect smile, and starts to eat the shit out of it.

I watch until the plane moves me out of range, then keep watching from my comm, renting super-expensive sat time on Dad's account.

The roofs go first, along with the road surfaces, then the floors below, and then structural integrity is a thing of past and they fall to pieces like gingerbread, furniture tumbling rolypoly away, everything edged with rough fractal fringe.

Dad's greyfaced and clueless when I land. All he knows is that something made the plane very sick. He's worried and wants to hug me.

I totter down the stairway that a guy in a jumpsuit rolled up, ears still ringing from the wind and my big boom. I'm almost down the step when a little Process-troll scurries up and says something in his ear.

I know what it is, because he's never looked so pissed at me in all my life.

I'm a friggin' *genius*.

*This cycle of stories— "Shadow of the Mothaship," "Home Again, Home Again,"
and "The Super Man and the Bugout"—were the first time I ever recycled a
world in my fiction. Half the fun of writing something new is inventing a new place
and new people and new problems to explore. Even though these stories are related,
they're all very different in tone and timeline, all meant to stand on their own.*

The inspiration for the stylistic games in this piece was E. L. Doctorow's Book
of Daniel, *which is, in turn, loosely based on the life of Abbie Hoffman—as well
as the story of the Rosenbergs, the couple executed in the 1950s for allegedly
selling nuclear secrets to the Soviets.*

*I read Doctorow's novel on holidays in Cuba, while I was learning to SCUBA
dive, and his narrative trick of switching to the third person every time the narrator came to something too personal to reveal in the first person blew me away. I
outlined this story while I was taking those first dives, clambering around the hulls
of sunken fishing boats and slowly descending the walls of reefs.*

*NB: E. L. Doctorow is not my father or anything. Family legend has it that
my paternal grandfather's great-uncle was E. L.'s grandfather. My folks bounced
this off of E. L. after a reading and he seemed to think that it was plausible
enough.*

Home Again, Home Again

The kids in my local bat-house breathe heavy metals, and their gelatinous bodies quiver nauseously during our counseling sessions, and for all that, they reacted just like I had when I told them I was going away for a while—with hurt and betrayal, and they aroused palpable guilt in me.

It goes in circles. When I was sixteen, and The Amazing Robotron told me he needed to go away for a while, but he'd be back, I did everything I could to make him guilty. Now it's me, on a world far from home, and a pack of snot-nosed jellyfish kids have so twisted my psyche that they're all I can think of when I debark the shuttle at Aristide Interplanetary, just outside my dirty ole Toronto.

The customs officer isn't even human, so it feels like just another R&R, another halting conversation carried on in ugly trade-speak, another bewilderment of queues and luggage carousels. Outside: another spaceport, surrounded by the variegated hostels for the variegated tourists, and bipeds are in bare majority.

I can think of it like that.

I can think of it as another spaceport.

I can think of it like another trip.

The thing he can't think of it is, is a homecoming. That's too hard for this weak vessel.

He's very weak.

Look at him. He's eleven, and it's the tencennial of the Ascension of his homeworld—dirty blue ball, so unworthy, yet—inducted into the Galactic fraternity and the infinite compassion of the bugouts.

The foam, which had been confined to just the newer, Process-enclaves before the Ascension, has spread, as has the cult of the Process For Lasting Happiness. Process is, after all, why the dirty blue ball was judged and found barely adequate for membership. Toronto, which had seen half its inhabitants emigrate on open-ended tours of the wondrous worlds of the bugout domain, is full again. Bursting. The whole damn planet is accreting a layer of off-world tourists.

It's a time of plenty. Plenty of cheap food and plenty of cheap foam structures, built as needed, then dissolved and washed away when the need disappears. Plenty of healthcare and education. Plenty of toys and distractions and beautiful, haunting bugout art. Plenty, in fact, of everything, except space.

He lived in a building that is so tall, its top floors are perpetually damp with clouds. There's a nice name for this building, inscribed on a much-abused foam sculpture in the central courtyard. No one uses the nice name. They call it by the name that the tabloids use, that the inhabitants use, that everyone but the off-world counselors use. They call it the bat-house.

Bats in the belfry. Batty. Batshit.

I hated it when they moved us into the bat-house. My parents gamely tried to explain why we were going, but they never understood, no more than any human could. The bugouts had a test, a scifi helmet you wore, and it told you whether you were normal, or batty. Some of our neighbors were clearly batshit: the woman who screamed all the time, about the bugs and the little niggers crawling over her flesh; the couple who ate dogturds off the foam sidewalk with lip-smacking relish; the guy who thought he was Nicola Tesla.

I don't want to talk about him right now.

His parents' flaw—whatever it was—was too subtle to detect without the scifi helmet. They never knew for sure what it was. Many of the bats were in the same belfry: part of the bugouts' arrogant compassion held that a couple never knew which one of them was defective, so his family never knew if it was his nervous, shy mother, or his loud, opinionated father who had doomed them to the quarantine.

His father told him, in an impromptu ceremony before he slid his keycard into the lock on their new apt in the belfry: "Chet, whatever they say, there's nothing wrong with us. They have no right to put us here." He knelt to look the skinny ten-year-old right in the eye. "Don't worry, kiddo. It's not for long—we'll get this thing sorted out yet." Then, in a rare moment of tenderness, one that stood out in Chet's memory as the last of such, his father gathered him in his arms, lifted him off his feet in a fierce hug. After a moment, his mother joined the hug, and Chet's face was buried in the spot where both of their shoulders met, smelling their smells. They still smelled like his parents then, like his old house on the Beaches, and for a moment, he knew his father was right, that this couldn't possibly last.

A tear rolled down his mother's cheek and dripped in his ear. He shook his shaggy hair like a dog and his parents laughed, and his father wiped away his mother's tear and they went into the apt, grinning and holding hands.

Of course, they never left the belfry after that.

I can't remember what the last thing my mother said to me was. Do I remember her tucking me in and saying, "Good night, sleep tight, don't let the bedbugs bite," or was that something I saw on a vid? Was it a nervous command to wipe my shoes on the way in the door? Was her voice soft and sad, as it sometimes is in my memories, or was it brittle and angry, the way she often seemed after she stopped talking, as she banged around the tiny, two-room apt?

I can't remember.

My mother fell away from speech like a half-converted parishioner falling away from the faith: she stopped visiting the temple of verbiage in dribs and drabs, first missing the regular sermons—the daily niceties of *good morning* and *good night* and *be careful, Chet*—then neglecting the major holidays, the *Watch outs!* and the *Ouchs!* and the answers to direct questions.

My father and I never spoke of it, and I didn't mention it to the other wild kids in the vertical city with whom I spent my days getting in what passed for trouble around the bat-house.

I did mention it to my counselor, The Amazing Robotron, so-called for the metal exoskeleton he wore to support his fragile body in Earth's hard gravity. But he didn't count, then.

The reason that Chet can't pinpoint the moment his mother sealed her lips is because he was a self-absorbed little rodent in those days.

Not a cute freckled hellion. A miserable little shit who played hide-and-seek with the other miserable little shits in the bat-house, but played it violently, hide-and-seek-and-break-and-enter, hide-and-seek-and-smash-and-grab. The lot of them are amorphous, indistinguishable from each other in his memory, all that remains of all those clever little brats is the lingering impression of loud, boasting voices and sharp little teeth.

The Amazing Robotron was a fool in little Chet's eyes, an easy-to-bullshit, ineffectual lump whose company Chet had to endure for a mandatory hour every other day.

"Chet, you seem distr-acted to-day," The Amazing Robotron sid in his artificial voice.

"Yah. You know. Worried about, uh, the future." Distracted by Debbie Carr's purse, filched while she sat in the sixty-eighth floor courtyard, talking with her stupid girlie friends. Debbie was the first girl from the gang to get tits, and now she didn't want to hang out with them anymore, and her purse was stashed underneath the base of a hollow planter outside The Amazing Robotron's apt, and maybe he could sneak it out under his shirt and find a place to dump it and sort through its contents after the session.

"What is it about the fu-ture that wo-rries you?" The Amazing Robotron was as unreadable as a pinball machine, something he resembled. Underneath, he was a collection of whip-like tentacles with a knot of sensory organs in the middle.

"You know, like, the whole friggin' thing. Like if I leave here when I'm eighteen, will my folks be okay without me, and like that."

"Your pa-rents are able to take care of them-selves, Chet. You must con-cern your-self with you, Chet. You should do something con-struct-tive with your wo-rry, such as de-ciding on a ca-reer that will ful-fill you when you leave the Cen-ter." The Center was the short form for the long, nice name that no one ever used to describe the bat-house.

"I thought, like, maybe I could be, you know, a spaceship pilot or something."

"Then you must stu-dy math-e-mat-ics and phy-sics. If you like, Chet, I can re-quest ad-vanced in-struct-tion-al mat-e-rials for you."

"Sure, that'd be great. Thanks, Robotron."

"You are wel-come, Chet. I am glad to help. My own par-ent was in a Cen-ter on my world, you know. I un-der-stand how you feel. There is still time re-main-ing in your ses-sion. What else would you like to dis-cuss?"

"My mother doesn't talk anymore. Nothing. Why is that?"

"Your mo-ther is. . . ." The Amazing Robotron fumbled for a word, buried somewhere deep in the hypnotic English lexicon baked into its brain. "Your mo-ther has a prob-lem, and she needs your aff-ec-tion now more than e-ver. What-ev-er rea-son she has for her si-lence, it is not you. Your mo-ther and fa-ther love you, and dream of the day when you leave here and make your own way through the gal-ax-y."

Of course his parents loved him, he supposed, in an abstract kind of way. His mother, who hadn't worn anything but a bathrobe in months, whose face he couldn't picture behind his eyes but whose bathrobe he could visualize in its every rip and stain and fray. His father, who seemed to have forgotten how to groom himself, who spent his loud days in one of the bat-house's workshops, drinking beer with his buddies while they played with the arc welders. His parents loved him, he knew that.

"OK, right, thanks. I've gotta blow, 'K?"

"All-right. I will see you on Thurs-day, then?"

But Chet was already out the door, digging Debbie Carr's purse from under the planter, then running, doubled over the bulge it made in his shirt, hunting for a private space in the anthill.

The entire north face of the bat-house was eyeless, a blind, windowless expanse of foam that seemed to curve as it approached infinity.

Some said it was an architectural error, others said it was part of the bat-house's heating scheme. Up in nosebleed country, on the 120th level, it was almost empty: sparsely populated by the very battiest bats, though as more and more humans were found batty, they pushed inexorably upwards.

Chet rode the lift to the 125th floor and walked casually to the end of the hallway. At this height, the hallways were bare foam, without the long-wear carpet and fake plants that adorned the low-altitude territories. He walked as calmly as he could to the very end of the northern hall, then hunkered down in the corner and spilled the purse.

Shit, but Debbie Carr was going girlie. The pile was all tampons and makeup and, ugh, a spare bra. A spare bra! I chuckled, and kept sorting. There were three pennies, enough to buy six chocolate bars in the black-market tuck-shop on the 75th floor. A clever little pair of folding scissors, their blades razor-sharp. I was using them to slit the lining of the purse when the door to 12525 opened, and the guy who thought he was Nicola Tesla emerged.

My palms slicked with guilty sweat, and the pile of Debbie's crap, set against the featureless foam corridor, seemed to scream its presence. I spun around, working my body into the corner, and held the little scissors like a dagger in my fist.

The guy who thought he was Nicola Tesla was clearly batty. He was wearing boxer-shorts and a tailcoat and had a halo of wild, greasy hair and a long, tangled beard, but even if he'd been wearing a suit and tie and had a trip to the barber's, I'd have known he was batty the minute I laid eyes on him. He didn't walk, he shambled, like he'd spent a long, long time on meds. His eyes, set in deep black pits of sleeplessness, were ferociously crazy.

He turned to stare at me.

"Hello, sonny. Do you like to swim?"

I stood in my corner, mute, trapped.

"I have an ocean in my apt. Maybe you'd like to try it? I used to love to swim in the ocean when I was a boy."

My feet moved without my willing them. An ocean in his apt? My feet wanted to know about this.

I entered his apt, and even my feet were too surprised to go on.

He had the biggest apt I'd ever seen. It spanned three quarters of the length of the bat-house, and was five storeys high. The spots where he'd dissolved the foam walls away with solvent were rough and uneven, and rings of foam encircled each of the missing storeys above. I couldn't imagine getting that much solvent: it was more tightly controlled than plutonium, the subject of countless action-adventure vids.

At one end of the apt stood a collection of tall, spiny apparatus, humming with electricity and sparking. They were remarkable, but their impact was lost in what lay at the other end.

The guy who thought he was Nicola Tesla had an ocean in his apt. It was a clear aquarium tank, fifteen meters long and nearly seventeen high, and eight meters deep. It was dominated by a massive, baroque coral reef, like a melting castle with misshapen brains growing out of it.

Schools of fish—bright as jellybeans—darted through the ocean's depths, swimming in and out of the softly waving plants. A thousand neon tetra, a flock of living quicksilver sewing needles, turned 90 degrees in perfect unison, then did it again, and again, and again, describing a neat, angular box in the water.

"Isn't it beautiful? I'm using it in one of my experiments, but I also find it very *calming*."

I hail a pedicab and the kids back on my adopted homeworld, with their accusing, angry words and stares vanish from my mind. The cabbie is about nineteen and muscular as hell, legs like treetrunks, clipped into the pedals. A flywheel spins between him and me, and his brakes store his momentum up in it every time he slows. On the two-hour ride into downtown Toronto, he never once comes to a full stop.

I've booked a room at the Royal York. I can afford it—the stipend I receive for the counseling work has been slowly accumulating in my bank account.

Downtown is all foam now, and "historical" shops selling authentic Earth crapola: reproductions of old newspapers, reproductions of old electronics, reproductions of old clothes and old food and other discarded cultural detritus. I see tall, clacking insect-creatures with walkman headphones across their stomachs. I see squat, rocky creatures smearing pizza slices onto their digestive membranes. I see soft, slithering creatures with Toronto Blue Jays baseball hats suspended in their jelly.

The humans I see are dressed in unisex coveralls, with discreet comms on their wrists or collars, and they don't seem to notice that their city is become a bestiary.

The cabby isn't even out of breath when we pull up at the Royal York, which, thankfully, is still clothed in its ancient dressed stone. We point our comms at each other and I squirt some money at him, adding a generous tip. His face, which had been wildly animated while he dodged the traffic on the long ride is a stony mask now, as though when at rest he entered a semiconscious sleep mode.

The doorman is dressed in what may or may not be historically accurate costume, though what period it is meant to represent is anyone's guess. He carries my bag to the check-in and I squirt more money at him. He wishes that I have a nice stay in Toronto, and I wish it, too.

At the check-in, I squirt my ID and still more money at the efficient young woman in a smart blazer, and another babu in period costume—those shoes look painful—carries my bag to the lift and presses the button.

We wait in strained silence and the lift makes its achingly slow progress towards us. There are no elevators on the planet I live on now—the wild gravity and wilder windstorms don't permit buildings of more than one story—but even if there were, they wouldn't be like this lift, like a human lift, like one of the fifty that ran the vertical length of the bat-house.

I nearly choke as we enter that lift. It has the smell of a million transient guests, aftershaves and perfumes and pheromones, and the stale recirc air I remember so well. I stifle the choke into my fist, fake a cough, and feel a self-consciousness I didn't know I had.

I'm worried that the babu knows that I grew up in the bathouse.

Now I can't make eye-contact with him. Now I can't seem to stand naturally, can't figure out where a not-crazy puts his hands and where a not-crazy puts his eyes. Little Chet and his mates liked to terrorize people in the lifts, play "Who farted" and "I'm gonna puke" and "I have to pee" in loud sing-songs, just to watch the other bats squirm.

The guy who thought he was Nicola Tesla thought that these games were unfunny, unsophisticated and unappetizing and little Chet stopped playing them.

I squirt extra money at the babu, after he opens my windows and shows me the shitter and the vid's remote.

I unpack mechanically, my meager bag yielding more-meager clothes. I'd thought I'd buy more after earthfall, since the spaceports' version of human apparel wasn't, very. I realize that I'm wearing the same clothes I left Earth in, lo those years before. They're hardly the worse for wear—when I'm in my exoskeleton on my new planet, I don't bother with clothes.

The ocean seemed too fragile to be real. All that caged water, held behind a flimsy-seeming sheet of clear foam, the corners joined with strips of thick gasket-rubber. Standing there at its base, Chet was terrified that it would burst and drown him—he actually felt the push of water, the horrid, dying wriggles of the fish as they were washed over his body.

"Say there, son. Hello?"

Chet looked up. Nicola Tesla's hair was standing on end, comically. He realized that his own long, shaggy hair was doing the same. The whole room felt electric.

"Are you all right?" He had a trace of an accent, like the hint of garlic in a salad dressing, an odd way of stepping on his vowels.

"Yeah, yeah, fine. I'm fine," Chet said.

"I am pleased to hear that. What is your name, son?"

"Chet. Affeltranger."

"I'm pleased to meet you. My name is Gaylord Ballozos, though that's not who I am. You see, I'm the channel for Nicola Tesla. Would you like to see a magic trick?"

Chet nodded. He wondered who Nicola Tesla was, and filed away the name Gaylord for making fun of, later. In doing so, he began to normalize the experience, to structure it as a story he could tell the other kids, after. The guy, the ocean, the hair. Gaylord.

A ball of lightning leapt from Tesla/Ballozos's fingertips and danced over their heads. It bounced around the room furiously, then stopped to hover in front of Chet. His clothes stood away from his body, snapping as though caught in a windstorm. Seen up close, the ball was an infinite pool of shifting electricity, like an ocean of energy. Tentatively, he reached out to touch it, and Tesla shouted "Don't!" and the ball whipped up and away, spearing itself on the point of one of the towers on the opposite side of the room.

It vanished, leaving a tangy, sharp smell behind.

The story Chet had been telling in his mind disappeared with it. He stood, shocked speechless.

The guy who thought he was Nicola Tesla chuckled a little, then started to laugh, actually doubling over and slapping his thighs.

"You can't *imagine* how long I've waited to show that trick to someone! Thank you, young Mr. Affeltranger! A million thanks to you, for your obvious appreciation."

Chet felt a giggle welling up in him, and he did laugh, and when his lips came together, a spark of static electricity leapt from their seam to his nose and made him jump, and laugh all the harder.

The guy came forward and pumped his arm in a dry handshake. "I can see that you and I are kindred spirits. You will have to come and visit again, very soon, and I will let you see more of my ocean, and maybe let you see 'Old Sparky,' too. Thank you, thank you, thank you, for dropping in."

And he ushered Chet out of his apt and closed the door, leaving him in the featureless hallway of the 125th storey.

I had never been as nervous as I was the following Thursday, when my regular appointment with The Amazing Robotron rolled around again. I hadn't spoken of the guy who thought he was

Nicola Tesla to any of my gang, and of course not to my parents, but somehow, I felt like I might end up spilling to The Amazing Robotron.

I don't know why I was worried. The guy hadn't asked me to keep it a secret, after all, and I had never had any problem holding my tongue around The Amazing Robotron before.

"Hel-lo, Chet. How have you been?"

"I've been OK."

"Have you been stud-y-ing math-e-mat-ics and phys-ics? I had the supp-le-ment-al mat-e-rials de-liv-er-ed to your apt yes-ter-day."

"No, I haven't. I don't think I wanna be a pilot no more. One of my buds tole me that you end up all fugged up with time an' that, that you come home an' it's the next century an' everyone you know is dead."

"That is one thing that hap-pens to some ex-plor-a-tor-y pilots, Chet. Have you thought a-bout any o-ther poss-i-bil-i-ties?"

"Kinda. I guess." I tried not to think about the 125th story and the ocean. I was thinking so hard, I stopped thinking about what I was saying to The Amazing Robotron. "Maybe I could be a coun-selor, like, and help kids."

The Amazing Robotron turned into a pinball machine again, an unreadable and motionless block. Silent for so long I thought he was gone, dead as a sardine inside his tin can. Then, he twitched both of his arms, like he was shivering. Then his robot-voice came out of the grille on his face. "I think that you would be a ve-ry good coun-sel-or, Chet."

"Yeah?" I said. It was the first time that The Amazing Robotron had told me he thought I'd be good at anything. Hell, it was the first time he'd expressed *any* opinion about anything I'd said.

"Yes, Chet. Be-ing a coun-sel-or is a ve-ry good way to help your-self un-der-stand what we have done to you by put-ting you in the Cen-ter."

I couldn't speak. My Mom, before she fell silent, had often spoken about how unfair it was for me to be stuck here, because of something that she or my father had done. But my father never seemed to notice me, and the teachers on the vid made a point of not mentioning the bat-house—like someone trying hard not to notice a stutter or a wart, and you *knew* that the best you could hope for from them was pity.

"Be-ing a coun-sel-or is ve-ry hard, Chet. But coun-sel-ors sometimes get a spec-ial re-ward. Some-times, we get to help. Do you re-ally want to do this?"

"Yeah. Yes. I mean, it sounds good. You get to travel, right?"

The Amazing Robotron's idiot-lights rippled, something I came to recognize as a chuckle, later. "Yes. Tra-vel is part of the job. I sug-gest that you start by ex-am-in-ing your friends. See if you can fi-gure out why they do what they do."

I've used this trick on my kids. What do I know about their psy-chology? But you get one, you convince it to explain the rest to you. It helps. Counselors are always from another world—by the time the first generation raised in a bat-house has grown old enough, there aren't any bats' children left to counsel on their homeworld.

I take room-service, pizza and beer in an ice-bucket: pretentious, but better than sharing a dining-room with the menagerie. Am I becoming a racist?

No, no. I just need to focus on things human, during this vacation.

The food is disappointing. It's been years since I lay awake at night, craving a slice and a brew and a normal gravity and a life away from the bats. Nevertheless, the craving remained, buried, and resurfaced when I went over the room-service menu. By the time the dumbwaiter in my room chimed, I was practically drooling.

But by the time I take my second bite, it's just pizza and a brew.

I wonder if I will ever get to sleep, but when the time comes, my eyes close and if I dream, I don't remember it.

I get up and dress and send up for eggs and real Atlantic salmon and brown toast and a pitcher of coffee, then find myself unable to eat any of it. I make a sandwich out of it and wrap it in napkins and stuff it into my day-pack along with a water-bottle and some sun-block.

It's a long walk up to the bat-house, but I should make it by nightfall.

Chet was up at 6h the next morning. His mom was already up, but she never slept that he could tell. She was clattering around the kitchen in her housecoat, emptying the cupboards and then re-stacking their contents for the thousandth time. She shot him a look of something between fear and affection as he pulled on his shorts and a t-shirt, and he found himself hugging her waist. For a second, it felt like she softened into his embrace, like she was going to say something, like it was normal, and then she picked up a plate and rubbed it with a towel and put it back into the cupboard.

Chet left without saying a word.

The bat-house breathed around him, a million farts and snores and whispered words. A lift was available almost before he took his finger off the summon button. "125," he said.

Chet walked to the door of the guy who thought he was Nicola Tesla and started to knock, then put his hands down and sank down into a squat, with his back against it.

He must have dozed, because the next thing he knew, he was tipping over backwards into the apt, and the guy who thought he was Nicola Tesla was standing over him, concerned.

"Are you all right, son?"

Chet stood, dusted himself off and looked at the floor. "Sorry, I didn't want to disturb you . . ."

"But you wanted to come back and see more. Marvelous! I applaud your curiosity, young sir. I have just taken the waters—perhaps you would like to try?" He gestured at the ocean.

"You mean, swim in it?"

"If you like. Myself, I find a snorkel and mask far superior. My set is up on the rim, you're welcome to them, but I would ask you to chew a stick of this before you get in." He tossed Chet a pack of gum. "It's an invention of my own—chew a stick of that, and you can *not* transmit any nasty bugs in your saliva for forty-eight hours. I hold a patent for it, of course, but my agents report that it has been met with crashing indifference in the Great Beyond."

Chet had been swimming before, in the urinary communal pools on the tenth and fifteenth levels, horsing around naked with his mates. Nudity was not a big deal for the kids of the bat-house—the kind of adult who you wouldn't trust in such circumstances didn't end up in bat-houses—the bugouts had a different place for them.

"Go on, lad, give it a try. It's simply marvelous, I tell you!"

Unsteadily, Chet climbed the spiral stairs leading up to the tank, clutching the handrail, chewing the gum, which fizzed and sparked in his mouth. At the top, there was a small platform. Self-consciously, he stripped, then pulled on the mask and snorkel that hung from a peg.

"Tighten the straps, boy!" the guy who thought he was Nicola Tesla shouted, from far, far below. "If water gets into the mask, just push at the top and blow out through your nose!"

Chet awkwardly lowered himself into the water. It was warm—blood temperature—and salty, and it fizzled a little on his skin, as though it, too, were electric.

He kept one hand on the snorkel, afraid that it would tip and fill with water, and then, slowly, slowly, relaxed on his belly, mask in the water, arms by his side.

My god! It was like I was flying! It was like all the dreams I'd ever had, of flying, of hovering over an alien world, of my consciousness taking flight from my body and sailing through the galaxy.

My hands were by my sides, out of view of the mask, and my legs were behind me. I couldn't see any of my body. My view stretched 8m down, an impossible, dizzying height. A narrow, elegant angelfish swam directly beneath me, and tickled my belly with one of its fins as it passed under.

I smiled, a huge grin, and it broke the seal on my mask, filling it with water. Calmly, as though I'd been doing it all my life, I pressed the top of my mask to my forehead and blew out through my nose. My mask cleared of water.

I floated.

The only sound was my breathing, and distant, metallic *pink!*s from the ocean's depths. A school of iridescent purple fish swam past me, and I lazily kicked out after them, following them to the edge of the coral reef that climbed the far wall of the ocean. When I reached it, I was overwhelmed by its complexity, millions upon millions of tiny little suckers depending from weird branches and misshapen brains and stone roses.

I held my breath.

And I heard nothing. Not a sound, for the first time in all the time I had been in the bat-house—no distant shouts and mutters. I was alone, in a vast, personal silence, in a private ocean. My pulse beat under my skin. Tiny fish wriggled in the coral, tearing at the green fuzz that grew over it.

Slowly, I turned around and around. The ocean-wall that faced into the apt was silvered on this side, reflecting back my little pale body to me. My head pounded, and I finally inhaled, and the sound of my breathing, harsh through the snorkel, rang in my ears.

I spent an age in the water, holding my breath, chasing the fish, disembodied, a consciousness on tour on an alien world.

The guy who thought he was Nicola Tesla brought me back. He waited on the rim of the tank until I swam near enough for him to touch, then he tapped me on the shoulder. I stuck my head up, and he said, "Time to get out, boy, I need to use the ocean."

Reluctantly, I climbed out. He handed me a towel.

I felt like I was still flying, atop the staircase on the ocean's edge. I felt like I could trip slowly down the stairs, never quite touching them. I pulled on my clothes, and they felt odd to me.

Carefully, forcing myself to grip the railing, I descended. The guy who thought he was Nicola Tesla stood at my side, not speaking, allowing me my reverie.

My hair was drying out, and starting to raise skywards, and the guy who thought he was Nicola Tesla went over to his apparatus and flipped a giant knife switch. The ocean stirred, a puff of sand rose from its bottom, and then, the coral on the ocean's edge *moved*.

It squirmed and danced and writhed, startling the fish away from it, shedding layers of algae in a green cloud.

"It's my latest idea. I've found the electromagnetic frequencies that the various coral resonate on, and by using those as a carrier wave, I can stimulate them into tremendously accelerated growth. Moreover, I can alter their electromagnetic valences, so that, instead of calcium salts, they use other minerals as their building-blocks."

He grinned hugely, and seemed to want Chet to say something. Chet didn't understand any of it.

"Well, don't you see?"

"Nuh."

"I can use coral to concentrate trace gold and platinum and any other heavy-metal you care to name out of the seas. I can prospect in the very water itself!" He killed the switch. The coral stopped their dance abruptly, and the new appendages they'd grown dropped away, tumbling gracefully to the ocean's floor. "You see? Gold, platinum, lead. I dissolved a kilo of each into the water last night, microscopic flakes. In five minutes, my coral has concentrated it all."

The stumps where the minerals had dropped away were jagged and sharp, and painful looking.

"It doesn't even harm the fish!"

Chet's playmates seemed as strange as fish to him. They met up on the 87th level, where there was an abandoned apt with a faulty lock. Some of them seemed batty themselves, standing in corners, staring at the walls, tracing patterns that they alone could see. Others seemed too confident ever to be bats—they shouted and boasted to each other, got into shoving matches that escalated into knock-out brawls and then dissolved into giggles. Chet found himself on the sidelines, an observer.

One boy, whose father hung around the workshops with Chet's father, was industriously pulling apart the warp of the carpet, rolling it into a ball. When the ball reached a certain size, he snapped the loose end, tucked it in and started another.

A girl whose family had been taken to the bat-house all the way from a reservation near Sioux Lookout was telling loud lies about home, about tremendous gun-battles fought out with the Ontario Provincial Police and huge, glamorous casinos where her mother had dealt blackjack to millionaire high-rollers, who tucked thousand dollar tips into her palm. About her bow and arrow and her rifle and her horses. Nobody believed her stories, and they made fun of her behind her back, but they listened when she told them, spellbound.

What was her name, anyway?

There were two boys, one followed the other everywhere. The followee was tormenting the follower, as usual, smacking him in the back of the head, then calling him a baby, goading him into hitting back, dodging easily, and retaliating viciously.

Chet thought that he understood some of what was going on. Maybe he'd be able to explain it to The Amazing Robotron.

I never thought I'd say this, but I miss my exoskeleton. My feet ache, my legs ache, my ass aches, and I'm hot and thirsty and my waterbottle is empty. I'm not even past Bloor Street, not even a tenth of the way to the bat-house.

The Amazing Robotron seemed thoughtful as I ratted out my chums. "So, I think they need each other. The big one needs the little one, to feel important. The little one needs the big one, so that he can feel useful. Is that right?"

"It is ve-ry per-cep-tive, Chet. When I was young, I had a sim-i-lar friend-ship with an-other. It—no, *she*—was the lit-tle one, and I was the big one. Her pa-rent died be-fore we came of age, and she left the Cen-ter, and when she came back to visit, a long time la-ter, we were re-ver-sed—I felt smal-ler but good, and spec-ial be-cause she told me all a-bout the out-side."

Something clicked inside me then. I saw myself inside The Amazing Robotron's exoskeleton, and he in my skin, our roles reversed. It lasted no longer than a lightning flash, but in that flash, I suddenly knew that I could talk to The Amazing Robotron, and that he would understand.

I felt so smart all of a sudden. I felt like The Amazing Robotron and I were standing outside the bat-house, *in* it but not *of* it, and we shared a secret insight into the poor, crazy bastards we were cooped up with.

"I don't really like anyone here. I don't like my Dad—he's always shouting, and I think he's the reason we ended up here. He's batshit—he gets angry too easy. And my Mom is batshit now, even if she wasn't batshit before, because of him. I don't feel like their son. I feel like I just share an apt with these two crazy people I don't like very much. And none of my mates are any good, either. They're all either like my Dad—loud and crazy, or like my Mom, quiet and crazy. Everyone's crazy."

"That may be true, Chet. But you can still like cra-zy peo-ple."

"Do *you* like 'em?"

The Amazing Robotron's idiot lights rippled. *Gotcha*, I thought.

"I do not like them, Chet. They are loud and cra-zy and they only think of them-selves."

I laughed. It was so refreshing not to be lied to. My skin was all tight from the dried saltwater, and that felt good, too.

"My Dad, the other day? He came home and was all, 'this is a conspiracy to drive us out of our house. It's because we bought a house with damn high ceilings. Some big damn alien wanted to live there, so they put us here. It's because I did such a good job on the ceilings!' Which is so stupid, 'cause the ceilings in our old house weren't no higher than the ceilings here, and besides, Dad screwed up all the plaster when he was trying to fix it up, and it was always cracking.

"And then he starts talking about what's really bugging him, which is that some guy at the workshop took his favorite drill and he couldn't finish his big project without it. So he got into a fight with the guy, and got the drill and then he finished his big, big project, and brought it home, and you know what it was? A *pencil-holder*! We don't even *have* any pencils! He is so screwed up."

And The Amazing Robotron's lights rippled again, and a huge weight lifted from my shoulders. I didn't feel ashamed of the mani-acs that gave me life—I saw them as pitiful subjects for my obser-vations. I laughed again, and that must have been the most I'd laughed since they put us in the bat-house.

I'm getting my sea-legs. I hope. My mouth is pasty, and salty, and sweat keeps running down into my eyes. I never even began to realize how much support the exoskeleton's jelly-suspension lent me.

But I've made it to Eglinton, and that's nearly a third of the way, and to celebrate, I stop in at a coffee-shop and drink a whole pitcher of lemonade while sitting by the air-conditioner.

I got the word that they were tearing down the bat-house only two weeks ago. The message came by priority email from The Amazing Robotron: all the bats were dead, or enough of them any-way that the rest could be relocated to less expensive quarters. It was barely enough notice to get my emergency leave application in, to book a ticket back to Earth, and to finally become a murderer all the way.

Damn, I hope I know what I'm doing.

The guy who thought he was Nicola Tesla told me all kinds of stories, and I was sure he was lying to me, but when I checked out the parts of his story that I could, they all turned out to be true.

"I don't actually *need* to be here. I've come here to get away from all the treachery, the deceit, the filthy pursuit of the dollar. As though I need more money! I invented foam! Oh, sure, the Process likes to take credit for it, but if you look up the patent, guess who owns it?

"Master Affeltranger, you may not realize it to look at me, but I have some *very* important friends, out there in the Great Beyond. With important friends, you can make a whole block of apts simply disappear from the record-books. You can make tremendous energy consumption vanish, likewise."

He spoke as he tinkered with his apparatus, which hummed alarmingly and occasionally sent a tortured arc of electricity into the guy who thought he was Nicola Tesla's chest.

It happened three times in a row, and he stamped his foot in frustration, and said, "Oh, *do* cut it out," apparently to one of his machines.

I'd been jumping every time he got zapped, but this time, I had to giggle. He whirled on me. "I am not trying to be *amusing*. One thing you people never realize is that the current has a *will*, it has a *mind*, and you have to keep it in check with a firm hand."

I shook my head a little, not understanding. He waved a hand at me, frustrated, and said, "Oh, go have a swim. I don't have time to argue with a child."

I climbed into the ocean, and the silence embraced me, and the water tingled with electricity, and my consciousness floated away from my body and soared over an alien world. Like a broken circuit, I disconnected from the world around me.

Chet's father came home with a can of beer in his hand and the rest of the six-pack in his gut. He walked over to the vid, where Chet was researching the life of Nicola Tesla, which took forever, since he had to keep linking back to simple tutorials on physics, history, and electrical engineering.

Chet's father stooped and took the remote out of Chet's hands and opened up a bookmarked docu-drama about the coming of the bugouts. Chet opened his mouth to protest, and his father shouted him down before he could speak. "Not one word, you hear me? Not! One! Word! I've had a shithole day and I wanna relax."

Chet's mother dropped a plastic tumbler, which bounced twice, and rolled to Chet's toe. He stepped over it, walked out the door, and took the elevator to the 125th floor.

Chet burst into the guy who thought he was Nicola Tesla's apt and screamed. Nicola Tesla was strapped into a heavy wooden chair, with a metal hood over his head. Arcs of electricity danced over his body, and he jerked and thrashed against the leather straps that bound his limbs. Unthinking, Chet ran forward and grabbed the buckle that bound his wrist, and a giant's fist smashed into him, hurling him across the room.

When he came to, the electric arcs were gone, but the guy who thought he was Nicola Tesla was motionless in his straps, under his hood.

Carefully, Chet came to his feet, and saw that the toe of his right sneaker had been blown out, leaving behind charred canvas. His foot hurt—burned.

He hobbled to the chair and gingerly prodded it, then jerked his hand back, though he hadn't been shocked. He bit his lip and stared. The wood was quite weathered and elderly, though it had been oiled and had a rich, well-cared-for finish. The leather straps were nightmarishly thick, gripping the guy who thought he was Nicola Tesla at the bicep and wrist, at the thigh and calf and ankle. Livid bruises were already spreading at their edges.

Chet was struck by a sudden urge to climb into the ocean and *stay* there. Just *stay* there.

Under the hood, the guy who thought he was Nicola Tesla groaned. Chet gave an involuntary squeak and jumped a little. The guy who thought he was Nicola Tesla's body snapped tense. "Who's there?" he said, his voice muffled by the hood.

"It's me, Chet."

"Chet? Damn. Damn, damn, damn." His right hand bent nearly double at the wrist and teased the buckle of the strap free. With one hand free, the guy who thought he was Nicola Tesla quickly undid the straps on his upper body, then lifted away the hood. He pointedly did not look at Chet as he doubled over and undid the straps on his legs and ankles.

Gingerly, he stood and stretched, then sighed tremendously.

"Chet, Chet, Chet. I hope I didn't frighten you too badly. This is Old Sparky, an exact replica of the electric chair at Sing-Sing Prison in New York. Edison, thief and charlatan that he was, insisted that his DC current was safer than my AC, and they built a chair that used my beautiful current to execute criminals, by the hundreds.

"Nicola Tesla and I became one when I was eight years old, and I received a tremendous shock from an electrified fence. I was stuck to it, glued by the current, and after a few moments, I just relaxed into the current—befriended it, if you will. That's when the spirit of Nicola Tesla, a-wandering through the wires for all the years since his death, infused my body.

"So now I use Old Sparky here to recharge—please forgive the expression—my connection with the current. I once spent eight years in the chair, when I needed to disappear for a while. When I woke, I hadn't aged at all—I didn't even need to shave! What do you think of that?"

Chet was staring in horror at him. "You electrocute yourself? On purpose?"

"Why, yes! Think of it as a trick I do, if it makes you feel better. I could show you how to do it . . ." he trailed off, but a look of hunger had passed over his face.

I get all kinds of access to bat-house records from the vid in my apt on my new world. No one named Gaylord Ballozos ever lived in any bat-house. Apt 12525, and the five above it, were never occupied. The records say that the locks have never been used, the doors never opened. It won't be searched when they evacuate the bat-house.

That's what the records say, anyway.

Electricity gives me the willies. The zaps of static from the dry air of the FTL I took home to Earth made me scream, little-boy squeaks that made the other passengers jump.

I don't remember that it was ever this hot in Toronto, even in the summer. The sky is all overcast, so maybe it's a temperature inversion. Up here at Steeles Avenue, I'm so dehydrated that I spend a whole dime on a magnum of still water and power-chug it, though you're not supposed to drink that way. Almost there.

The other kids in the abandoned apt on the 87th floor ignored me. They'd been paying less and less attention to me, ever since I started spending my afternoons up on 125, and I was getting a reputation as a keener for all the time I spent with The Amazing Robotron.

That suited me fine; the corner of the gutted kitchen was as private a space as I was going to find in the bat-house. I had the apparatus that Nicola Tesla had given me plugged into the AC outlet under the sink. I closed my eyes and breathed deeply, concentrating on the moments after my breath left my chest, that calm like the ocean's silence. Smoothly, I reached out and grasped the handle of the apparatus and squeezed.

The first time I tried this, under Nicola Tesla's supervision, I'd jerked my hand away and squeezed it between my legs as soon as the current shot through me. Now, though, I could keep squeezing, slowly increasing the voltage and amperage, relaxing into the involuntary tension in my muscles.

I'd gotten so good at it that I'd started using the timer—I could lean into the current forever without it. I had it set for three hours, but when the current died, it felt like no time at all had passed. I probed around my consciousness for any revelation, but no spirit had come into my body during the exercise. The guy who thought he was Nicola Tesla didn't know if there were any other spirits in the wire, but it stood to reason that if there was one, there had to be more.

I stood, and felt incredibly calm and balanced and centered and I floated past the other kids. It was time for my session with The Amazing Robotron.

"Chet, how are you fee-ling?"

"I'm well, thank you." Nicola Tesla spoke well and carefully, and I'd started to ape him.

"And what would you like to dis-cuss to-day?"

"I don't really have anything to talk about, honestly. Everything is fine."

"That is good. Do you have any new ob-ser-va-tions about your friends?"

"I'm sorry, no. I haven't been paying much attention lately."

"Why hav-en't you?"

"It just doesn't interest me, sorry."

"Why does-n't it in-ter-est you?"

"I just don't care about them, to be frank."

The Amazing Robotron was absolutely still for a moment. "Are things well with your par-ents, too?"

"The same as always. I think they've found their niches." *Find your niche* was an expression I'd pirated from the guy who thought he was Nicola Tesla. I was very proud of it.

"In that case, why don't we end this mee-ting?"

I was surprised. The Amazing Robotron always demanded his full hour. "I'll see you on Wednesday, then?"

"I'm af-raid not, Chet. I will be gone for a few months—I have to re-turn home. There will be a sub-sti-tute coun-sel-or arri-ving next Monday."

My calm center shattered. Sweat sprang out on my palms. "What? You're leaving? How can you be leaving?"

"I'm so-rry, Chet. There is an em-er-gen-cy at home. I'll be back as soon as I can."

"Frick that! How can you go? What'll I do if you don't come back?

You're the only one I can talk to!"

"I'm so-rry, Chet. I have to go."

"If you gave a shit, you'd stay. You can't just leave me here!" I knew as I said it that it didn't make any sense, but a picture sprang into my mind, one that I'd been carrying without knowing it for a long time: The Amazing Robotron and me as an adult, walking away from the bat-house, with suitcases, leaving together, forever. I felt a sob hiccough in my throat.

"I will re-turn, Chet. I did-n't wish to up-set you."

"Frick that! I don't give a shit if you come back, asshole."

Chet went straight to 87 and plugged in to the apparatus. He didn't set the timer, and he stayed plugged in for nearly two days, when two fighting boys tumbled into him and knocked his hand away. He was centered and numb again, and didn't have any sense of the intervening time. He didn't even have to pee. He wondered if he was trying to commit suicide.

He checked his comm and got the date, noticed with distant surprise that it was two days later, and wandered up to 125.

The guy who thought he was Nicola Tesla shouted a distant "Come in" when Chet tapped on the door. He was playing with his ocean again. Chet felt his hair float up off his shoulders. He stopped and watched the coral squirm and dance.

"I spent nearly two days on the apparatus," Chet said.

"Eh? Very good, very good. You're progressing nicely."

"My counselor has left. He had to go home."

"Yes? Well, there you are."

"What were your parents like?"

"Nicola Tesla's father was a bishop, and his mother was an illiterate, though she was a gifted memnist and taught me much about visualization."

"No, I mean *your* parents. Mister and Missus Ballozos. What were *they* like?"

The guy who thought he was Nicola Tesla shut down the ocean and watched the lumps of ore tumble to the sand. "Why do you want to know about *them?* Are you having some sort of trouble at home?" he asked impatiently, not looking away from the ocean.

"No reason," Chet said. "I have to go home now."

"Yes, fine."

"The hell have you been, boy?" Chet's father said, when he came through door. His father was in front of the vid, wearing shorts and a filthy t-shirt, holding the remote in one hand. Chet's mother was sitting at the window, staring out into the clouds.

"Out. Around. I'm okay, okay?"

"It's not okay. You can't just run around like some kind of animal. Sit the hell down and tell me where you've been. Your counselor was here looking for you."

"Robotron? He was here?"

"Yes he was here! And I had to tell him I didn't know where my damn kid was! How do you think that makes me look? You know how worried your mother was?"

Chet's mother didn't stir from her post by the window, but she flinched when Chet's father spoke. Chet swallowed hard.

"What did he want?"

"Never mind that! Sit the hell down and tell me where you've been and what the hell you thought you were doing!"

Chet sat beside his father and stared at his hands. He knew he could outwait his father. After half an hour, Chet's father turned the vid on. Four long hours later, he switched it off, and went to bed.

Chet's mother finally turned away from the now-dark window. She reached into the pocket of her grimy bathrobe and withdrew an envelope and handed it to Chet, then turned and went to the apt's other room to sleep.

My name was on the outside of the envelope, in rough script, written with awkward exoskeleton manipulators. I broke its seal, and it folded out into a single flat sheet of paper.

DEAR CHET, it began. At the bottom of it was a complex scrawl that I recognized from the front of The Amazing Robotron's exoskeleton. It must be some kind of signature.

DEAR CHET,

I AM SORRY TO HAVE TO LEAVE YOU SO SUDDENLY, AND WITHOUT ANYONE ELSE TO TALK TO. THERE IS AN EMERGENCY AT MY HOME, BUT I WOULDN'T GO IF I DIDN'T BELIEVE THAT YOU WERE ABLE TO HANDLE MY ABSENCE. YOU ARE A VERY PERCEPTIVE AND STRONG YOUNG MAN, AND YOU WILL BE ABLE TO MANAGE IN MY ABSENCE. I WILL BE BACK, YOU KNOW.

YOU WILL BE ALL RIGHT. I PROMISE.

THIS ISN'T EASY FOR ME TO DO, EITHER. IT MAY BE
THAT I AM THE ONLY ONE YOU CAN TALK TO HERE AT
THE CENTER. IT IS LIKEWISE TRUE THAT YOU ARE
THE ONLY ONE I CAN TALK TO.

I WILL MISS YOU, MY FRIEND CHET.

The writing was childish, with many line-outs and corrections.
Reading it, I heard it not in The Amazing Robotron's halting
mechanical speech, but in my own voice.

I didn't cry. I held the letter tight in my hand, as tight as I ever
held the apparatus, and leaned into it, like it was a source of
strength.

They haven't even started work on the bat-house. There are
bugout saucers hovering all around it, with giant foam-solvent
tanks mounted under their bellies. A small crowd has gathered.

I take off my jacket and lay it on the strip of grass by the sidewalk across the street from the bat-house. I pull off my soaked t-
shirt and feel a rare breeze across my chest, as soothing as a kiss on
a fevered forehead. I ball up the shirt, then lay down on my jacket,
using the shirt as a pillow.

The bat-house is empty, its eyes staring blind, vertical to infinity.
The grotty sculpture out front is gone already, and with it, the sign
with the polite, never-used name. It is now just the bat-house.

I check my comm. The dissolving of the bat-house is scheduled
for less than an hour from now.

The new counselor was no damn good. It wore a different
exoskeleton, a motorized gurney on wheels with three buzzing
antigrav manipulators that floated constantly around the apt, tasting the air. It called itself "Tom." I didn't call it anything, and I lim-
ited my answers to it to monosyllables.

The next time I came on the guy who was Nicola Tesla in his
chair, the letter was in my pocket. I took a long swim in the ocean,
and then I stripped off my mask and spit out the snorkel, took a deep
breath and dove until my ears felt like they were going to burst. I

stared at my reflection in the silvered wall of the tank. Through the distortion of the water and the sting of the salt, my body was indistinct and clothed in quicksilver, surrounded by schools of alien, darting fish. I didn't recognize myself, but I didn't take my eyes away until my lungs were ready to burst and I resurfaced.

The guy who thought he was Nicola Tesla was still thrashing away at his straps when I climbed down from the ocean's top. At one side of Old Sparky, there was a timer, like the one on my apparatus, and a knife-switch for timed and untimed sessions.

I stared at him. My life unrolled before me, a life distanced and remote from the world around me, a life trapped in my own deepening battiness. Before I could think about what I was doing, I flipped the switch from "Timed" to "untimed." I took one last look at the ocean, looked again at Nicola Tesla, my friend and seducer, stuck to his chair until someone switched it off again, and left the 125th floor.

I took the apparatus apart in the kiddy workshop, stripped it to a collection of screws and wires and circuit boards, then carefully smashed each component with a hammer until it was in thousands of tiny pieces.

It took me two days to do it right, and not a moment passed when I didn't nearly run upstairs and switch off Tesla's chair.

And not a moment passed when I didn't visualize Tesla's wrath, his betrayal, his anger, when I unbuckled him.

And not a moment passed when I didn't wish I could plug in the apparatus, swim in the ocean, take myself away from the world and the world away from me.

The Amazing Robotron returned at the end of the second day.

"Chet, I am glad to see you a-gain."

I bit my lip and choked on tears of relief. "I need to leave here, Robotron. I can't stay another minute. Please, get me out of here. I'll do anything. I'll run away. Get me out, get me out, get me out!" I was babbling, sniveling and crying, and I begged all the harder.

"Why do you want to leave right now?"

"I—I can't take it anymore. I can't *stand* being here. I'd rather be in prison than in here anymore."

"When I was young, I left the Cen-ter I was rais-ed in to attend coun-sel-ing school. You are near-ly old e-nough to go now. May-be your pa-rents would let you go?"

I knew he had found the only way out.

I started work on my father. I wheedled and begged and demanded, and he just laughed. For three whole days, I used begging as a way to avoid thinking of Tesla. For three days, my father shook his head.

· I cried myself to sleep and wallowed in my guilt every night, and when I woke, I cried more. I stopped leaving the apt. I stopped eating. My mother and I sat all day, staring out the window. I stopped talking.

One morning, after my father had left, I dragged a stool to the window and pressed my face against it. My mother clattered around behind me.

"Go," my mother said.

I gave a squeak and turned around. My mother had folded my clothes in a neat pile and had laid a canvas bag beside it. She had the vid remote in her hand, and on the screen was a waiver for me to go to school. We locked eyes for a moment, and I moved to go to her, but she turned and stormed into the kitchen and started to clean the cupboards, silent again.

I left that day.

The saucers lift off to-the-second on-time. The crowd, which has grown, sighs collectively as the saucers disappear over the haze, then a fine mist of solvent rains down on our heads. It's as salty as sea-water, and the bat-house trembles as it begins to melt. Streams of salty water course down its sides.

The top of the building comes into view, the saucers chasing it down as it dissolves, spraying a steady blast of solvent.

I tense as the building's top reaches what I estimate to be 150. My calves bunch and my breath catches in my chest. I feel like I'm drowning, and the building's top crawls downwards, and my feet are sloshing to the ankles in dissolved foam, that runs off into the sewers.

I stay tense until the building's top is far beneath what *must* be 125, then I exhale in a whoof of air. My head spins, and I brace my hands against my thighs. I'm not looking up when it happens, as a result.

The first sign is when the great tide of green, scummy, plant-stinking water courses down over us, soaking us to the skin, blinding me and sending me reeling in reverie. Did I see hunks of dead, petrified coral crashing around me, or did I imagine it?

A brief second later the building's top emits a bolt of lightning that broke even Tesla's record for man-made lightning, recorded at nearly a kilometer in length. A clap of thunder accompanies it, louder than any sound I have ever heard, and it its wake I am perfectly deaf, submerged in silence.

The finger of lightning crawls through space like a broken-back rattler, and my hair rises from my shoulders. In the presence of so much current, I should be petrified, but it is magnificent. The finger seeks and seeks, then contacts one of the saucers and literally blasts it out of the sky. It plummets in slow-motion, and as it does, the building's top descends even further, and I *swear* I see the chair falling from the building's edge, and the man strapped inside it had not aged a day in all the lifetimes gone by.

Chet's comm died somewhere in the lightning strike, but the emergency crews that took him away and looked in his ears and poked him in the chest andgave him pills take him back to the Royal York in a saucer, bridging the distance in a few minutes, touching down on Front Street. The Royal York's doorman doesn't bat an eye as he gets the door for him.

The elevator ride is fine. He is still wrapped in the silence of his deafness, but it's a comforting, *centering* silence.

Once Chet is back in his room, he fires up the vid and starts writing a letter to The Amazing Robotron.

I was a Red Diaper Baby. My parents were and are Trotskyists, and I grew up in "The Movement." When they told me, at the age of five, that I was going to march in my aunt's wedding I reportedly leapt to my feet and started picketing the living-room, carrying an imaginary placard, chanting "Not the Church and not the State/Women must control their fate!"

Movement politics—the intersection of a commitment to justice and all the human follies of power-hunger, avarice, jealousy and pride—are a fascinating source of personal drama and tension.

I started out wanting to write a story about a Jewish Super Man, someone truer to Supe's roots. Siegel and Shuster, Superman's creators, were both Jewish, both from Toronto. I started noodling with the idea of the Super Man being raised in the Gaza Strip, the Jewish stretch of Bathurst Street in Toronto where my father and mother were raised.

I found myself wondering about a Super Man raised in the Canadian tradition of "Peace, Order and Good Government" instead of "Life, Liberty and the Pursuit of Happiness," and came around to a kind of lefty Super Man, a Canadian Super Man, balanced on the seesaw of Judaic guilt and intellectualism and the invincibility of a Super Man.

A Super Man is tough to write about. He's immortal, he's impervious, he's nigh-omnipotent. How do you create dramatic tension about such a person? What danger can he be in? The Super Man cries out for a more-powerful being to pour the heat on. Who better to out-super the Super Man than the bugouts?

The Super Man and the Bugout

"Mama, I'm *not* a super-villain," Hershie said for the millionth time. He chased the last of the gravy on his plate with a hunk of dark rye, skirting the shriveled derma left behind from his kishka. Ever since the bugouts had inducted Earth into their Galactic Federation, promising to end war, crime, and corruption, he'd found himself at loose ends. His adoptive Earth-mother, who'd named him Hershie Abromowicz, had talked him into meeting her at her favorite restaurant in the heart of Toronto's Gaza Strip.

"Not a super-villain, he says. Listen to him: mister big-stuff. Well, smartypants, if you're not a super-villain, what was that mess on the television last night then?"

A busboy refilled their water, and Hershie took a long sip, staring off into the middle distance. Lately, he'd taken to avoiding looking at his mother: her infra-red signature was like a landing-strip for a coronary, and she wouldn't let him take her to one of the bugout clinics for nanosurgery.

Mrs.. Abromowicz leaned across the table and whacked him upside the head with one hand, her big rings clicking against the temple of his half-rim specs. Had it been anyone else, he would have caught her hand mid-slap, or at least dodged in a superfast blur, quicker than any human eye. But his mama had let him know

182

what she thought of *that* sass before his third birthday. Raising super-infants requires strict, *loving* discipline. "Hey, wake up! Hey! I'm talking to you! What was that mess on television last night?"

"It was a demonstration, mama. We were protesting. We want to dismantle the machines of war—it's in the Torah, mama. Isaiah: they shall beat their swords into ploughshares and their spears into pruning hooks. Tot would have approved."

Mrs. Abromowicz sucked air between her teeth. "Your father never would have approved of *that*."

That was the action last night. It had been his idea, and he'd tossed it around with the movement people who'd planned the demo: they'd gone to an army-surplus store and purchased hundreds of decommissioned rifles, their bores filled with lead, their firing pins defanged. He'd flown above and ahead of the demonstration, in his traditional tights and cape, dragging a cargo net full of rifles from his belt. He pulled them out one at a time, and bent them into balloon-animals—fanciful giraffes, wiener-dogs, bumble-bees, poodles—and passed them out the crowds lining Yonge Street. It had been a boffo smash hit. And it made great TV.

Hershie Abromowicz, Man from the Stars, took his mother's hands between his own and looked into her eyes. "Mama, I'm a grown man. I have a job to do. It's like . . . like a calling. The world's still a big place, bugouts or no bugouts, and there's lots of people here who are crazy, wicked, with their fingers on the triggers. I care about this planet, and I can't sit by when it's in danger."

"But why all of a sudden do you have to be off with these *meshuggenahs*? How come you didn't *need* to be with the crazy people until now?"

"Because there's a *chance* now. The world is ready to rethink itself. Because —" The waiter saved him by appearing with the check. His mother started to open her purse, but he had his debit card on the table faster than the eye could follow. "It's on me, Ma."

"Don't be silly. I'll pay."

"I *want* to. Let me. A son should take his mother out to lunch once in a while."

She smiled, for the first time that whole afternoon, and patted his cheek with one manicured hand. "You're a good boy, Hershie,

I know that. I only want that you should be happy, and have what's best for you."

Hershie, in tights and cape, was chilling in his fortress of solitude when his comm rang. He checked the callerid and winced: Thomas was calling, from Toronto. Hershie's long-distance bills were killing him, ever since the Department of Defense had cut off his freebie account.

Not to mention that talking to Thomas inevitably led to more trouble with his mother.

He got up off of his crystalline recliner and flipped the comm open, floating up a couple of meters. "Thomas, what's up?"

"Supe, didja see the reviews? The critics *love* us!"

Hersh held the comm away from his head and sighed the ancient, put-upon Hebraic sigh of his departed stepfather. Thomas Aquino Rusk liked to play at being a sleazy Broadway producer, his "plays" the eye-catching demonstrations he and his band of merry shit-disturbers hijacked.

"Yeah, it made pretty good vid, all right." He didn't ask why Thomas was calling. There was only one reason he *ever* called: he'd had another idea.

"You'll never guess why I called."

"You've had an idea."

"I've had an idea!"

"Really."

"You'll love it."

Hershie reached out and stroked the diamond-faceted coffins that his birth parents lay in, hoping for guidance. His warm fingers slicked with melted hoarfrost, and as they skated over the crypt, it sang a pure, high crystal note like a crippled flying saucer plummeting to the earth. "I'm sure I will, Thomas."

As usual, Thomas chose not to hear the sarcasm in his voice. "Check this out—DefenseFest 33 is being held in Toronto in March. And the new keynote speaker is the Patron Ik'spir Pat! The friggin' head friggin' bugout! His address is 'Galactic History and Military Tactics: a Strategic Overview.'"

"And this is a good thing?"

"Ohfuckno. It's terrible, terrible, of course. The bugouts are selling us out. Going over to the Other Side. Just awful. But think of
the possibilities!"

"But think of the possibilities? Oy." Despite himself, Hershie
was smiling. Thomas always made him smile.

"You're smiling, aren't you?"

"Shut up, Thomas."

"Can you make a meeting at the Belquees for 18h?"

Hershie checked his comm. It was 1702h. "I can make it."

"See you there, buddy." Thomas rang off.

Hershie folded his comm, wedged it in his belt, and stroked his
parents' crypt, once more, for luck.

Hershie loved the commute home. Starting at the Arctic Circle, he
flew up and up and up above the highest clouds, then flattened out
his body and rode the currents home, eeling around the wet frozen
cloudmasses, slaloming through thunderheads, his critical faculties
switched off, flying at speed on blind instinct alone.

He usually made visual contact with the surface around Barrie,
just outside of Toronto, and he wasn't such a goodiegoodie that he
didn't feel a thrill of superiority as he flew over the cottage-country
commuters stuck in the end-of-weekend traffic, skis and snowmo-
biles strapped to their roofs.

The Belquees had the best Ethiopian food and the worst Ethiopian
decor in town. Successive generations of managers had added their
own touches—tiki-lanterns, textured wallpaper, framed photos of
Haile Selassie, tribal spears and grass dolls—and they'd accreted in
layers, until the net effect was of an African rummage sale. But
man, the food was good.

Downstairs was a banquet room whose decor consisted of mate-
rial too ugly to be shown upstairs, with a stage and a disco ball. It
had been a regular meeting place for Toronto's radicals for more
than fifty years, the chairs worn smooth by generations of left-
wing buttocks.

Tonight, it was packed. At least fifty people were crammed
around the tables, tearing off hunks of tangy rice-pancake and

scooping up vegetarian curry with them. Even before he saw Thomas, his super-hearing had already picked his voice out of the din and located it. Hershie made a beeline for Thomas's table, not making eye-contact with the others—old-guard activists who still saw him as a tool of the war-machine.

Thomas licked his fingers clean and shook his hand. "Supe! Glad you could make it! Sit, sit." There was a general shuffling of coats and chairs as the other people at the table cleared a space for him. Thomas was already pouring him a beer out of one of the pitchers on the table.

"Geez, how many people did you invite?"

Tina, a tiny Chinese woman who could rhyme "Hey hey, ho ho" and "One, two, three, four" with amazing facility said, "Everyone's here. The Quakers, the commies, a couple of councilors, the vets, anyone we could think of. This is gonna be *huge*."

The food was hot, and the different curries and salads were a symphony of flavors and textures. "This is terrific," he said.

"Best Ethiopian outside of Addis Ababa," said Thomas.

Better than Addis Ababa, Hershie thought, but didn't say it. He'd been in Addis Ababa as the secret weapon behind Canada's third and most ill-fated peacekeeping mission there. There hadn't been a lot of restaurants open then, just block after block of bombed-out buildings, and tribal warlords driving around in tacticals, firing randomly at anything that moved. The ground CO sent him off to scatter bands of marauders while the bullets spanged off his chest. He'd never understood the tactical significance of those actions—still didn't— but at the time, he'd been willing to trust those in authority.

"Good food," he said.

An hour later, the pretty waitress had cleared away the platters and brought fresh pitchers, and Hershie's tights felt a little tighter. One of the Quakers, an ancient, skinny man with thin grey hair and sharp, clever features stood up and tapped his beer-mug. Gradually, conversation subsided.

"Thank you," he said. "My name is Stewart Pocock, and I'm here from the Circle of Friends. I'd like us all to take a moment to say a silent thanks for the wonderful food we've all enjoyed."

There was a nervous shuffling, and then a general bowing of heads and mostly silence, broken by low whispers."

"Thomas, I thought *you* called this meeting," Hershie whispered.

"I did. These guys always do this. Control freaks. Don't worry about it," he whispered back.

"Thank you all. We took the liberty of drawing up an agenda for this meeting."

"They *always* do this," Thomas said.

The Quakers led them in a round of introductions, which came around to Hershie. "I'm, uh, The Super Man. I guess most of you know that, right?" Silence. "I'm really looking forward to working on this with you all." A moment of silence followed, before the next table started in on its own introductions.

"Time," Louise Pocock said. Blissfully. At last. The agenda had ticks next to INTRODUCTION, BACKGROUND, STRATEGY, THE DAY, SUPPORT AND ORGANIZING and PUBLICITY. Thomas had hardly spoken a word through the course of the meeting. Even Hershie's alien buttocks were numb from sitting.

"It's time for the closing circle. Please, everybody, stand up and hold hands." Many of the assembled didn't bother to stifle their groans. Awkwardly, around the tables and the knapsacks, they formed a rough circle and took hands. They held it for an long, painful moment, then gratefully let go.

They worked their way upstairs and outside. The wind had picked up, and it blew Hershie's cape out on a crackling horizontal behind him, so that it caught many of the others in the face as they cycled or walked away.

"Supe, let's you and me grab a coffee, huh?" Thomas said, without any spin on it at all, so that Hershie knew that it wasn't a casual request.

"Yeah, sure."

The cafe Thomas chose was in a renovated bank, and there was a private room in the old vault, and they sat down there, away from prying eyes and autograph hounds.

"So, you pumped?" Thomas said, once they had they ordered coffees.

"After *that* meeting? Yeah, sure."

Thomas laughed, a slightly patronizing but friendly laugh. "That was a *great* meeting. Look, if those guys had their way, we'd have about a march a month, and we'd walk slowly down a route that we had a permit for, politely asking people to see our point of view. And in between, we'd have a million meetings like this, where we come up with brilliant ideas like, 'Let's hand out fliers next time.'

"So what we do is, go along with them. Give them enough rope to hang themselves. Let 'em have four or five of those, until everyone who shows up is so bored, they'll do *anything*, as long as its not that.

"So, these guys want to stage a sit-in in front of the convention center. Bo-ring! We wait until they're ready to sit down, then we start playing music and turn it into a *dance-in*. Start playing movies on the side of the building. Bring in a hundred secret agents in costume to add to it. They'll never know what hit 'em."

Hershie squirmed. These kinds of Machiavellian shenanigans came slowly to him. "That seems kind of, well, disingenuous, Thomas. Why don't we just hold our own march?"

"And split the movement? No, this is much better. These guys do all the postering and phoning, they get a good crowd out, this is their natural role. Our natural role, my son," he placed a friendly hand on Hershie's caped shoulder, "is to see to it that their efforts aren't defeated by their own poverty of imagination. They're the feet of the movement, but we're its *laugh*." Thomas pulled out his comm and scribbled on its surface. "*They're the feet of the movement, but we're its laugh*, that's great, that's one for the memoirs."

Hershie decided he needed to patrol a little to clear his head. He scooped trash and syringes from Grenadier Pond. He flew silently through High Park, ears cocked for any muggings.

Nothing.

He patrolled the Gardner Expressway next and used his heat vision to melt some black ice.

Feeling useless, he headed for home.

He was most of the way up Yonge Street when he heard the siren. A cop car, driving fast, down Jarvis. He sighed his father's sigh and rolled east, heading into Regent Park, locating the dopplering siren. He touched down lightly on top of one of the ugly, squat tenements, and skipped from roof to roof, until he spotted the cop. He was beefy, with the traditional moustache and the flak vest that they all wore on downtown patrol. He was leaning against the hood of his cruiser, panting, his breath clouding around him.

A kid rolled on the ground, clutching his groin, gasping for breath. His infrared signature throbbed painfully between his legs. Clearly, he'd been kicked in the nuts.

The cop leaned into his cruiser and lowered the volume on his radio, then, without warning, kicked the kid in the small of the back. The kid rolled on the ice, thrashing painfully.

Before Hershie knew what he was doing, he was hovering over the ice, between the cop and the kid. The cateyes embedded in the emblem on his chest glowed in the streetlamps. The cop's eyes widened so that Hershie could see the whites around his irises.

Hershie stared. "What do you think you're doing?" he said, after a measured silence.

The cop took a step back and slipped a little on the ice before catching himself on his cruiser.

"Since when do you kick unarmed civilians in the back?"

"He—he ran away. I had to catch him. I wanted to teach him not to run."

"By inspiring his trust in the evenhandedness of Toronto's Finest?" Hershie could see the cooling tracks of the cruiser, skidding and weaving through the projects. The kid had put up a good chase. Behind him, he heard the kid regain his feet and start running. The cop started forward, but Hershie stopped him with one finger, dead center in the flak jacket.

"You can't let him get away!"

"I can catch him. Trust me. But first, we're going to wait for your backup to arrive, and I'm going to file a report."

A *Sun* reporter arrived before the backup unit. Hershie maintained stony silence in the face of his questions, but he couldn't stop the man from listening in on his conversation with the old constable who showed up a few minutes later, as he filed his report. He found the kid a few blocks away, huddled in an alley, hand pressed to the small of his back. He took him to Mount Sinai's emerg and turned him over to a uniformed cop.

The hysterical *Sun* headlines that vilified Hershie for interfering with the cop sparked a round of recriminating voicemails from his mother, filled with promises to give him such a *zetz* in the head when she next saw him. He folded his tights and cape and stuffed them in the back of his closet and spent a lot of time in the park for the next few weeks. He liked to watch the kids play-ing, a United Nations in miniature, parents looking on amiably, stymied by the language barrier that their kids hurdled with ease.

On March first, he took his tights out of the overstuffed hall closet and flew to Ottawa to collect his pension.

He touched down on the Parliament Hill and was instantly sur-rounded by high-booted RCMP constables, looking slightly pan-icky. He held his hands up, startled. "What gives, guys?"

"Sorry, sir," one said. "High security today. One of Them is speaking in Parliament."

"Them?"

"The bugouts. Came down to have a chat about neighborly relations. Authorized personnel only today."

"Well, that's me," Hershie said, and started past him.

The constable, looking extremely unhappy, moved to block him. "I'm sorry sir, but that's not you. Only people on the list. My orders, I'm afraid."

Hershie looked into the man's face and thought about hurtling skywards and flying straight into the building. The man was only doing his job, though. "Look, it's payday. I have to go see the min-ister of defense. I've been doing it every month for *years*."

"I know that sir, but today is a special day. Perhaps you could return tomorrow?"

"Tomorrow? My rent is due *today*, sergeant. Look, what if I comm his office?"

"Please, sir, that would be fine." The sergeant looked relieved.

Hershie hit a speed dial and waited. A recorded voice told him that the office was closed, the minister at a special session.

"He's in session. Look, it's probably on his desk—I've been coming here for years; really, this is ridiculous."

"I'm sorry. I have my orders."

"I don't think you could stop me, sergeant."

The sergeant and his troops shuffled their feet. "You're probably right, sir. But orders are orders."

"You know, sergeant, I retired a full colonel from the Armed Forces. I *could* order you to let me past."

"Sorry sir, no. Different chain of command."

Hershie controlled his frustration with an effort of will. "Fine then. I'll be back tomorrow."

The building super wasn't pleased about the late rent. He threatened Hershie with eviction, told him he was in violation of the lease, quoted the relevant sections of the Tenant Protection Act from memory, then grudgingly gave in to Hershie's pleas. Hershie had half a mind to put his costume on and let the man see what a *real* super was like.

But his secret identity was sacrosanct. Even in the era of Pax Aliena, the Super Man had lots of enemies, all of whom had figured out, long before, that even the invulnerable have weaknesses: their friends and families. It terrified him to think of what a bitter, obsolete, grudge-bearing terrorist might do to his mother, to Thomas, or even his old high-school girlfriends.

For his part, Thomas refused to acknowledge the risk; he'd was more worried about the Powers That Be than mythical terrorists.

The papers the next day were full of the overnight cabinet shuffle in Ottawa. More than half the cabinet had been relegated to the back benches, and many of their portfolios had been eliminated or amalgamated into the new "Superportfolios": Domestic Affairs, Trade, and Extraterrestrial Affairs.

The old minister of defense, who'd once had Hershie over for Thanksgiving dinner, was banished to the lowest hell of the back-bench. His portfolio had been subsumed into Extraterrestrial Affairs, and the new minister, a young up-and-comer named

Woolley, wasn't taking Hershie's calls. Hershie called Thomas to see
if he could loan him rent money.

Thomas laughed. "Chickens coming home to roost, huh?" he
said.

"What's that supposed to mean?" Hershie said, hotly.

"Well, there's only so much shit-disturbing you can do before
someone sits up and takes notice. The Belquees is probably bugged,
or maybe one of the commies is an informer. Either way, you're
screwed. Especially with Woolley."

"Why, what's wrong with Woolley?" Hershie had met him in
passing at prime minister's office affairs, a well-dressed twenty-
nine-year-old. He'd seemed like a nice enough guy.

"What's *wrong* with him?" Thomas nearly screamed. "He's the
friggin' *antichrist*! He was the one that came up with the idea of
selling advertising on squeegee kids' t-shirts! He's heavily supported by private security outfits—he makes Darth Vader look like
a swell guy. That slicked-down, blow-dried asshole—"

Hershie cut him off. "OK, OK, I get the idea."

"No you don't, Supe! You don't get the half of it. This guy isn't
your average Liberal—those guys usually basic opportunists. He's a
zealot! He'd like to beat us with *truncheons*! I went to one of his
debates, and he showed up with a *baseball bat*! He tried to *hit me*
with it!"

"What were you doing at the time?"

"What does it matter? Violence is never an acceptable response.
I've thrown pies at better men than him —"

Hershie grinned. Thomas hadn't invented pieing, but his contri-
butions to the art were seminal. "Thomas, the man is a federal minister, with obligations. He can't just write me off he'll have to pay me."

"Sure, sure," Thomas crooned. "Of *course* he will—who ever
heard of a politician abusing his office to advance his agenda? I
don't know what I was thinking. I apologize."

Hershie touched down on Parliament Hill, heart racing. Thomas's
warning echoed in his head. His memories of Woolley were
already morphing, so that the slick, neat kid became feral, preda-
tory. The Hill was marshy and cold and gray, and as he squelched

up to the main security desk, he felt a cold ooze of mud infiltrate its way into his super-bootie. There was a new RCMP constable on duty, a turbanned Sikh. Normally, he felt awkward around the Sikhs in the Mounties. He imagined that their lack of cultural context made his tights and emblem seem absurd, that they evoked grins beneath the Sikhs' fierce moustaches. But today, he was glad the man was a Sikh, another foreigner with an uneasy berth in the Canadian military-industrial complex. The Sikh was expressionless as Hershie squirted his clearances from his comm to the security desk's transceiver. Imperturbably, the Sikh squirted back directions to Woolley's new office, just a short jaunt from the exalted heights of the prime minister's office.

The minister's office was guarded by: a dignified antique door that had the rich finish of wood that has been buffed daily for two centuries; an RCMP constable in plainclothes; a young, handsome receptionist in a silk navy power-suit; a slightly older office manager whose heart-stopping beauty was only barely restrained by her chaste blouse and skirt; and, finally, a pair of boardroom doors with spotless brass handles and a retinal scanner.

Each obstacle took more time to weather than the last, so it was nearly an hour before the office manager stared fixedly into the scanner until the locks opened with a soft clack. Hershie squelched in, leaving a slushy dribble on the muted industrial-grade brown carpet.

Woolley knelt on the stool of an ergonomic work-cart, enveloped in an articulated nest of displays, comms, keyboards, datagloves, immersive headsets, stylii, sticky notes and cup-holders. His posture, hair and expression rivaled one-another for flawlessness.

"Hello, hello," he said, giving Hershie's hand a dry, firm pump. He smelled of expensive talc and leather car interiors.

He led Hershie to a pair of stark Scandinavian chairs whose polished lead undersides bristled with user-interface knobs. The old minister's tastes had run to imposing oak desks and horsehair club-chairs, and Hershie felt a moment's disorientation as he sank into the brilliantly functional sitting-machine. It chittered like a roulette wheel and shifted to firmly support him.

"Thanks for seeing me," Hershie said. He caught his reflection in the bulletproof glass windows that faced out over the Rideau

Canal, and felt a flush of embarrassment when he saw how clown-ish his costume looked in the practical environs.

Woolley favored him with half a smile and stared sincerely with eyes that were widely spaced, clever and hazel, surrounded by smile lines. The man fairly oozed charisma. "I should be thanking you. I was just about to call you to set up a meeting."

Then why haven't you been taking my calls? Hershie thought. Lamely, he said, "You were?"

"I was. I wanted to touch base with you, clarify the way that we were going to operate from now on."

Hershie felt his gorge rise. "From now on?"

"I phrased that badly. What I mean to say is, this is a new cabi-net, a new Ministry. It has its own modus operandi."

"How can it have its own modus operandi when it was only created last night?" Hershie said, hating the petulance in his voice.

"Oh, I like to keep lots of contingency plans on hand—the time to plan for major changes is far in advance. Otherwise, you end up running around trying to get office furniture and telephones installed when you need to be seizing opportunity."

It struck Hershie how *finished* the office was—the staff, the systems, the security. He imagined Woolley hearing the news of his appointment and calling up files containing schematics, purchase orders, staff requisitions. It wasn't exactly devious, but it certainly teetered on the meridian separating *planning* and *plotting*.

"Well, you certainly seem to have everything in order."

"I've been giving some thought to your payment arrangement. Did you know that there's a whole body of policy relating to your pension?"

Hershie nodded, not liking where this was going.

"Well, that's just not sensible," Woolley said, sensibly. "The Canadian government already has its own pension apparatus: we make millions of direct-deposits every day, for welfare, pensions, employment insurance, mothers' allowance. We're up to our armpits in payment infrastructure. And having you fly up to Ottawa every month, well, it's ridiculous. This is the twenty-first century—we have better ways of moving money around.

"I've been giving it some thought, and I've come up with a solution that should make everything easier for everyone. I'm going to transfer your pension to the Canada Pension Plan offices; they'll make a monthly deposit directly to your account. I've got the paperwork all filled out here; all you need to do is fill in your banking information and your Social Insurance Number."

"But I don't have a Social Insurance Number or a bank account," Hershie said. Of course, Hershie Abromowicz had both, but the Super Man didn't.

"How do you pay taxes, then?" Woolley had a dangerous smile.

"Well, I —" Hershie stammered. "I don't! I'm tax-exempt! I've never had to pay taxes or get a bank account—I just take my checks to the Canadian Union of Public Employees' Credit Union and they cash them for me. It's the *arrangement*."

Woolley shook his head. "Who told you you were tax-exempt?" he asked, wonderingly. "*No one* is tax-exempt, except Status Indians. As to not having a bank account, well, you can open an account at the CUPE Credit Union and we'll make the deposits there. But not until this tax status matter is cleared up. You'll have to talk to Revenue Canada about getting a SIN, and get that information to Canada Pensions."

"I *pay taxes!* Through my secret identity."

"But does this . . ." he made quote marks with his fingers, "*secret identity* declare your pension income?"

"Of course I don't! I have to keep my secret identity a *secret!*" His voice was shrill in his own ears. "It's a *secret identity*. I served in the forces as the Super Man, so I get paid as the Super Man. Tax exempt, no bank accounts, no SIN. Just a check, every month."

Woolley leaned back and clasped his hands in his lap. "I know that's how it used to be, but what I'm trying to tell you today is that arrangement, however longstanding, however well-intentioned, wasn't proper—or even *legal*. It had to end some time. You're retired now—you don't need your *secret identity*," again with the finger-quotes. "If you already have a SIN, you can just give it to me, along with your secret identity's bank information, and we can have your pension processed in a week or two."

"*A week or two*?" Hershie bellowed. "I need to pay my *rent*! That's not how it works!"

Woolley stood, abruptly. "No sir, that *is* how it works. I'm trying to be reasonable. I'm trying to expedite things for you during this time of transition. But you need to meet me halfway. If you could give me your SIN and account information right now, I could speed things up considerably, I'm sure. I'm willing to make that effort, even though things are very busy here."

Hershie toyed with the idea of demolishing the man's office, turning his lovely furniture into molten nacho topping, and finishing up by leaving the man dangling by his suit from the CN Tower's needle. But his mother would kill him. "I can't give you my secret identity," Hershie said, pleadingly. "It's a matter of national security. I just need enough to pay my rent."

Woolley stared at the ceiling for a long, long time. "There is one thing," he said.

"Yes?" Hershie said, hating himself for the note of hope in his voice.

"The people at DefenseFest 33 called my office yesterday, to see if I'd appear as a guest speaker with the Patron Ik'spir Pat. I had to turn them down, of course—I'm far too busy right now. But I'm sure they'd be happy to have a veteran of your reputation in that slot, and it carries a substantial honorarium. I could call them for you and give them your comm . . .?"

Hershie thought of Thomas, and of the rent, and of his mother, and of all the people at the Belquees who'd stared mistrustfully at him. "Have them call me," he sighed. "I'll talk to them."

He got to his feet, the toe of his boot squelching out more dirt pudding.

"Hershie?"

"Yes, mama?" She'd caught him on the way home, flying high over the fleabag motels on the old Highway 2.

"It's Friday," she said.

Right. Friday. He told her he'd come for dinner, and that meant getting there before sunset. "I'll be there," he said.

"Oh, it's not important. It's just me. Don't hurry on my account—after all, you'll have thousands of Shabbas dinners with your mother. I'll live forever."

"I said I'll be there."

"And don't wear that costume," she said. She hated the costume. When the Department of Defense had issued it to him, she'd wanted to know why they were sending her boy into combat wearing red satin panties.

"I'll change."

"That's a good boy," she said. "I'm making brisket."

By the time he touched down on the roof of his building, he knew he'd be late for dinner. He skimmed down the elevator shaft to the tenth floor and ducked out to his apartment, only to find the door padlocked. There was a note from the building super tacked to the peeling green paint. Among other things, it quoted the codicil from the Tenant Protection Act that allowed the super to padlock the door and forbade Hershie, on penalty of law, from doing anything about it.

Hershie's super-hearing picked up the sound of a door opening down the hallway. In a blur, he flew up to the ceiling and hovered there, pressing himself flat on the acoustic tile. One of his neighbors, that guy with the bohemian attitude who always seemed to be laughing at poor, nebbishy Hershie Abromowicz, made his way down the hall. He paused directly below Hershie's still, hovering form, reading the note on the door while he adjusted the collar of his ski-vest. He smirked at the note and got in the elevator.

Hershie let himself float to the ground, his cheeks burning.

Damn it, he didn't have *time* for this. Not for any of it. He considered the padlock for a moment, then snapped the hasp with his thumb and index finger. Moving through the apartment with super-human speed, he changed into a pair of nice slacks, a cable-knit sweater his mother had given him for his last birthday, a tweedy jacket and a woolen overcoat. Opening a window, he took flight.

"Thomas, I *really* can't talk right now," he said. His mother was angrily drumming her rings on the table's edge. Abruptly, she grabbed the bowl of cooling soup from his place setting and carried it into the kitchen. She hadn't done this since he was a kid, but it still inspired the same panicky dread in him—if he wasn't going to eat his dinner, she wasn't going to leave it.

"Supe, we *have* to talk about this. I mean, DefenseFest is only a week away. We've got things to do!"

"Look, about DefenseFest . . ."

"Yes?" Thomas had a wary note in his voice.

Hershie's mother reappeared with a plate laden with brisket, tsimmis, and kasha. She set it down in front of him.

"We'll talk later, OK?" Hershie said.

"But what about DefenseFest?"

"It's complicated," Hershie began. His mother scooped up the plate of brisket and headed back to the kitchen. She was muttering furiously. "I have to go," he said and closed his comm.

Hershie chased his mother and snatched the plate from her as she held it dramatically over the sink disposal. He held up his comm with the other hand and made a show of powering it down.

"It's off, mama. Please, come and eat."

"I've been thinking of selling the house," she said, as they tucked into slices of lemon pound cake.

Hershie put down his fork. "Sell the house?" While his father hadn't exactly *built* the house with his own hands, he had sold his guts out at his discount menswear store to pay for it. His mother had decorated it, but his father's essence still haunted the corners.

"Why would you sell the house?"

"Oh, it's too big, Hershie. I'm just one old lady, and it's not like there're any grandchildren to come and stay. I could buy a condo in Florida, and there'd be plenty left over for you."

"I don't need any money, mama. I've got my pension."

She covered his hands with hers. "Of course you do, bubbie. But fixed incomes are for old men. You're young, you need a nest egg, something to start a family with." Her sharp eyes, sunk into motherly pillows of soft flesh, bored into him. He tried to keep his gaze light and carefree. "You've got money problems?" she said, at length.

Hershie scooped up a forkful of pound-cake and shook his head. His mother's powers of perception bordered on clairvoyance, and he didn't trust himself to speak the lie outright. He looked around the dining room, furnished with faux chinoise screens, oriental rugs, angular art-glass chandeliers.

"Tell mama," she said.

He sighed and finished the cake. "It's the new minister. He won't give me my pension unless I tell him my secret identity."

"So?" his mother said. "You're so ashamed of your parents, you'd rather starve than tell the world that their bigshot hero is Hershie Abromowicz? I, for one wouldn't mind—finally, I could speak up when my girlfriends are going on about their sons the lawyers."

"Mom!" he said, feeling all of eight years old. "I'm not ashamed and you know it. But if the world knew who I was, well, who knows what kind of danger you'd be in? I've made some powerful enemies, mama."

"Enemies, shmenemies," she said, waving her hands. "Don't worry yourself on my account. Don't make me the reason that you end up in the cold. I'm not helpless you know. I have Mace."

Hershie thought of the battles he'd fought: the soldiers, the mercenaries, the terrorists, the crooks and the super-crooks with their insane plots and impractical apparati. His mother was as formidable as an elderly Jewish woman with no grandchildren could be, but she was no match for automatic weapons. "I can't do it, mama. It wouldn't be responsible. Can we drop it?"

"Fine, we won't talk about it anymore. But a mother *worries*. You're sure you don't need any money?"

He cast about desperately for a way to placate her. "I'm fine. I've got a speaking engagement lined up."

There was a message waiting on his comm when he powered it back up. A message from a relentlessly cheerful woman with a chirpy Texas accent, who identified herself as the programming coordinator for DefenseFest 33. She hoped he would return her call that night.

Hershie hovered in a dark cloud over the lake, the wind blowing his coat straight back, holding the comm in his hand. He squinted through the clouds and distance until he saw his apartment building, a row of windows lit up like teeth, his darkened window a gap in the smile. He didn't mind the cold, it was much colder in his fortress of solitude, but his apartment was more than warmth. It was his own shabby, homey corner of the hideously expensive city. On the flight from his mother's, he'd found an old-style fifty-dollar bill, folded neatly and stuck in the breast pocket of his overcoat.

He returned the phone call.

The super wasn't happy about being roused from his sitcoms, but he grudgingly allowed Hershie to squirt the rent money at his comm. He wanted to come up and take the padlock, but Hershie talked him into turning over the key, promising to return it in the morning.

His apartment was a little one-bedroom with a constant symphony of groaning radiators. Every stick of furniture in it had been rescued from curbsides while Hershie flew his night patrols, saving chairs, sofas and even a scarred walnut armoire from the trashman.

Hershie sat at the round formica table and commed Thomas.

"It's me," he said.

"What's up?"

He didn't want to beat around the bush. "I'm speaking at DefenseFest. Then I'm going on tour, six months, speaking at military shows. It pays well. Very well." Very, very well—well enough that he wouldn't have to worry about his pension. The US-based promoters had sorted his tax status out with the IRS, who would happily exempt him, totally freeing him from entanglements with Revenue Canada. The cheerful Texan had been *glad* to do it.

He waited for Thomas's trademark stream of vitriol. It didn't come. Very quietly, Thomas said, "I see."

"Thomas," he said, a note of pleading in his voice. "It's not my choice. If I don't do this, I'll have to give Woolley my secret identity—he won't give me my pension without my Social Insurance Number."

"Or you could get a job," Thomas said, the familiar invective snarl creeping back.

"I just told you, I can't give out my SIN!"

"So have your secret identity get a job. Wash dishes!"

"If I took a job," Hershie said, palms sweating, "I'd have to give up flying patrols—I'd have to stop fighting crime."

"*Fighting crime?*" Thomas's voice was remorseless. "What *crime?* The bugouts are taking care of crime—they're making plans to shut down the *police*! Supe, you've been obsoleted."

"I know," Hershie said, self-pitying. "I know. That's why I got involved with you in the first place—I need to have a *purpose*. I'm the Super Man!"

"So your purpose is speaking to military shows? Telling the world that it still needs its arsenals, even if the bugouts have made war obsolete? Great purpose, Supe. Very noble."

He choked on a hopeless sob. "So what can I do, Thomas? I on't want to sell out, but I've got to *eat*."

"Squeeze coal into diamonds?" he said. It was teasing, but not nasty teasing. Hershie felt his tension slip: Thomas didn't hate him.

"Do you have any idea how big a piece of coal you have to start with to get even a one-carat stone? Trust me—someone would notice if entire coalfaces started disappearing."

"Look, Supe, this is surmountable. You don't have to sell out. You said it yourself, you're the Super Man—you have responsibilities. You have duties. You can't just sell out. Let's sleep on it, huh?"

Hershie was so very, very tired. It was always hardest on him when the Earth's yellow sun was hidden; the moon was a paltry substitute for its rejuvenating rays. "Let's do that," he said. "Thanks, Thomas."

DefenseFest 33 opened its doors on one of those incredibly bright March days when the snow on the ground throws back lumens sufficient to shrink your pupils to microdots. Despite the day's brightness, a bitterly cold wind scoured Front Street and the Metro Convention Center.

From a distance, Hershie watched demonstration muster out front of the Eaton Center, a few kilometers north, and march down to Front Street, along their permit-proscribed route. The turnout was good, especially given the weather: about 5,000 showed up with wooly scarves and placards that the wind kept threatening to tear loose from their grasp.

The veterans marched out front, under a banner, in full uniform. Next came the Quakers, who were of the same vintage as the veterans, but dressed like elderly English professors. Next came three different Communist factions, who circulated back and forth, trying to sell each other magazines. Finally, there came the rabble: Thomas's group of harlequin-dressed anarchists; high-school students with packsacks who industriously commed their browbeaten classmates who'd elected to stay at their desks; "civilians" who'd seen a notice and come out, and tried gamely to keep up with the chanting.

The chanting got louder as they neared the security cordon around the convention center. The different groups all mingled as they massed on the opposite side of the barricades. The Quakers and the vets sang "Give Peace a Chance," while Thomas and his cohort prowled around, distributing materiel to various trusted individuals.

The students hollered abuse at the attendees who were trickling into the convention center in expensive overcoats, florid with expense-account breakfasts and immaculately groomed.

Hershie's appearance silenced the crowd. He screamed in over the lake, banked vertically up the side of the CN Tower, and plummeted downward. The demonstrators set up a loud cheer as he skimmed the crowd, then fell silent and aghast as he touched down on the *opposite* side of the barricade, with the convention-goers. A cop in riot-gear held the door for him and he stepped inside. A groan went up from the protestors, and swelled into a wordless, furious howl.

Hershie avoided the show's floor and headed for the green room. En route, he was stopped by a Somali general who'd been acquitted by a War Crimes tribunal, but only barely. The man greeted him like an old comrade and got his aide to snap a photo of the two of them shaking hands.

The green room was crowded with coffee-slurping presenters who pecked furiously at their comms, revising their slides. Hershie drew curious stares when he entered, but by the time he'd gotten his Danish and coffee, everyone around him was once again bent over their work, a field of balding cabbages anointed with high-tech hair-care products.

Hershie's palms were slick, his alien hearts throbbing in counterpoint. His cowlick wilted in the aggressive heat shimmering out of the vent behind his sofa. He tried to keep himself calm, but by the time a gofer commed him and squirted directions to the main ballroom, he was a wreck.

Hershie commed into the feed from the demonstration in time to see the Quakers sit, en masse, along the barricade, hands intertwined, asses soaking in the slush at the curbside. The cops watched them impassively, and while they were distracted, Thomas gave a signal to his crew, who hastily unreeled a stories-high smartscreen, the gossamer fabric snapping taut in the wind as it unfurled over the convention center's facade.

The cops were suddenly alert, moving, but Thomas was careful to keep the screen on his side of the barricade. Tina led a team of high-school students who spread out a solar collector the size and consistency of a parachute. It glinted in the harsh sun.

Szandor hastily cabled a projector/loudhailer apparatus to the collector. Szandor's dog nipped at his heels as he steadied and focused the apparatus on the screen, and Szandor plugged his comm into it and powered it up.

There was a staticky pop as the speakers came to life, loud enough to be heard over the street noise. The powerful projector beamed its image onto the screen, bright even in the midday glare.

There were hoots from the crowd as they recognized the feed: a live broadcast of the keynote addresses in the Center. The Patron Ik'spir Pat's hoverchair prominent. The camera lingered on the Patron's eyes, the only part of him visible from within the chair's masking infrastructure. They were startling, silvery orbs, heavy-lidded and expressionless.

The camera swung to Hershie. Szandor spat dramatically and led a chorus of hisses.

Hershie hastily closed his comm and cleared his throat, adjusted his mic, and addressed the crowd.

"Uh . . ." he said. His guts somersaulted. Time to go big or go home.

"Hi." That was better. "Thanks. I'm the Super Man. For years, I worked alongside UN Peacekeeping forces around the world. I hoped I was doing good work. Most of the time, I suppose I may have been."

He caught the eye of Brenda, the cheerful Texan who'd booked him in. She looked uneasy.

"There's one thing I'm certain of, though: it's that the preparation for war has never led to anything *but* war. With this show, you ladies and gentlemen are participating in a giant conspiracy to commit murder. Individually, you may not be evil, but collectively, you're the most amoral supervillain I've ever faced."

Brenda was talking frantically into her comm. His mic died. He simply expanded his mighty diaphragm and kept on speaking, his voice filling the ballroom.

"I urge you to put this behind you. We've entered into a new era in human history. The good Patron here offers the entire universe; you scurry around, arranging the deaths of people you've never met.

"It's a terribly, stupid, mindless pursuit. You ought to be ashamed of yourselves."

With that, Hershie stepped away from the podium and walked out of the ballroom.

The camera tracked him as he made his way back through the convention center, out the doors. He leapt the barricade and settled in front of the screen. The demonstrators gave him a standing ovation, and Thomas gravely shook his hand. The handshake was repeated on the giant screen behind them, courtesy of the cameraman, who had gamely vaulted the barricade as well.

The crowd danced, hugged each other, laughed. Szandor's dog bit him on the ass, and he nearly dropped the projector.

He recovered in time to nearly drop it again, as the Patron Ik'spir Pat's hoverchair glided out the center's doors and made a beeline for Hershie.

Hershie watched the car approach with nauseous dread. The Patron stopped a few centimeters from him, so they were almost eyeball-to-eyeball. The hoverchair's PA popped to life, and the Patron spoke, in the bugouts' thrilling contralto.

"Thank you for your contribution," the bugout said. "It was refreshing to have another perspective presented."

Hershie tried for a heroic nod. "I'm glad you weren't offended."

"On the contrary, it was stimulating. I shall have to speak with the conference's organizers; this format seems a good one for future engagements."

Hershie felt his expression slipping, sliding towards slack-jawed incredulity. He struggled to hold it, then lost it entirely when one of the Patron's silvery eyes drooped closed in an unmistakable wink.

"Hi, mama."

"Hershie, I just saw it on the television."

He cringed back from his comm as he shrank deeper into the corner of the Belquees that he'd moved to when his comm rang.

"Mama, it's all right. They've signed me for the full six months. I'll be fine—"

"Of course you'll be fine, bubbie. But would it kill you to brush your hair before you go on television in front of the whole world? Do you want everyone to think your mother raised a slob?"

Hershie smiled. "I will, mama."

"I know you will, bubbie. You're a very good-looking man, you know. But no one wants to marry a man with messy hair."

"I know, mama."

"Well, I won't keep you. Do you think you could come for dinner on Friday? I know you're busy, but your old mother won't be here forever."

He sighed his father's sigh. "I'll be there, mama."

I wrote this story especially for this collection, during a week-long writer's retreat at an arts-center on Toronto Island in July 2002. It's the first solo story I've completed since I went to work for the Electronic Frontier Foundation (www.eff.org) in March 2002 (I've been working on novels and collaborations, which really eat into the short-story writing time).

We're teetering along the brink of a steep cliff. The entrenched copyright interests—Hollywood studios, the recording industry, even writers' groups—are running around in a blind panic at the thought that new technology will undermine their businesses. These groups have excellent lobbyists, and they're pushing for extraordinary powers in Congress and in standards-bodies. Each of these initiatives undercuts such fundamental liberties as freedom of speech, and many require technologists to kowtow to Hollywood, getting approval from the studio technophobes before any new tech can be shipped.

Worst of all, these initiatives undermine the basic fair-use freedoms that all artists rely on to make their work. The copyright maximalists will tell you that there's no reason for works to ever enter the public domain, that there are no circumstances under which making an unauthorized copy of a work is justifiable.

But we all stand on the shoulders of giants. The public domain—a rich commons whence we can all fish for ideas, phrases and texts for use in our work—is just a small fraction of this ecology. The stories in the book are derived works, tales made out of the bits and pieces of the stories that the writers who inspired me wrote.

I don't write a lot of fictional polemic—nonfiction polemic is basically my day-job—but this piece all but demanded that I write it. It's unflinchingly nerdy—I'm thinking of inventing a new genre called "NerdcOre" to accommodate it—but there are plenty of unflinching nerds whom I hope it will speak to.

OwnzOred

Ten years in the Valley, and all Murray Swain had to show for it was a spare tire, a bald patch, and a life that was friendless and empty and maggoty-rotten. His only ever California friend, Liam, had dwindled from a tubbaguts programmer-shaped potato to a living skeleton on his death-bed the year before, herpes blooms run riot over his skin and bones in the absence of any immunoresponse. The memorial service featured a framed photo of Liam at his graduation, his body was donated for medical science.

Liam's death really screwed things up for Murray. He'd gone into one of those clinical depression spirals that eventually afflicted all the aging bright young coders he'd known during his life in tech. He'd get misty in the morning over his second cup of coffee and by the midafternoon blood-sugar crash, he'd be weeping silently in his cubicle, clattering nonsensically at the keys to disguise the disgusting snuffling noises he made. His wastebasket overflowed with spent tissues and a rumor circulated among the evening cleaning-staff that he was a compulsive masturbator. The impossibility of the rumor was immediately apparent to all the other coders on his floor who, pr0n-hounds that they were, had explored the limits and extent of the censoring proxy that sat at the headwaters of the office network. Nevertheless, it was gleefully repeated in the collegial fratmosphere of his workplace and wags kept dumping their collections of conference-snarfed hotel-sized bottles of hand-lotion on his desk.

The number of bugs per line in Murray's code was 500 percent that of the overall company average. The QA people sometimes just sent his code back to him (From: qamanager@globalsemi.com To: mswain@globalsemi.com Subject: Your code ... Body: ... sucks) rather than trying to get it to build and run. Three weeks after Liam died, Murray's team leader pulled his commit privileges on the CVS repository, which meant that he had to grovel with one of the other coders when he wanted to add his work to the project.

Two months after Liam died, Murray was put on probation.

Three months after Liam died, Murray was given two weeks' leave and an email from HR with contact info for an in-plan shrink who could counsel him. The shrink recommended Cognitive Therapy, which he explained in detail, though all Murray remembered ten minutes after the session was that he'd have to do it every week for years, and the name reminded him of Cognitive Dissonance, which was the name of Liam's favorite stupid Orange County garage band.

Murray returned to Global Semiconductor's Mountain View headquarters after three more sessions with the shrink. He badged in at the front door, at the elevator, and on his floor, sat at his desk and badged in again on his PC.

From: tvanya@globalsemi.com To: mswain@globalsemi. com Subject: Welcome back! Come see me ... Body: ... when you get in.

Tomas Vanya was Murray's team lead, and rated a glass office with a door. The blinds were closed, which meant: dead Murray walking. Murray closed the door behind him and sighed a huge heave of nauseated relief. He'd washed out of Silicon Valley and he could go home to Vancouver and live in his parents' basement and go salmon fishing on weekends with his high-school drinking buds. He didn't exactly love Global Semi, but shit, they were number three in a hot, competitive sector where Moore's Law drove the cost of microprocessors relentlessly downwards as their speed rocketed relentlessly skyward. They had four billion in the bank, a healthy share price, and his options were above water, unlike the poor fucks at Motorola, number four and falling. He'd washed out of the nearly-best, what the fuck, beat spending his prime years in Hongcouver writing government-standard code for the Ministry of Unbelievable Dullness.

Even the number-two chair in Tomas Vanya's office kicked major ergonomic azz. Murray settled into it and popped some of the controls experimentally until the ess of his spine was cushioned and pinioned into chiropractically correct form. Tomas unbagged a Fourbucks Morning Harvest muffin and a venti coconut Frappucino and slid them across his multi-tiered Swedish Disposable Moderne desque.

"A little welcome-back present, Murray," Tomas said. Murray listened for the sound of a minimum-wage security guard clearing out his desk during this exit-interview-cum-breakfast-banquet. He wondered if Global Semi would forward-vest his options and mentally calculated the strike price minus the current price times the number of shares times the conversion rate to Canadian Pesos and thought he could maybe put down 25 percent on a two bedroom in New Westminster.

"Dee-licious and noo-tritious," Murray said and slurped at the frappe.

"So," Tomas said. "So."

Here it comes, Murray thought, and sucked up a brain-freezing mouthful of frou-frou West Coast caffeine delivery system. G0nz0red. Fi0red. Sh17canned. Thinking in leet-hacker crap made it all seem more distant.

"It's really great to see you again," Tomas said. "You're a really important part of the team here, you know?"

Murray restrained himself from rolling his eyes. He was fired, so why draw it out? There'd been enough lay-offs at Global Semi, enough boom and bust and bust and bust that it was a routine, they all knew how it went.

But though Murray was an on Air Canada jet headed for

Vangroover, Tomas wasn't even on the damned script. "You're sharp and seasoned. You can communicate effectively. Most techies can't write worth a damn, but you're good. It's rare."

Ah, the soothing sensation of smoke between one's buttocks. It was true that Murray liked to write, but there wasn't any money in it, no glory either. If you were going to be a writer in the tech world, you'd have to be—

"You've had a couple weeks off to reassess things, and we've been reassessing, too. Coding, hell, most people don't do it for very long. Especially assembler, Jesus, if you're still writing assembler after five years, there's something, you know, *wrong*. You end up in management or you move horizontally. Or you lose it." Tomas realized that he'd said the wrong thing and blushed.

Aw, shit.

"Horizontal movement. That's the great thing about a company this size. There's always somewhere you can go when you burn out on one task."

No, no, no.

"The Honorable Computing initiative is ready for documentation, Murray. We need a tech writer who can really *nail it*."

A tech writer. Why not just break his goddamned fingers and poke his eyes out? Never write another line of code, never make the machine buck and hum and make his will real in the abstract beauty of silicon? Tech writers were coders' janitors, documenting the plainly self-evident logic of APIs and code-structures, niggling over punctuation and grammar and friggin' stylebooks, like any of it *mattered*—human beings could parse English, even if it wasn't well-formed, even if you had a comma-splice or a dangling participle.

"It's a twelve month secondment, a change of pace for you and a chance for us to evaluate your other strengths. You go to four weeks' vacation and we accelerate your vesting and start you with a new grant at the same strike price, over twenty-four months."

Murray did the math in his head, numbers dancing. Four weeks' vacation—that was three years ahead of schedule, not that anyone that senior ever used his vacation days, but you could bank them for retirement or, a-hem, exit strategy. The forward vesting meant that he could walk out and fly back to Canada in three weeks if he hated it and put *thirty* percent down on a two-bedroom in New West.

And the door was closed and the blinds were drawn and the implication was clear. Take this job or shove it.

He took the job.

A month later he was balls-deep in the documentation project and feeling, you know, not horrible. The Honorable Computing initiative was your basic Bond-villain world-domination horseshit, of course, but it was technically sweet and it kept him from misting over and bawling. And they had cute girls on the documentation floor, liberal arts/electrical engineering double-majors with abs you could bounce a quarter off of who were doing time before being promoted up to join the first cohort of senior female coders to put their mark on the Valley.

He worked late most nights, only marking the passing of five PM by his instinctive upwards glance as all those fine, firm rear ends walked past his desk on their way out of the office. Then he went into night mode, working by the glow of his display and the emergency lights until the custodians came in and chased him out with their vacuum cleaners.

One night, he was struggling to understand the use-cases for Honorable Computing when the overhead lights flicked on, shrinking his pupils to painful pinpricks. The cleaners clattered in and began to pointedly empty the wastebins. He took the hint, grabbed his shoulderbag and staggered for the exit, badging out as he went.

His car was one of the last ones in the lot, a hybrid Toyota with a lot of dashboard geek-toys like a GPS and a back-seat DVD player, though no one ever rode in Murray's back seat. He'd bought it three months before Liam died, cashing in some shares and trading in the giant gas-guzzling SUV he'd never once taken off-road.

As he aimed his remote at it and initiated the cryptographic handshake—i.e., unlocked the doors—he spotted the guy leaning against the car. Murray's thumb jabbed at the locking button on the remote, but it was too late: the guy had the door open and he was sliding into the passenger seat.

In the process of hitting the remote's panic button, Murray managed to pop the trunk and start the engine, but eventually his thumb mashed the right button and the car's lights strobed and the horn blared. He backed slowly towards the office doors, just as the guy found the dome-light control and lit up the car's interior and Murray got a good look at him.

It was Liam.

Murray stabbed at the remote some more and killed the panic button. Jesus, who was going to respond at this hour in some abandoned industrial park in the middle of the Valley anyway? The limp-dick security guard? He squinted at the face in the car.

Liam. Still Liam. Not the skeletal Liam he'd last seen rotted and intubated on a bed at San Jose General. Not the porcine Liam he'd laughed with over a million late-night El Torito burritos. A fit, healthy, *young* Liam, the Liam he'd met the day they both started at Global Semi at adjacent desks, Liam fresh out of Cal Tech and fit from his weekly lot-hockey game and his weekend dirtbike rides in the hills. Liam-prime, or maybe Liam's younger brother or something.

Liam rolled down the window and struck a match on the passenger-side door, then took a Marlboro Red from a pack in his shirt pocket and lit it. Murray walked cautiously to the car, his thumb working on his cellphone, punching in the numbers 9-1-1 and hovering over "SEND." He got close enough to see the scratch the match-head had left on the side-panel and muttered "*fuck*" with feeling.

"Hey dirtbag, you kiss your mother with that mouth?" Liam said. It *was* Liam.

"You kiss *your* mother after I'm through with her mouth?" Murray said, the rote of old times. He gulped for air.

Liam popped the door and got out. He was ripped, bullish chest and cartoonish wasp-waist, rock-hard abs through a silvery club-shirt and bulging thighs. A body like that, it's a full-time job, or so Murray had concluded after many failed get-fit initiatives involving gyms and retreats and expensive home equipment and humiliating early-morning jogs through the sidewalk-free streets of Shallow Alto.

"Who the fuck are you?" Murray said, looking into the familiar eyes, the familiar smile-lines and the deep wrinkle between Liam's eyes from his concentration face. Though the night was cool, Murray felt runnels of sweat tracing his spine, trickling down between his buttocks.

"You know the answer, so why ask? The question isn't who, it's *how*. Let's drive around a little and I'll tell you all about it."

Liam clapped a strong hand on his forearm and gave it a companionable squeeze. It felt good and real and human.

"You can't smoke in my car," Murray said.

"Don't worry," Liam said. "I won't exhale."

Murray shook his head and went around to the driver's side. By the time he started the engine, Liam had his seatbelt on and was poking randomly at the on-board controls. "This is pretty rad. You told me about it, I remember, but it sounded stupid at the time. Really rad." He brought up the MP3 player and scrolled through Murray's library, adding tracks to a mix, cranking up the opening crash of an old, old, old punk Beastie Boys song. "The speakers are for shit, though!" he hollered over the music.

Murray cranked the volume down as he bounced over the speed bumps, badged out of the lot, and headed for the hills, stabbing at the GPS to bring up some roadmaps that included the private roads way up in the highlands.

"So, do I get two other ghosts tonight, Marley, or are you the only one?"

Liam found the sunroof control and flicked his smoke out into the road. "Ghost, huh? I'm meat, dude, same as you. Not back from the dead, just back from the *mostly dead*." He did the last like Billy Crystal as Miracle Max in *The Princess Bride*, one of their faves. "I'll tell you all about it, but I want to catch up on your shit first. What are you working on?"

"They've got me writing docs," Murray said, grateful of the car's darkness covering his blush.

"Awwww," Liam said. "You're shitting me."

"I kinda lost it," Murray said. "Couldn't code. About six months ago. After."

"Ah," Liam said.

"So I'm writing docs. It's a sideways promotion and the work's not bad. I'm writing up Honorable Computing."

"What?"

"Sorry, it was after your time. It's a big deal. All the semiconductor companies are in on it: Intel, AMD, even Motorola and Hitachi. And Microsoft—they're hardcore for it."

"So what is it?"

Murray turned onto a gravel road, following the tracery on the glowing GPS screen as much as the narrow road, spiraling up and up over the sparse lights of Silicon Valley. He and Liam had had a million bullshit sessions about tech, what was vaporware and what was killer, and now they were having one again, just like old times. Only Liam was dead. Well, if it was time for Murray to lose his shit, what better way than in the hills, great tunes on the stereo, all alone in the night?

Murray was warming up to the subject. He'd wanted someone he could really chew this over with since he got reassigned, he'd wanted Liam there to key off his observations. "OK, so, the Turing Machine, right? Turing's Universal Machine. The building-block of modern computation. In Turing's day, you had all these specialized machines: a machine for solving quadratics, a machine for calculating derivatives, and so on. Turing came up with the idea of a machine that could configure itself to be any specialized machine, using symbolic logic: software. Included in the machines that you can simulate in a Turing Machine is another Turing Machine, like Java or VMWare. With me?"

"With you."

"So this gives rise to a kind of existential crisis. When your software is executing, how does it know what its execution environment is? Maybe it's running on a Global Semi Itanium clone at 1.6 gigahertz, or maybe it's running on a model of that chip, simulated on a Motorola G5 RISC processor."

"Got it."

"Now, forget about that for a sec and think about Hollywood. The coked-up Hollyweird fatcats hate Turing Machines. I mean, they want to release their stuff over the Internet, but they want to deliver it to you in a lockbox. You get to listen to it, you get to watch it, but only if they say so, and only if you've paid. You can buy it over and over again, but you can never own it. It's scrambled—encrypted—and they only send you the keys when you satisfy a license server that you've paid up. The keys are delivered to a secure app that you can't fuxor with, and the app locks you out of the video card and the sound card and the drive while it's decrypting the stream and showing it to you, and then it locks everything up again once you're done and hands control back over to you."

Liam snorted. "It is to laugh."

"Yeah, I know. It's bullshit. It's Turing Machines, right? When the software executes on your computer, it has to rely on your computer's feedback to confirm that the video card and the sound card are locked up, that you're not just feeding the cleartext stream back to the drive and then to 10,000,000 pals online. But the 'computer' it's executing on could be simulated inside another computer, one that you've modified to your heart's content. The 'video card' is a simulation; the 'sound card' is a simulation. The computer is a brain in a bottle, it's in the Matrix, it can't trust its senses because you're in control, it's a Turing Machine nested inside another Turing Machine."

"Like Descartes."

"What?"

"You gotta read your classics, bro. I've been catching up over the past six months or so, doing a *lot* of reading. Mostly free e-books from the Gutenberg Project. Descartes' *Meditations* are some heavy shiznit. Descartes starts by saying that he wants to figure out some stuff about the world, but he can't, right, because in order to say stuff about the world, he needs to trust his senses, but his senses are wrong all the time. When he dreams, his senses deliver full-on THX all-digital IMAX, but none of it's really *there*. How does he know when he's dreaming or when he's awake? How does he know when he's experiencing something or imagining it? How does he know he's not a brain in a jar?"

"So, how does he know?" Murray asked, taking them over a reservoir on a switchback road, moonlight glittering over the still water, occulted by fringed silhouettes of tall California pines.

"Well, that's where he pulls some religion out of his ass. Here's how it goes: God is good, because part of the definition of God is goodness. God made the world. God made me. God made my senses. God made my senses *so that I could experience the goodness of his world.* Why would God give me bum senses? QED, I can trust my senses."

"It *is* like Descartes," Murray said, accelerating up a new hill.

"Yeah?" Liam said. "Who's God, then?"

"Crypto," Murray said. "Really good, standards-defined crypto. Public ciphersystems whose details are published and understood. AES, RSA, good crypto. There's a signing key for each chip fab— ours is in some secret biometrics-and-machineguns bunker under some desert. That key is used to sign *another* key that's embedded in a tamper-resistant chip—"

Liam snorted again.

"No, really. Not tamper-*proof,* obviously, but tamper-*resistant*— you'd need a tunneling microscope or a vat of freon to extract the keys from the chip. And every chip has its own keys, so you'd need to do this for every chip, which doesn't, you know, *scale.* So there's this chip full of secrets, they call the Fritz chip, for Fritz Hollings, the Senator from Disney, the guy who's trying to ban computers so that Hollywood won't go broke. The Fritz chip wakes up when you switch on the machine, and it uses its secret key to sign the operating system—well, the boot-loader and the operating system and the drivers and stuff—so now you've got a bunch of crypto-graphic signatures that reflect the software and hardware configuration of your box. When you want to download *Police Academy 6,* your computer sends all these keys to Hollywood cen-tral, attesting to the operating environment of your computer. Hollywood decides on the fly if it wants to trust that config, and if it does, it encrypts the movie, using the keys you've sent. That means that you can only unscramble the movie when you're run-ning that Fritz chip, on that CPU, with that version of the OS and that video driver and so on."

"Got it: so if the OS and the CPU and so on are all
'Honorable'"—Liam described quote-marks with his index
fingers—"Then you can be sure that the execution environment is
what the software expects it to be, that it's not a brain in a vat.
Hollywood movies are safe from napsterization."

They bottomed out on the shore of the reservoir and Murray
pulled over. "You've got it."

"So basically, whatever Hollywood says, goes. You can't fake an
interface, you can't make any uses that they don't authorize. You
know that these guys sued to make the VCR illegal, right? You
can't wrap up an old app in a compatibility layer and make it work
with a new app. You say Microsoft loves this? No fucking wonder,
dude—they can write software that won't run on a computer running Oracle software. It's your basic Bond-villain —"

"— world-domination horseshit. Yeah, I know."

Liam got out of the car and lit up another butt, kicked loose
stones into the reservoir. Murray joined him, looking out over the
still water.

"Ring Minus One," Liam said, and skipped a rock over the oily-
black surface of the water, getting four long bounces out of it.

"Yeah." Murray said. Ring Zero, the first registers in the processor, was where your computer checked to figure out how to start
itself up. Compromise Ring Zero and you can make the computer
do anything—load an alternate operating system, turn the whole
box into a brain-in-a-jar, executing in an unknown environment.
Ring Minus One, well, that was like God-code, space on another,
virtual processor that was unalterable, owned by some remote
party, by LoCal and its entertainment giants. Software was released
without any copy-prevention tech because everyone knew that
copy-prevention tech *didn't work*. Nevertheless, Hollywood was
always chewing the scenery and hollering, they just didn't believe
that the hairfaces and ponytails didn't have some seekrit tech that
would keep their movies safe from copying until the heatdeath of
the universe or the expiry of copyright, whichever came last.

"You run this stuff," Liam said, carefully, thinking it through, like
he'd done before he got sick, murdered by his need to feed speed-
balls to his golden, tracked-out arm. "You run it and while you're

watching a movie, Hollywood 0wnz your box." Murray heard
the zero and the zee in 0wnz. Hacker-speak for having total control. No one wants to be 0wnz0red by some teenaged script-kid-
die who's found some fresh exploit and turned it loose on your
computer.

"In a nutsack. Gimme a butt."

Liam shook one out of the pack and passed it to Murray, along
with a box of Mexican strike-anywhere matches. "You're back on
these things?" Liam said, a note of surprise in his voice.

"Not really. Special occasion, you being back from the dead and
all. I've always heard that these things'd kill me, but apparently
being killed isn't so bad—you look great."

"Artful segue, dude. You must be burning up with curiosity."

"Not really," Murray said. "Figgered I'm hallucinating. I haven't
hallucinated up until now, but back when I was really down, you
know, clinical, I had all kinds of voices muttering in my head,
telling me that I'd fucked up, it was all fucked up, crash the car into
the median and do the world a favor, whatever. You get a little better from that stuff by changing jobs, but maybe not all the way
better. Maybe I'm going to fill my pockets with rocks and jump in
the lake. It's the next logical step, right?"

Liam studied his face. Murray tried to stay deadpan, but he felt
the old sadness that came with the admission, the admission of guilt
and weakness, felt the tears pricking his eyes. "Hear me out first,
OK?" Liam said.

"By all means. It'd be rude not to hear you out after you came
all the way here from the kingdom of the dead."

"Mostly dead. Mostly. Ever think about how all the really good
shit in your body—metabolism, immunoresponse, cognition—it's
all in Ring Minus One? Not user-accessible? I mean, why is it that
something like wiggling your toes is under your volitional control,
but your memory isn't?"

"Well, that's complicated stuff—heartbeat, breathing,
immunoresponse, memory. You don't want to forget to breathe,
right?"

Liam hissed a laugh. "Horse-sheeit," he drawled. "How complicated is moving your arm? How many muscle-movements in a

smile? How many muscle-movements in a heartbeat? How complicated is writing code versus immunoresponse? Why when you're holding your breath can't you hold it until you don't want to hold it anymore? Why do you have to be a fucking Jedi Master to stop your heart at will?"

"But the interactions—"

"More horseshit. Yeah, the interactions between brain chemistry and body and cognition and metabolism are all complicated. I was a speed-freak, I know all about it. But it's not any more complicated than any of the other complex interactions you master every day—wind and attack and spin when someone tosses you a ball; speed and acceleration and vectors when you change lanes; don't even get me started on what goes on when you season a soup. No, your body just isn't *that* complicated—it's just hubris that makes us so certain that our meat-sacks are transcendently complex.

"We're simple, but all the good stuff is 0wned by your autonomic systems. They're like conditional operators left behind by a sloppy coder: while x is true, do y. We've only had the vaguest idea what x is, but we've got a handle on y, you betcha. Burning fat, for example." He prodded Murray's gut-overhang with a long finger. Self-consciously, Murray tugged his JavaOne gimme jacket tighter.

"For forty years now, doctors have been telling us that the way to keep fit is to exercise more and eat less. That's great fucking advice, as can be demonstrated by the number of trim, fit residents of Northern California that can be found waddling around any shopping mall off Interstate 101. Look at exercise, Jesus, what could be stupider? Exercise doesn't burn fat, exercise just satisfies the condition in which your body is prepared to burn fat off. It's like a computer that won't boot unless you restart it twice, switch off the monitor, open the CD drive and stand on one foot. If you're a luser, you do all this shit every time you want to boot your box, but if you're a leet hax0r like you and me, you just figure out what's wrong with the computer and *fix it*. You don't sacrifice a chicken twice a day, you 0wn the box, so you make it dance to your tune.

"But your meat, it's not under your control. You know you have to exercise for 20 minutes before you start burning any fat at all? In other words, the first twenty minutes are just a goddamned waste of time. It's sacrificing a chicken to your metabolism. Eat less, exercise more is a giant chicken-sacrifice, so I say screw it. I say, you should be super-user in your own body. You should be leet as you want to be. Every cell in your body should be end-user modifiable."

Liam held his hands out before them, then stretched and stretched and stretched the fingers, so that each one bent over double. "Triple jointed, metabolically secure, cognitively large and *in charge*. I 0wn, dude."

Liam fished the last cig out of the pack, crumpled it and tucked it into a pocket. "Last one," he said. "Wanna share?"

"Sure," Murray said, dazedly. "Yeah," he said, taking the smoke and bringing it to his lips. The tip, he realized too late, was dripping with saliva. He made a face and handed it back to Liam. "Aaagh! You juiced the filter!"

"Sorry," Liam said, "Talking gets my spit going. Where was I? Oh, yeah, I 0wn. Want to know how it happened?"

"Does it also explain how you ended up not dead?"

"Mostly dead. Indeed it does."

Murray walked back to the car and lay back on the hood, staring at the thin star-cover and the softly swaying pine-tops. He heard Liam begin to pace, heard the cadence of Liam's thinking stride, the walk he fell into when he was on a roll.

"Are you sitting comfortably?" Liam said. "Then I shall begin."

The palliatives on the ward were abysmal whiners, but they were still better than the goddamned church volunteers who came by to patch-adams at them. Liam was glad of the days when the dementia was strong, morphine days when the sun rose and set in a slow blink and then it was bedtime again.

Lucky for him, then, that lucid days were fewer and farther between. Unlucky for him that his lucid days, when they came, were filled with the G-Men.

The G-Men had come to him in the late days of his tenure on the palliative ward. They'd wheeled him into a private consultation room and given him a cigarette that stung the sores on his lips, tongue and throat. He coughed gratefully.

"You must be the Fed," Liam said. "No one else could green-light indoor smoking in California." Liam had worked for the Fed before. Work in the Valley and you end up working for the Fed, because when the cyclic five-year bust arrives, the only venture capital that's liquid in the US is military research green—khaki money. He'd been seconded twice to biometrics-and-machineguns bunkers where he'd worked on need-to-know integration projects for Global Semi's customers in the Military-Industrial Simplex.

The military and the alphabet soup of Fed cops gave birth to the Valley. After WWII, all those shipbuilder engineers and all those radar engineers and all those radio engineers and the tame academics at Cal Tech and Cal and Stanford sorta congealed, did a bunch of startups and built a bunch of crap their buds in the Forces would buy.

Khaki money stunted the Valley. Generals didn't need to lobby in Congress for bigger appropriations. They just took home black budgets that were silently erased from the books, aerosolized cash that they misted over the eggheads along Highway 101. Two generations later, the Valley was filled with techno-determinists, swaggering nerd squillionaires who were steadfastly convinced that the money would flow forever and ever amen.

Then came Hollywood, the puny $35 billion David that slew the $600 billion Goliath of tech. They bought Congresscritters, had their business-models declared fundamental to the American way of life, extended copyright ad [inifinitum|nauseam] and generally kicked the shit out of tech in DC. They'd been playing this game since 1908, when they sued to keep the player piano off the market, and they punched well above their weight in the legislative ring. As the copyright police began to crush tech companies throughout the Valley, khaki money took on the sweet appeal of nostalgia, strings-free cash for babykiller projects that no one was going to get sued over.

The Feds that took Liam aside that day could have been pulled from a fiftieth anniversary revival of *Nerds and Generals*. Clean-cut, stone-faced, prominent wedding-bands. The Feds had never cared for Liam's jokes, though it was his trackmarks and not his punchlines that eventually accounted for his security clearance being yanked. These two did not crack a smile as Liam wheezed out his pathetic joke.

Instead, they introduced themselves gravely. Col. Gonzalez—an MD, with caduceus insignia next to his silver birds—and Special Agent Fredericks. Grateful for his attention, they had an offer to make him.

"It's experimental, and the risks are high. We won't kid you about that."

"I appreciate that," Liam wheezed. "I like to live dangerously. Give me another smoke, willya?"

Col. Gonzalez lit another Marlboro Red with his brass Zippo and passed him a sheaf of papers. "You can review these here, once we're done. I'm afraid I'll have to take them with me when we go, though."

Liam paged through the docs, passing over the bio stuff and nodding his head over the circuit diagrams and schematics. "I give up," he said. "What does it all do?"

"It's an interface between your autonomic processes and a microcontroller."

Liam thought about that for a moment. "I'm in," he said.

Special Agent Fredericks' thin lips compressed a hair and his eyes gave the hintiest hint of a roll. But Col. Gonzalez nodded to himself. "All right. Here's the protocol: tomorrow, we give you a bug. It's a controlled mutagen that prepares your brainstem so that it can emits and receives weak electromagnetic fields that can be manipulated with an external microcontroller. In subjects with effective immunoresponse, the bug takes less than one percent of the time—"

"But if you're dying of AIDS, that's not a problem," Liam said and smiled until some of the sores at the corners of his mouth cracked and released a thin gruel of pus. "Lucky fucking me."

"You grasp the essentials," the Colonel said. "There's no surgery involved. The interface regulates immunoresponse in the region of the insult to prevent rejection. The controller has a serial connector that connects to a PC that instructs it in respect of the governance of most bodily functions."

Liam smiled slantwise and butted out. "God, I'd hate to see the project you developed this shit for. Zombie soldiers, right? You can tell me, I've got clearance."

Special Agent Fredericks shook his head. "Not for three years, you haven't. And you never had clearance to get the answer to that question. But once you sign here and here and here, you'll *almost* have clearance to get *some* of the answers." He passed a clipboard to Liam.

Liam signed, and signed, and signed. "Autonomic processes, right?"

Col. Gonzalez nodded. "Correct."

"Including, say, immunoresponse?"

"Yes, we've had very promising results in respect of the immune system. It was one of the first apps we wrote. Modifies the genome to produce virus-hardened cells and kick-starts production of new cells."

"Yeah, until some virus out-evolves it," Liam said. He knew how to debug vaporware.

"We issue a patch," the Colonel said.

"I write good patches," Liam said.

"We know," Special Agent Fredericks said, and gently prized the clipboard from his fingers.

The techs came first, to wire Liam up. The new bug in his system broadened his already-exhaustive survey of the ways in which the human body can hurt. He squeezed his eyes tight against the morphine rush and lazily considered the possibility of rerouting pain to a sort of dull tickle.

The techs were familiar Valley-dwellers, portly and bedecked with multitools and cellular gear and wireless PDAs. They handled him like spoiled meat, with gloves and wrinkled noses, and talked shop over his head to one another.

Colonel Gonzalez supervised, occasionally stepping away to liaise with the hospital's ineffectual medical staff.

A week of this—a week of feeling like his spine was working its way out of his asshole, a week of rough latex hands and hacker jargon—and he was wheeled into a semi-private room, surrounded by louche oatmeal-colored commodity PCs—no keyboards or mice, lest he get the urge to tinker.

The other bed was occupied by Joey, another Silicon Valley needle-freak, a heroin addict who'd been a design engineer for Apple, figuring out how to cram commodity hardware into stylish gumdrop boxen. Joey and Liam croaked conversation between themselves when they were both lucid and alone. Liam always knew when Joey was awake by the wet hacking coughs he wrenched out of his pneumonia-riddled lungs. Alone together, ignored by the mad scientists who were hacking their bodies, they struck up a weak and hallucinogenic camaraderie.

"I'm not going to sleep," Joey said, in one timeless twilight.

"So don't sleep, shit," Liam said.

"No, I mean, ever. Sleep, it's like a third of your life, 20, 30 years. What's it good for? It resets a bunch of switches, gives your brain a chance to sort through its buffers, a little oxygenation for your tissues. That stuff can all take place while you're doing whatever you feel like doing, hiking in the hills or getting laid. Make 'em into cron jobs and nice them down to the point where they just grab any idle cycles and do their work incrementally."

"You're crazy. I like to sleep," Liam said.

"Not me. I've slept enough in this joint, been on the nod enough, I never want to sleep another minute. We're getting another chance, I'm not wasting a minute of it." Despite the braveness of his words, he sounded like he was half-asleep already.

"Well, that'll make *them* happy. All part of a good super-soldier, you know."

"Now who's crazy?"

"You don't believe it? They're just getting our junkie asses back online so they can learn enough from us to field some mean, lean, heavily modified fighting-machines."

"And then they snuff us. You told me that this morning. Yesterday? I still don't believe it. Even if you're right about why they're doing this, they're still going to want us around so they can monitor the long-term effects."

"I hope you're right."

"You know I am."

Liam stared into the ceiling until he heard Joey's wet snores, then he closed his eyes and waited for the fever dreams.

Joey went critical the next day. One minute, he was snoring away in bed while Liam watched a daytime soap with headphones. The next minute, there were twenty people in the room: nurses, doctors, techs, even Col. Gonzalez. Joey was doing the floppy dance in the next bed, the OD dance that Liam had seen once or twice, danced once or twice on an Emergency Room floor, his heart pounding the crystal meth mambo.

Someone backhanded Liam's TV and it slid away on its articulated arm and yanked the headphones off his head, ripping open the scabs on the slowly healing sores on his ears. Liam stifled a yelp and listened to the splashing sounds of all those people standing ankle-deep in something pink and bad-smelling, and Liam realized it was watery blood and he pitched forward and his empty stomach spasmed, trying to send up some bile or mucous, clicking on empty.

Colonel Gonzales snapped out some orders and two techs abandoned their fretting over one of the computers, yanked free a tangle of roll-up, rubberized keyboards and trackballs and USB cables, piled them on the side of Liam's gurney, snapped up the guard rails and wheeled him out of the room.

They crashed through a series of doors before hitting a badge-point. One tech thought he'd left his badge back in the room on its lanyard (he hadn't—he'd dropped it on the gurney and Liam had slipped it under the sheets), the other one wasn't sure if his was in one of his many pockets. As they frisked themselves, Liam stole his skeletal hand out from under the covers, a hand all tracked out with collapsed IV veins and yellowing fingernails, a claw of a hand.

The claw shook as Liam guided it to a keyboard, stole it under the covers, rolled it under the loose meat of his thigh.

"Need to know?" Liam said, spitting the words at Col. Gonzalez. "If I don't need to know what happened to Joey, who the fuck does?"

"You're not a medical professional, Liam. You're also not cleared. What happened to Joey was an isolated incident, nothing to worry about."

"Horseshit! You can tell me what happened to Joey or not, but I'll find out, you goddamned betcha."

The Colonel sighed and wiped his palms on his thighs. He looked like shit, his brush-cut glistening with sweat and scalp-oil, his eyes bagged and his youthful face made old with exhaustion lines. It had been two hours since Joey had gone critical—two hours of lying still with the keyboard nestled under his thigh, on the gurney in the a locked room, until they came for him again. "I have a lot of work to do yet, Liam. I came to see you as a courtesy, but I'm afraid that the courtesy is at a close." He stood.

"Hey!" Liam croaked after him. "Gimme a fucking cigarette, will you?"

Once the Colonel was gone, Liam had the run of the room. They'd mopped it out and disinfected it and sent Joey's corpse to an Area 51 black ops morgue for gruesome autopsy, and there was only half as much hardware remaining, all of it plugged back into the hard pucker of skin on the back of Liam's neck.

Cautiously, Liam turned himself so that the toes of one foot touched the ground. Knuckling his toes, he pushed off towards the computers, the gurney's wheels squeaking. Painfully, arthritically, he inched to the boxes, then plugged in and unrolled the keyboard.

He hit the spacebar and got rid of the screen-saver, brought up a login prompt. He'd been stealthily shoulder-surfing the techs for weeks now, and had half a dozen logins in his brain. He tapped out the login/pass combination and he was in.

The machine was networked to a CVS repository in some bunker, so the first thing he did was login to the server and download all the day's commits, then he dug out the READMEs. While everything was downloading, he logged into the tech's email account and found Col. Gonzalez's account of Joey's demise.

It was encrypted with the group's shared key as well as the tech's key, but he'd shoulder-surfed both, and after three tries, he had cleartext on the screen.

Hydrostatic shock. The membranes of all of Joey's cells had ruptured simultaneously, so that he'd essentially burst like a bag of semi-liquid Jell-O. Preliminary indications were that the antiviral cellular modifications had gone awry due to some idiosyncrasy of

Joey's "platform"—his physiology, in other words—and that the "fortified" cell-membranes had given way disastrously and simultaneously.

A ghoulish giggle escaped Liam's lips. Venture capitalists liked to talk about "Liquidity events"—times in the life of a portfolio company when the investors get to cash out: acquisition and IPO, basically. Liam had always joked that the VCs needed adult diapers to cope with their liquidity events, but now he had a better one. Joey had experienced the ultimate liquidity event.

The giggle threatened to rise into a squeal as he contemplated a liquidity event of his own, so he swallowed it and got into the READMEs and the source code.

He wasn't a biotech, wasn't a medical professional, but neither were the coders who'd been working on the mods that were executing on his "platform" at that very moment. In their comments and data-structures and READMEs, they'd gone to great pains to convert medical jargon to geekspeak, so that Liam was actually able to follow most of it.

One thing he immediately gleaned is that his interface was modifying his cells to be virus-hardened as slowly as possible. They wanted a controlled experiment, data on every stage of the recovery—if a recovery was indeed in the cards.

Liam didn't want to wait. He didn't even have to change the code—he just edited a variable in the config file and respawned the process. Where before he'd been running at a pace that would reverse the course of HIV in his body in a space of three weeks, now he was set to be done in three *hours*. What the fuck—how many chances was he going to get to screw around after they figured out that he'd been tinkering?

Manufacturing the curative made him famished. His body was burning a lot of calories, and after a couple hours he felt like he could eat the ass out of a dead bear. Whatever was happening was happening, though! He felt the sores on his body dry up and start to slough off. He was hungry enough that he actually caught himself peeling off the scabby Corn Flakes and eating them. It grossed him out, but he was *hungry*.

His only visitor that night was a nurse, who made enough noise with her trolley on the way down the hall that he had time to balance the keyboard on top of the monitor and knuckle the bed back into position with his toes. The nurse was pleased to hear that he had an appetite and obligingly brought him a couple of supper-trays—the kitchen had sent up one for poor Joey, she explained.

Once Liam was satisfied that she was gone, he returned to his task with a renewed sense of urgency. No techs and no docs and no Colonel for six hours now—there must be a shitload of paperwork and fingerpointing over Joey, but who knew how long it would last?

He stuffed his face, nailing about three thousand calories over the next two hours, poking through the code. Here was a routine for stimulating the growth of large muscle-groups. Here was one for regenerating fine nerves. The enhanced reflexes sounded like a low-cal option, too, so he executed it. It was all betaware, but as between a liquidity event, a slow death on the palliative ward and a chance at a quick cure, what the fuck, he'd take his chances.

He was chuckling now, going through the code, learning the programmers' style and personality from their comments and variable names. He was so damned hungry, and the muscles in his back and limbs and ass and gut all felt like they were home to nests of termites.

He needed more food. He gingerly peeled off the surgical tape holding on controller and its cable. Experimentally, he stood. His inner ear twirled rollercoaster for a minute or two, but then it settled down and he was actually erect—upright—well, both, he could cut glass with that boner, it was the first one he'd had in a year—and *walking!*

He stole out into the hallway, experiencing a frisson of delight and then the burning ritual humiliation of any person who finds himself in a public place wearing a hospital gown. His bony ass was hanging out of the back, the cool air of the dim ward raising goose-pimples on it.

He stepped into the next room. It was dusky-dark, the twilight of a hospital nighttime, and the two occupants were snoring in contratime. Each had his (her? it was too dark to tell) own nightstand, piled high with helium balloons, Care Bears, flowers and baskets of nuts, dried fruits and chocolates. Saliva flooded Liam's mouth. He tiptoed across to each nightstand and held up the hem of his gown, then grinched the food into the pocket it made.

Stealthily, he stole his way down the length of the ward, emptying fruit-baskets, boxes of candy and chocolate, leftover dinner trays. By the time he returned to his room, he could hardly stand. He dumped the food out on the bed and began to shovel it into his face, going back through the code, looking for obvious bugs, memory leaks, buffer overruns. He found several and recompiled the apps, accelerating the pace of growth in his muscles. He could actually feel himself bulking up, feel the tone creeping back into his flesh.

He'd read the notes in the READMEs on waste heat and the potential to denature enzymes, so he stripped naked and soaked towels in a quiet trickle of ice-water in the small sink. He kept taking breaks from his work to wring out the steaming towels he wrapped around his body and wet them down again.

The next time he rose, his legs were springy. He parted the slats of the blinds and saw the sun rising over the distant ocean and knew it was time to hit the road, jack.

He tore loose the controller and its cable and shut down the computer. He undid the thumbscrews on the back of the case and slid it away, then tugged at the sled for the hard-disk until it sprang free. He ducked back out into the hall and quickly worked his way through the rooms until he found one with a change of men's clothes neatly folded on the chair—ill-fitting tan chinos and a blue Oxford shirt, the NoCal yuppie uniform. He found a pair of too-small penny-loafers too and jammed his feet into the toes. He dressed in his room and went through the wallet that was stuck in the pants pocket. A couple hundred bucks' worth of cash, some worthless plastic, a picture of a heavyset wife and three chubby kids. He dumped all the crap out, kept the cash, snatched up the drive-sled and booted, badging out with the tech's badge.

"How long have you been on the road, then?" Murray asked. His mouth tasted like an ashtray and he had a mild case of the shakes.

"Four months. I've been breaking into cars mostly. Stealing laptops and selling them for cash. I've got a box at the rooming-house with the hard drive installed, and I've been using an e-gold account to buy little things online to help me out."

"Help you out with *what?*"

"Hacking—duh. First thing I did was reverse-engineer the inter-face bug. I wanted a safe virus I could grow arbitrary payloads for in my body. I embedded the antiviral hardening agent in the vec-tor. It's a sexually transmissible *wellness*, dude. I've been barebacking my way through the skankiest crack-hoes in the Tenderloin, playing Patient Zero, infecting everyone with the Cure."

Murray sat up and his head swam. "You did what?"

"I cured AIDS. It's going around, it's catching, you might already be a winner."

"Jesus, Liam, what the fuck do you know about medicine? For all you know, your cure is worse than the disease—for all you know, we're all going to have a—'liquidity event' any day now!"

"No chance of that happening, bro. I isolated the cause of that early on. This medical stuff is just *not that complicated*—once you get over the new jargon, it's nothing you can't learn as you go with a little judicious googling. Trust me. You're soaking in it."

It took Murray a moment to parse that. "You infected *me?*"

"The works—I've viralized all the best stuff. Metabolic con-trollers, until further notice, you're on a five-cheeseburger-a-day diet; increased dendrite density; muscle-builders. At-will pain-dampeners. You'll need those—I gave you the interface, too."

A spasm shot up Murray's back, then down again.

"It was on the cigarette butt. You're cancer-immune, by-the-by. I'm extra contagious tonight." Liam turned down his collar to show Murray the taped lump there, the dangling cable that disap-peared down his shirt, connecting to the palmtop strapped to his belt.

Murray arched his back and mewled through locked jaws.

Liam caught his head before it slammed into the Toyota's hood. "Breathe," he hissed. "Relax. You're only feeling the pain because you're choosing not to ignore it. Try to ignore it, you'll see. It kicks azz."

"I needed an accomplice. A partner in crime. I'm underground, see? No credit-card, no ID. I can't rent a car or hop a plane. I needed to recruit someone I could trust. Naturally, I thought of you."

"I'm flattered," Murray sarcased around a mouthful of double-bacon cheeseburger with extra mayo.

"You should be, asshole," Liam said. They were at Murray's one-bedroom techno-monastic condo: shit sofa, hyper-ergonomic chairs, dusty home theatre, computers everywhere. Liam drove them there, singing into the wind that whipped down from the sunroof, following the GPS's sterile Eurobabe voice as it guided them back to the anonymous shitbox building where Murray had located his carcass for eight years.

"Liam, you're a pal, really, my best friend ever, I couldn't be happier that you're alive, but if I could get up I would fucking *kill you*. You *raped me*, asshole. Used my body without my permission."

"You see it that way now, but give it a couple weeks, it'll, ah, grow on you. Trust me. It's rad. So, call in sick for the next week—you're going to need some time to get used to the mods."

"And if I don't?"

"Do whatever you want, buddy, but I don't think you're going to be in any shape to go to work this week—maybe not next week either. Tell them it's a personal crisis. Take some vacation days. Tell 'em you're going to a fat-farm. You must have a shitload of holidays saved up."

"I do," Murray said. "I don't know why I should use them, though."

"Oh, this is the best vacation of all, the Journey thru Innerspace. You're going to love it."

Murray hadn't counted on the coding.

Liam tunneled into his box at the rooming house and dumped its drive to one of the old laptops lying around Murray's apartment. He set the laptop next to Murray while he drove to Fry's Electronics to get the cabling and components he needed to make the emitter/receiver for the interface. They'd always had a running joke that you can build *anything* from parts at Fry's, but when Liam invoked it, Murray barely cracked a smile. He was stepping through the code in a debugger, reading the comments Liam had left behind as he'd deciphered its form and function.

He was back in it. There was a runtime that simulated the platform and as he tweaked the code, he ran it on the simulator and checked out how his body would react if he executed it for real. Once he got a couple of liquidity events, he saw that Liam was right, they just weren't that hard to avoid.

The API was great, there were function calls for just about everything. He delved into the cognitive stuff right off, since it was the area that was rawest, that Liam had devoted the least effort to. At-will serotonin production. Mnemonic perfection. Endorphin production, adrenalin. Zen master on a disk. Who needs meditation and biofeedback when you can do it all in code?

Out of habit, he was documenting as he went along, writing proper tutorials for the API, putting together a table of the different kinds of interaction he got with different mods. Good, clear docs, ready for printing, able to be slotted in as online help in the developer toolkit. Inspired by Joey, he began work on a routine that would replace all the maintenance chores that the platform did in sleep-mode, along with a subroutine that suppressed melatonin and all the other circadian chemicals that induced sleep.

Liam returned from Fry's with bags full of cabling and soldering guns and breadboards. He draped a black pillowcase over a patch of living-room floor and laid everything out on it, wires and strippers and crimpers and components and a soldering gun, and went to work methodically, stripping and crimping and twisting. He'd taken out his own connector for reference and he was comparing them both, using a white LED torch on a headband to show him the pinouts on the custom end.

"So I'm thinking that I'll clone the controller and stick it on my head first to make sure it works. You wear my wire and I'll burn the new one in for a couple days and then we can swap. OK?"

"Sure," Murray said, "Whatever." His fingers rattled on the keys.

"Got you one of these," Liam said and held up a bulky Korean palmtop. "Runs Linux. You can cross-compile the SDK and all the libraries for it; the compiler's on the drive. Good if you want to run an interactive app"—an application that changed its instructions based on output from the platform—"and it's stinking cool, too. I fucking *love* gear."

"Gear's good," Murray agreed. "Cheap as hell and faster every time I turn around."

"Well, until Honorable Computing comes along," Liam said. "That'll put a nail in the old coffin."

"You're overreacting."

"Naw. Just being realistic. Open up a shell, OK? See at the top, how it says 'tty'? The kernel thinks it's communicating with a printer. Your shell window is a simulation of a printer, so the kernel knows how to talk to it—it's got plenty of compatibility layers between it and you. If the guy who wrote the code doesn't want you to interface with it, you can't. No emulation, that's not 'honorable.' Your box is 0wned."

Murray looked up from his keyboard. "So what do you want me to do about it, dead man?"

"Mostly dead," Liam said. "Just think about it, OK? How much money you got in your savings account?"

"Nice segue. Not enough."

"Not enough for what?"

"Not enough for sharing any of it with you."

"Come on, dude, I'm going back underground. I need fifty grand to get out of the country—Canada, then buy a fake passport and head to London. Once I'm in the EU, I'm in good shape. I learned German last week, this week I'm doing French. The dendrite density shit is the shit."

"Man und zooperman," Murray said. "If you're zo zooper, go and earn a buck or two, OK?"

"Come on, you know I'm good for it. Once this stuff is ready to go—"

"What stuff?"

"The codebase! Haven't you figured it out yet? It's a startup! We go into business in some former-Soviet Stan in Asia or some African kleptocracy. We infect the locals with the Cure, then the interface, and then we sell 'em the software. It's *viral marketing*, gettit?"

"Leaving aside CIA assassins, if only for the moment, there's one gigantic flaw in your plan, dead-man."

"I'm all aflutter with anticipation."

"There's no fucking revenue opportunity. The platform spreads for free—it's already out there, you've seeded it with your magic undead super-cock. The hardware is commodity hardware, no margin and no money. The controller can be built out of spare parts from Fry's—next gen, we'll make it WiFi, so that we're using commodity wireless chipsets and you can control the device from a distance—"

"—yeah, and that's why we're selling the software!" Liam hopped from foot to foot in a personal folk-dance celebrating his sublime cleverness.

"In Buttfuckistan or Kleptomalia. Where being a warez d00d is an honorable trade. We release our libraries and binaries and APIs and fifteen minutes later, they're burning CDs in every souk and selling them for ten cents a throw."

"Nope, that's not gonna happen."

"Why not?"

"We're gonna deploy on Honorable hardware."

"I am not hearing this." Murray closed the lid of his laptop and tore into a slice of double-cheese meat-lover's deep-dish pizza. "You are not telling me this."

"You are. I am. It's only temporary. The interface isn't Honorable, so anyone who reverse-engineers it can make his own apps. We're just getting ours while the getting is good. All the good stuff—say, pain-control and universal antiviral hardening—we'll make for free, viralize it. Once our stuff is in the market, the whole world's going to change, anyway. There'll be apps for happiness, cures for every disease, hibernation, limb-regeneration, whatever. Anything any human body has ever done, ever, you'll be able to do at-will. You think there's going to be anything recognizable as an economy once we're ubiquitous?"

Every morning, upon rising, Murray looked down at his toes and thought, "Hello toes." It had been ten years since he'd had regular acquaintance with anything south of his gut. But his gut was gone, tight as a drumhead. He was free from scars and age-marks and unsightly moles and his beard wouldn't grow in again until he asked it to. When he thought about it, he could feel the dull ache of the new teeth coming in underneath the ones that had grown discolored and chipped, the back molar with all the ugly amalgam fillings, but if he chose to ignore it, the pain simply went away.

He flexed the muscles, great and small, all around his body. His fat index was low enough to see the definition of each of those superbly toned slabs of flexible contained energy—he looked like an anatomy lesson, and it was all he could do not to stare at himself in the mirror all day.

But he couldn't do that—not today, anyway. He was needed back at the office. He was already in the shitter at work over his "unexpected trip to a heath-farm," and if he left it any longer, he'd be out on his toned ass. He hadn't even been able to go out for new clothes—Liam had every liquid cent he could lay hands on, as well as his credit-cards.

He found a pair of ancient, threadbare jeans and a couple of medium t-shirts that clung to the pecs that had grown up underneath his formerly sagging man-boobs and left for the office.

He drew stares on the way to his desk. The documentation department hummed with hormonal female energy, and half a dozen of his co-workers found cause to cruise past his desk before he took his morning break. As he greedily scarfed up a box of warm Krispy Kremes, his cellphone rang.

"Yeah?" he said. The caller-ID was the number of the international GSM phone he'd bought for Liam.

"They're after us," Liam said. "I was at the Surrey border-crossing and the Canadian immigration guy had my pic!"

Murray's heart pounded. He concentrated for a moment, then his heart calmed, a jolt of serotonin lifting his spirits. "Did you get away?"

"Of course I got away. Jesus, you think that the CIA gives you a phone call? I took off cross-country, went over the fence for the duty-free and headed for the brush. They shot me in the fucking leg—I had to dig the bullet out with my multitool. I'm sending in ass-loads of T-cells and knitting it as fast as I can."

Panic crept up Murray's esophagus, and he tamped it down. It broke out in his knees, he tamped it down. His balance swam, he stabilized it. He focused his eyes with an effort. "They *shot* you?"

"I think they were trying to wing me. Look, I burned all the source in 4,096-bit GPG ciphertext onto a couple of CDs, then zeroed out my drive. You've got to do the same, it's only a matter of time until they run my back-trail to you. The code is our only bargaining chip."

"I'm at work—the backups are at home, I just can't."

"Leave, asshole, like *now!* Go—get in your car and *drive*. Go home and start scrubbing the drives. I left a bottle of industrial paint-stripper behind and a bulk eraser. Unscrew every drive-casing, smash the platters and dump them in a tub with all the stripper, then put the tub onto the bulk-eraser—that should do it. Keep one copy, ciphertext only, and make the key a good one. Are you going?"

"I'm badging out of the lot, shit, shit, shit. What the fuck did you do to me?"

"Don't, OK? Just don't. I've got my own problems. I've got to go now. I'll call you later once I get somewhere."

He thought hard on the way back to his condo, as he whipped down the off-peak emptiness of Highway 101. Being a coder was all about doing things in the correct order: first *a;* then *b;* then, if *c* equals *d, e;* otherwise, *f.*

First, get home. Then set the stateful operation of his body for maximal efficiency: reset his metabolism, increase the pace of dendrite densification. Manufacture viralized anti-viral in all his serum. Lots of serotonin and at-will endorphin. Hard times ahead.

Next, encipher and back up the data to a removable. Did he have any CD blanks at home? With eidetic clarity, he saw the half-spent spool of generic blanks on the second shelf of the media totem.

Then trash the disks, pack a bag and hit the road. Where to?

He pulled into his driveway, hammered the elevator button a dozen times, then bolted for the stairs. Five flights later, he slammed his key into the lock and went into motion, executing the

plan. The password gave him pause—generating a 4,096 bit key
that he could remember was going to be damned hard, but then
he closed his eyes and recalled, with perfect clarity, the first five
pages of documentation he'd written for the API. His fingers rattled on the keys at speed, zero typos.

He was just dumping the last of the platters into the acid bath
when they broke his door down. Half a dozen big guys in martian
riot-gear, outsized science-fiction black-ops guns. One flipped up his
visor and pointed to a badge clipped to a D-ring on his tactical vest.

"Police," he barked. "Hands where I can see them."

The serotonin flooded the murky grey recesses of Murray's
brain and he was able to smile nonchalantly as he straightened from
his work, hands held loosely away from his sides. The cop pulled a
zap-strap from a holster at his belt and bound his wrists tight. He
snapped on a pair of latex gloves and untaped the interface on the
back of Murray's neck, then slapped a bandage over it.

"Am I under arrest?"

"You're not cleared to know that," the cop said.

"Special Agent Fredericks, right?" Murray said. "Liam told me
about you."

"Dig yourself in deeper, that's right. No one wants to hear from
you. Not yet, anyway." He took a bag off his belt, then, in a quick
motion, slid it over Murray's head, cinching it tight at the throat,
but not so tight he couldn't breathe. The fabric passed air, but not
light, and Murray was plunged into total darkness. "There's a gag
that goes with the hood. If you play nice, we won't have to use it."

"I'm nice, I'm nice," Murray said.

"Bag it all and get it back to the house. You and you, take him
down the back way."

Murray felt the bodies moving near him, then thick zap-straps
cinching his arms, knees, thighs and ankles. He tottered and tipped
backwards, twisting his head to avoid smacking it, but before he hit
the ground, he'd be roughly scooped up into a fireman's carry, resting on bulky body-armor.

As they carried him out, he heard his cellphone ring. Someone
plucked it off his belt and answered it. Special Agent Fredericks
said, "Hello, Liam."

Machineguns-and-biometrics bunkers have their own special signature scent, scrubbed air and coffee farts and ozone. They cut his clothes off and disinfected him, then took him through two airshowers to remove particulate that the jets of icy pungent Lysol hadn't taken care of. He was dumped on a soft pallet, still in the dark.

"You know why you're here," Special Agent Fredericks said from somewhere behind him.

"Why don't you refresh me?" He was calm and cool, heart normal. The cramped muscles bound by the plastic straps eased loose, relaxing under him.

"We found two CDs of encrypted data on your premises. We can crack them, given time, but it will reflect well on you if you assist us in our inquiries."

"Given about a billion years. No one can brute-force a 4,096-bit GPG cipher. It's what you use in your own communications. I've worked on military projects, you know that. If you could factor out the products of large primes, you wouldn't depend on them for your own security. I'm not getting out of here ever, no matter how much I cooperate."

"You've got an awfully low opinion of your country, sir." Murray thought he detected a note of real anger in the Fed's voice and tried not to take satisfaction in it.

"Why? Because I don't believe you've got magic technology hidden away up your asses?"

"No, sir, because you think you won't get just treatment at our hands."

"Am I under arrest?"

"You're not cleared for that information."

"We're at an impasse, Special Agent Fredericks. You don't trust me and I don't have any reason to trust you."

"You have every reason to trust me," the voice said, very close in now.

"Why?"

The hood over his tag was tugged to one side and he heard a sawing sound as a knife hacked through the fabric at the base of his skull. Gloved fingers worked a plug into the socket there.

"Because," the voice hissed in his ear, "Because I am *not* stimulating the pain center of your brain. Because I am not cutting off the blood-supply to your extremities. Because I am not draining your brain of all the serotonin there or leaving you in a vegetative state. Because I can do all of these things and I'm not."

Murray tamped his adrenals, counteracted their effect, relaxed back into his bonds. "You think you could outrace me? I could stop my heart right now, long before you could do any of those things." Thinking: *I am a total bad-azz, I am. But I don't want to die.*

"Tell him," Liam said.

"Liam?" Murray tried to twist his head toward the voice, but strong hands held it in place.

"Tell him," Liam said again. "We'll get a deal. They don't want us dead, they just want us under control. Tell him, OK?"

Murray's adrenals were firing at max now, he was sweating uncontrollably. His limbs twitched hard against his bonds, the plastic strapscutting into them, the pain surfacing despite his efforts. It hit him. His wonderful body was 0wnz0red by the Feds.

"Tell me, and you have my word that no harm will come to you. You'll get all the resources you want. You can code as much as you want."

Murray began to recite his key, all five pages of it, through the muffling hood.

Liam was fully clothed, no visual restraints. As Murray chafed feeling back into his hands and feet, Liam crossed the locked office with its grey industrial carpeting and tossed him a set of khakis and a pair of boxers. Murray dressed silently, then turned his accusing glare on Liam.

"How far did you get?"

"I didn't even make it out of the state. They caught me in Sebastopol, took me off the Greyhound in cuffs with six guns on me all the time."

"The disks?"

"They needed to be sure that you got rid of all the backups, that there wasn't anything stashed online or in a safe-deposit box, that they had the only copy. It was their idea."

"Did you really get shot?"

"I really got shot."

"I hope it really fucking hurt."

"It really fucking hurt."

"Well, good."

The door opened and Special Agent Fredericks appeared with a big brown bag of Frappuccinos and muffins. He passed them around.

"My people tell me that you write excellent documentation, Mr. Swain."

"What can I say? It's a gift."

"And they tell me that you two have written some remarkable code."

"Another gift."

"We always need good coders here."

"What's the job pay? How are the bennies? How much vacation?"

"As much as you want, excellent, as long as you want, provided we approve the destinations first. Once you're cleared."

"It's not enough," Murray said, upending twenty ounces of West Coast frou-frou caffeine delivery system on the carpeting.

"Come on, Murray," Liam said. "Don't be that way."

Special Agent Fredericks fished in the bag and produced another novelty coffee beverage and handed it to Murray. "Make this one last, it's all that's left."

"With all due respect," Murray said, feeling a swell of righteousness in his chest, in his thighs, in his groin, "Go fuck yourself. You don't 0wn me."

"They do, Murray. They 0wn both our asses." Liam said, staring into the puddle of coffee slurry on the carpet.

Murray crossed the room as fast as he could and smacked Liam, open palm, across the cheek.

"That will do," Special Agent Fredericks said, with surprising mildness.

"He needed smacking," Murray said, without rancor, and sat back down.

"Liam, why don't you wait for us in the hallway?"

"You came around," Liam said. "Everyone does. These guys 0wn."

"I didn't ask to share a room with you, Liam. I'm not glad I am. I'd rather not be reminded of that fact, so shut your fucking mouth before I shut it for you."

"What do you want, an apology? I'm sorry. I'm sorry I infected you, I'm sorry I helped them catch you. I'm sorry I fux0red your life. What can I say?"

"You can shut up anytime now."

"Well, this is going to be a *swell* living-arrangement."

The room was labeled "Officers' Quarters," and it had two good, firm queen-sized mattresses, premium cable, two identical stainless-steel dressers, and two good ergonomic chairs. There were junction boxes beside each desk with locked covers that Murray supposed housed Ethernet ports. All the comforts of home.

Murray lay on his bed and pulled the blankets over his head. Though he didn't need to sleep, he chose to.

For two weeks, Murray sat at his assigned desk, in his assigned cube, and zoned out on the screen-saver. He refused to touch the keyboard, refused to touch the mouse. Liam had the adjacent desk for a week, then they moved him to another office, so that Murray had solitude in which to contemplate the whirling star-field. He'd have a cup of coffee at 10:30 and started to feel a little sniffly in the back of his nose. He ate in the commissary at his own table. If anyone sat down at his table, he stood up and left. They didn't sit at his table. At 2PM, they'd send in a box of warm Krispy Kremes, and by 3PM, his blood-sugar would be crashing and he'd be sobbing over his keyboard. He refused to adjust his serotonin levels.

On the third Monday, he turned up at his desk at 9AM as usual and found a clipboard on his chair with a ball-point tied to it.

Discharge papers. Non-disclosure agreements. Cross-your-heart swears on pain of death. A modest pension. Post-It "Sign here" tabs had been stuck on here, here and here.

The junkie couldn't have been more than fifteen years old. She was death-camp skinny, tracked out, sitting cross-legged on a cardboard box on the sidewalk, sunning herself in the thin Mission noonlight. "Wanna buy a laptop? Two hundred bucks."

Murray stopped. "Where'd you get it?"

"I stole it," she said. "Out of a convertible. It looks real nice. One-fifty."

"Two hundred," Murray said. "But you've got to do me a favor."

"Three hundred, and you wear a condom."

"Not that kind of favor. You know the Radio Shack on Mission at 24th? Give them this parts list and come back here. Here's a $100 down-payment."

He kept his eyes peeled for the minders he'd occasionally spotted shadowing him when he went out for groceries, but they were nowhere to be seen. Maybe he'd lost them in the traffic on the 101. By the time the girl got back with the parts he'd need to make his interface, he was sweating bullets, but once he had the laptop open and began to rekey the entire codebase, the eidetic rush of perfect memory dispelled all his nervousness, leaving him cool and calm as the sun set over Mission.

From the sky, Africa was green and lush, but once the plane touched down in Mogadishu, all Murray saw was sere brown plains and blowing dust. He sprang up from his seat, laundering the sleep toxins in his brain and the fatigue toxins in his legs and ass as he did.

He was the first off the jetway and the first at the customs desk.

"Do you have any commercial or work-related goods, sir?"

"No sir," Murray said, willing himself calm.

"But you have a laptop computer," the customs man said, eyeballing his case.

"Oh, yeah. That. Can't ever get away from work, you know how it is."

"I certainly hope you find time to relax, sir." The customs man stamped the passport he'd bought in New York.

"When you love your work, it can be relaxing."

"Enjoy your stay in Somalia, sir."